T0065261

The Hands of Memory

Also by Michael Kaye

<u>Novels</u>

One Monday
Riddle
From The Cradle To The Grave
The Choice
Never The Light Of Day
The Feral Girls

<u>Poetry</u>

Covering The Cracks
Lovers And Losers

The Hands of Memory

A Novel By

MICHAEL KAYE

iUniverse

THE HANDS OF MEMORY

iUniverse books may be ordered through booksellers or by contacting:

iUniverse
1663 Liberty Drive
Bloomington, IN 47403
www.iuniverse.com
844-349-9409

Because of the dynamic nature of the Internet, any web addresses or links contained in this book may have changed since publication and may no longer be valid. The views expressed in this work are solely those of the author and do not necessarily reflect the views of the publisher, and the publisher hereby disclaims any responsibility for them.

Any people depicted in stock imagery provided by Getty Images are models, and such images are being used for illustrative purposes only. Certain stock imagery © Getty Images.

ISBN: 978-1-6632-1290-0 (sc)
ISBN: 978-1-6632-1291-7 (e)

Print information available on the last page.

iUniverse rev. date: 11/24/2020

This book is for Cindy Cerro-Conlon
She will know why

Acknowledgments

I owe my grateful and profound thanks to Amanda Ann Waite, BS, MHA, LNHA, the administrator of an upstate New York nursing home facility, for being generous with her time and professional knowledge. Any liberties I have taken with her advice are mine, not hers.

Sue Mason has my deep gratitude for sharing her extensive genealogy expertise, offering meaningful suggestions and pointing me in the right direction.

To Richard Drake, my heartfelt appreciation for his artistry on the front cover, which enhances the book beyond measure.

To my wife, Kristine, for her editing, technical expertise and continued support and love.

The days may come, the days may go,
but still the hands of memory weave
the blissful dreams of long ago.

George Cooper

Chapter One

If it's stories you want, then this is the place you need to go. Sure the folks there are old but they're the ones who've lived, laughed and cried. Take my advice, sweetheart, and spend some time with them. They'll give you everything you need to make your film.

As she drove through the entrance to *The Sweet and Comfy Nursing Home*, Ingrid Strauss well remembered the advice from her wise and feisty grandmother. She smiled as she recalled her grandmother's piercing eyes on her own when delivering her wisdom as though sent directly from the mountaintop.

Ingrid also knew the advice came with a veiled threat: *Everything you need is there, honey. Don't mess it up.*

The memory sent a shiver down Ingrid's spine, a jolt that made her realize just how important this project could turn out to be. As the recipient of this year's prestigious Murray Film Institute Award for documentary film making, Ingrid held in her hands not only her career but also a voice for those who didn't have a voice.

Her presentation to the selection committee focused on recording for posterity the lives of those who, though still alive, had now been mostly forgotten. The vision she shared with the members, a vision that convinced them to award Ingrid the $50,000 first prize, centered on the now lost contributions these featured men and women had made, in their own unique ways, to the world.

Talking to her own grandmother, listening to her fascinating, colorful stories of making her way from childhood to old age whilst dealing with a myriad of challenging, sometimes bewildering problems life threw her way, convinced Ingrid this was *the* documentary she just had to make.

Now, all her meticulous planning, all of the energy and effort she had put into bringing her conception to fruition, came down to this: driving through the entrance to *The Sweet and Comfy Nursing Home.*

"Hi, Ms. Strauss, I'm Sylvia Richards, the Administrator here. We talked on the phone. How are you?"

"I'm well, thanks," Ingrid responded, carefully, aware that getting off on the right foot with this woman was probably critical to the smooth running and success of the project.

"So excited, we are," Sylvia answered warmly, "to have you here. You've already created quite a buzz with our residents. Everyone's dying to meet you."

Ingrid immediately relaxed, grateful for the hospitable welcome.

"You're very gracious to allow me to come into your nursing home, Ms. Richards…"

"…Sylvia, please."

"Oh, sure…Sylvia. Ingrid, then…and I hope we won't cause too much disruption to the daily routine. We'll be as discreet as possible."

"Not to worry. Things can always do with a little shake up around here. I've already told my staff to afford you every reasonable consideration. You're free to go wherever you please and speak with whomever you like. As I've said, the residents are so excited you're here. They'll probably talk your ear off but, oh my, you'll hear some stories, believe me."

Ingrid laughed, happy to know about the prospective goldmine awaiting her.

"No film without them," she said, raising her eyebrows. "I just hope I'll be able to get them to be themselves and talk to me as though I'm an old friend."

"Ingrid," Sylvia answered with a grin, "don't worry. You're going to hear amazing stories from some truly remarkable people. Not only that but you'll also be stunned, surprised and probably brought to tears by some of the things they'll tell you. So…be prepared to have the Kleenex handy. Now, c'mon, let's go. I'll show you around. Time to get your feet wet."

The nursing home was less than ten years old and it was obvious a tremendous amount of thoughtful planning had gone into its design. Ingrid found it hard to immediately absorb the multitude of astonishing features, both aesthetic and practical. Her first impression was not of an institution as such but rather of a muted country club.

Pastel colors gave the communal rooms a warm, comforting feel, accented by paintings and photographs, many produced by the residents themselves. Vases of flowers and colorful pot plants brought an air of freshness and beauty that brightened otherwise empty spaces.

Ingrid was also struck by the sense of community wherever she went. Chatter among the residents was constant, seemingly amiable but never loud or obnoxious. There was calmness about the place, a sense that the folks who lived there really respected the institution and each other. It was an impressive start to her tour.

"This is one of our rec rooms," Sylvia enthused, ushering Ingrid into a large, open area full of mostly women busily attending to various arts and crafts. Easels, pots of paints, containers of multicolored beads, markers, string and a host of other materials littered the room like an ever changing kaleidoscope. The residents were bantering with each other but their intensity and seriousness matched the determination and pleasure etched into their faces.

"Wow, this is fantastic," Ingrid beamed. "They look like their having so much fun."

"Not only fun but competition, too. Twice a year we organize an art show, open to the public, where they choose best in show etc. Let me tell you, Ingrid," Sylvia slyly grinned, "cut throat doesn't even come close. Now, let me show you the exercise room."

Sylvia explained that this space was extensively used for a great number of activities.

"We have yoga three or four times a week. Some gentle aerobics, stretching and weights, and anything else you can think of. Believe me, no one here gets a chance to be a couch potato. We also have a half mile trail behind the main building for those who prefer a gentler kind of exercise, all under supervision, of course."

"I'm exhausted just hearing about all this," Ingrid joked.

"We also have movies three times a week, plus live performances from all sorts of companies: local schools, musical groups, ballet and light opera, even an Elvis impersonator, which is a huge hit with the girls. Oh, and there's bingo, too. Everybody loves their bingo. I'd be disowned if I ever took that away. This space seems to be the heart and soul of the place," Sylvia gushed.

"And I'm guessing you have a long waiting list. Right?"

"Yes and no. Yes, lots of folk have heard about us and want to come here. Unfortunately, we also have…how shall I put this delicately?... a constant turnover. Most of our residents are here for about five or six years, but we have several who've been with us for eight or more. C'mon, let's go meet Jack and Pearl."

They found Jack pottering around in the extensive flower and vegetable garden he created just outside the main entrance. In keeping with the other facilities, this plot was immaculate, colorful and inviting.

"Jack! Jack!" Sylvia yelled from a distance to warn him of their approach. "Got a minute to meet Ingrid? She's the one who's going to be making a film about you all."

Jack carefully put down his hoe, hitched up his pants and ambled over.

"Who d'you say she is?" Jack questioned, shielding his watery eyes from the sun. "I'm a little hard of hearing, missy," he continued, looking right at Ingrid.

"Ingrid Strauss, Mr…er…Mr…"

"Just Jack will do fine," he cut in quickly. "We don't stand on formalities around here, do we Sylvia?"

Sylvia shook her head in agreement.

"Not that I've noticed, Jack."

"This is amazing," Ingrid said, spreading her hands to indicate the vast garden. "You must really love being here, Jack."

"Growing things. That's what it's all about," Jack answered, proudly. "Whether it's plants or people, that's what it's all about."

"Jack's a retired school teacher, so he knows a little something about growing people."

"Yeah," he laughed, "if it's stories you want, I got a million. Tales of the tykes I call them. If you've got a few weeks I'd gladly spill the beans."

"Gonna hold you to that, Jack," Ingrid responded, nodding. "You may be just who I'm looking for."

"Any time. And, oh, I've a fresh bottle of bourbon in my room in case you're interested," Jack suggested, with a wink.

"Sounds too good to refuse," Ingrid offered, smiling. "Stories and whiskey...what could possibly go wrong?"

"And on that note," Sylvia interrupted, "we should let you get back to your flowers, Jack. Catch you later."

He gave each of the women a warm hug before strolling back to tend some more to his beloved garden.

"What a sweetie," Ingrid told Sylvia, as they made their way to meet Pearl in the small library.

"He is," agreed Sylvia. "And he's typical of most of the folks here."

"Most?" Ingrid queried. "You mean..."

"A few can be a tad difficult at times," explained Sylvia. "But I guess they keep us from becoming too complacent. Pearl's a prime example."

Actually, Ingrid was pleased to learn not all the residents were clones of Mary Poppins and Walt Disney. Her documentary needed to be real and alive, not sugary sweet and boring.

They found Pearl Lister peeling and slicing an apple in the far corner of the library. A couple of books were open in front of her but she seemed more intent on the apple than on reading.

She didn't look up as the two women approached and only acknowledged them when Sylvia gently called out her name.

"Oh, Sylvia, it's you. For one dreadful moment I thought it might be Josephine."

Sylvia ignored Pearl's seemingly unkind reference to a fellow resident.

"Pearl, I'd like to introduce Ingrid Strauss to you. She's going to be making a documentary about our happy home. Ingrid," she continued, "Pearl. She may give you a run for your money."

The three women laughed but Ingrid surmised there may have been more than a joke associated with Sylvia's comment.

"You're quite young to be hanging around a bunch of old people," Pearl said, as she continued eating her apple. "May I ask - why us?"

Ingrid sat down opposite Pearl, focusing intently on the older woman.

"You may and I'm happy to tell you," Ingrid began confidently, sure that she needed to stand up to Pearl from the get-go. "The documentary form of filmmaking is the most fascinating for me. I'm passionate about trying to tell true stories, whether they're about people's lives or important events.

"Although they're called 'projects' I don't look at them that way. For me it's about recording truthful history which will hopefully serve as an inspiration and a certain amount of understanding for the next generations.

"It's about preserving the past, its value and importance to our lives today. I want the stories I hope to hear to be reflective not only of times past but what we as a society can learn from them. Wisdom and lives well lived come from age and maturity. That's why I'm here, Pearl, to give a voice to people who matter, even if they don't think they do anymore."

"My. My," Pearl exclaimed, clearly impressed both with Ingrid's passion for her work and her intellect. "Well, I'm sure you'll bring a breath of fresh air. I expect Sylvia's already told you we are a diverse group from a mixture of backgrounds. If you can't get what you need from us then I doubt you could anywhere."

And with that, Pearl finished off her apple, took up a book and began reading.

"What's her story?" Ingrid asked, as they walked the halls on their way to the dining area for coffee.

Sylvia politely but firmly explained that she couldn't divulge personal information on the residents.

"What they tell you on their own accord is up to them. Besides, Ingrid, you need to hear their stories first hand."

"Of course," Ingrid nodded. "But who's Josephine and why was Pearl glad that it was us and not her back then?"

"Ah, Josephine," Sylvia remarked, as they settled down with their drinks. "Again, can't tell you much except to say she's a mutterer and a singer. Drives some of the other residents crazy the way she goes on and on."

"She talks a lot. Is that so bad?"

Sylvia shrugged.

"Only if you're around it all day long. But it's not only that. She's also… let's see if I can put this nicely…she's a tad theatrical."

"Really. How so?"

"Hand gestures. The way she carries herself. You get the picture. Not that any of it is put on. It's just the way she is. She's naturally this way."

"Interesting," Ingrid considered. "Has she been with you long?"

"I'd say about five or six years."

"May I ask how old she is?"

"Without looking it up I'd say around ninety. But she still looks good."

"Any family?"

"We're her family, but no one ever comes to visit, if that's what you mean?"

"Must be a lonely existence."

"Not our Josephine," Sylvia remarked, raising her eyebrows. "Life and soul of the party. But she must find things difficult in one sense, though."

"Oh? Why's that?"

"Well, you see, Ingrid, Josephine's our only black resident."

On their last stop around the nursing home, Sylvia took Ingrid to the Alzheimer and Dementia unit. Ingrid had no idea what to expect but was prepared to be dismayed and downhearted. In fact, the opposite happened.

They were met with brightness and smiles from residents, some who talked to them in their own way and seemed only happy to have visitors pay attention. Ingrid noticed Sylvia's natural repartee and the calm way she engaged each resident. They, in return, seemed so pleased to see her, reaching out to touch her hand or wave as she left them.

Ingrid made a mental note to ask Sylvia if she could arrange for a family member or two to speak with her on camera about their loved ones living with the disease. Since this unit was obviously such an integral part of the nursing home's function, Ingrid knew she had to include a section about it in her documentary.

Back in Sylvia's office after the tour was over, Ingrid respectfully inquired about Sylvia's background. She seemed awfully young to have all those responsibilities on her shoulders, and yet Ingrid was so impressed with her command of every area, together with her easy, outgoing interactions with all of the residents they'd met.

"Actually," Sylvia began, "I seem to have been at this for as long as I can remember. When I was a young teenager my grandparents unexpectedly moved to Florida. I was very, very close to them, so I was devastated when they went away. I don't think I stopped crying for days.

"Finally, my poor mother couldn't stand it any longer and suggested I go visit the folk at the local nursing home. I wasn't keen but I did it. And, to my great surprise, I loved it. They liked having a young kid around, while they gave me lots of laughs and a real sense of purpose.

"Long story short, I ended up volunteering until I graduated high school and moved away to college. But the experience stayed with me and I decided that environment was the right life path for me. I got my Bachelor's and then my Master's, all the while volunteering and doing intern work. I've been here six years and I love it."

"Well, I know I've only just met you, Sylvia," Ingrid said, proudly, "but as far as I can see this facility is lucky to have you at its head."

Later that evening, in the quiet of her apartment, Ingrid sketched out her plans for moving her project from the theoretical to the practical. She sipped her wine and ran her hand through her cropped, dark hair, as her mind raced in a dozen different directions.

What she'd seen and heard earlier in the day convinced her she had a potential *tour de force* of a documentary in her hands if she didn't screw it up.

She thought about Jack and Pearl and the dozen or so other residents she'd met and talked with. Most were interesting, funny and, most importantly, willing to share their pasts with her. She felt not only lucky but extremely privileged to be taken into their confidences. As much as she was giving them, Ingrid realized they were giving her so much more.

As she wrote and planned the themes of the documentary into the wee hours, a nagging thought kept popping into her head. *Josephine. Josephine.*

Josephine. Over and over this woman's name hammered into her brain like a persistent ache.

Ingrid hadn't even met her and yet here she was obsessing like her life depended upon it. *The only black person. Theatrical. Always muttering. Life and soul of the party.* Out of all the people she'd met or heard about that day, it was as if Ingrid needed to discover everything she could about Josephine. Was her story worthwhile telling? What happened to her in her ninety years on this earth? Would she even consider talking to a stranger?

Ingrid finally went to bed with all these thoughts still floating inside her head. She didn't know any of the answers but in the days and weeks to come she decided it was her duty and destiny to find out.

Chapter Two

They met accidentally, this twenty-five year old rookie filmmaker and a ninety-one year old black woman named Josephine Benson.

Ingrid began her preliminary research early the next day by joining some of the residents for breakfast. Most knew who she was and why she was there, so the conversations were light, friendly and interesting.

From the two dozen or so folk she spoke to Ingrid was able to assess the value and usefulness of their stories. Some went into great detail, while others skirted around obviously deeper, more personal events and situations. Ingrid thought these might hold the greatest promise; reluctance to divulge too much could possibly hide the most fascinating and private matters that shaped a particular life.

Her hand ached from the extensive note taking so she decided to take advantage of the half mile walking trail that Sylvia told her about yesterday. The weather, sunny but only moderately warm, allowed Ingrid to step out at a reasonable speedy pace. She was anxious to return to the residents but felt she needed a break to clear her head.

As she entered the monitored trail she noticed a small figure about a quarter mile ahead of her. At first, she thought it might be a child, perhaps a great grandchild, of one of the residents. It was only when she caught up to the figure that she realized the person must be Pearl Lister's nemesis, Josephine.

Ingrid studied the woman's features for a few seconds, surprised by the thick mop of silvery hair, bright, wide eyes and ebony skin that hardly showed a wrinkle. If this woman was ninety-one then it was a miracle.

Startled, Josephine stopped in her tracks, looking Ingrid up and down before cracking her face with the warmest of smiles.

Offering her hand, she said, "Josephine Benson, child. So very pleased to finally meet you. Walk with me a while."

Ingrid quickly fell into Josephine's pace, slightly nervous of what to expect next.

"Ingrid Strauss, Mrs. Benson. So happy to have this opportunity."

"*Ms.* Benson," Josephine corrected. "I never married. Came close once," she added, with more than a tinge of sadness. "What about you, child? You got yourself a husband?"

Ingrid screwed up her face in mock horror.

"Not for me right now. Too much other stuff I'm interested in."

"Yes, like us old folk here."

Ingrid nodded, before saying, "Exactly, although I don't mean to be rude."

As they walked, Ingrid noticed Josephine's particular and peculiar gait. It was as if she glided along the path rather than placing one foot in front of the other. Also conspicuous, and equally mesmerizing to Ingrid, was the way Josephine used her hands, gracefully gesturing all the time like butterflies flitting on the wind.

"You must be an educated person," Josephine speculated. "College, I expect."

"Film school. Four years of doing what I love. It was a dream."

"Doing what you love, eh? So wonderful for a young thing like you."

"I know I'm very lucky," Ingrid conceded. "That's why I want to give something back with my filmmaking."

They walked on in silence for a minute or two before Josephine stopped, turned and folded her arms.

"Child, you're just so curious to know what it must be like for me here with all these white friends of mine."

Ingrid stared back, tilting her head slightly.

"Actually, Ms. Benson, no I'm not. What I'm curious about is your life and how you finally ended up here."

Josephine chuckled at Ingrid's response.

"Well, now, that is a whole different story. How long you got, child?"

"As long as it takes, Ms. Benson. As long as it takes."

"Can I trust you?"

"Well, I'd like to put you on film so others can share in it."

"Not what I meant. Can I trust you to tell the truth?"

"Of course, but that cuts both ways," Ingrid suggested.

"Oh, I like you, child," Josephine chuckled again. "But you gonna have to work for your supper 'cause I'm not giving you an easy ride."

"The bumpier the better," Ingrid offered. "When can we start?"

"Let me think some more on all this. I may change my mind by morning."

Ingrid frowned.

"Then I'll hound you 'til you agree. I'm very persistent."

"Come see me in a few days," Josephine answered, peeling off the track and heading back to the main building. "You'll excuse me but I've got to get back and give that Pearl a hard time. She'll be missing me by now."

That evening Ingrid systematically entered her notes into her laptop. She categorized each of the residents' stories according to her own impressions of how well they fitted her definition of inspirational human narratives. There had to be hardship, failure, courage in the face of seemingly insurmountable odds and an indefatigable hopeful spirit.

Disappointingly, Ingrid found only a few that measured up to her criteria. But she'd only interviewed twenty-four residents so she was optimistic of discovering at least a handful more jewels in the mine.

And then she remembered Josephine Benson. For some reason, Ingrid knew for certain Josephine's story, whatever it was and whatever it contained, would be the *piece de resistance*. Her heart actually beat faster at the thought and promise of what Josephine might divulge. Would it be famine or feast? Would it be too difficult a story to film and convey its true meaning and relevance?

As she finally climbed into bed, exhausted but exhilarated, Ingrid well understood this documentary, this moment in her life, would probably define her for years to come. Scared but also excited, she slept well that night, confident in the knowledge of her ability to deliver everything she expected of herself and nothing less.

Over the next few days Ingrid conducted many more interviews, finally drawing a halt when the number reached fifty. She had to admit the sheer volume of stories was beginning to overwhelm her, and yet she marveled at the richness of the material as well as the variations and contrasts each remembrance brought to the table. She never imagined in her wildest dreams what treasure troves of memories would be revealed with such detailed precision and enthusiasm, even when those recollections sometimes recalled painful, turbulent or life-wrenching times. She regarded these residents as heroes not only for willingly sharing these difficulties but also for actually living through them and surviving.

As she was about to leave for the day Ingrid stopped by the library to visit Pearl. She felt particularly touched by some of the things Pearl had confided and wanted to thank her again.

Pearl was in her usual corner, this time munching from a tin of peanuts. As Ingrid approached, she heard Pearl loudly mutter, "Oh, for goodness sake, would you give it a rest for a while!"

Ingrid couldn't see anyone else around so assumed Pearl was talking to herself.

"Pearl, hi. Just dropped by to thank you again for your help. I absolutely loved your stories."

Pearl nodded, her face stern, almost angry.

"You're welcome. Hope you'll be able to use some of it."

"Of course. By the way, who were you talking to when I came in?"

Pearl sighed heavily.

"Her," she replied, nodding towards a tall shelf of books. "She's at it again. The woman never stops."

Ingrid glanced over but saw no one.

"It's Josephine!" Pearl said, angrily, as if Ingrid was too stupid to realize.

"Oh, okay. Is she disturbing you?"

"You might say that," Pearl answered, her voice snotty and mean. "Drivel. That's all it is. All day long. Mumbo jumbo. Nonsense. Aaaah, I can't stand it."

Ingrid took a couple of steps towards where Josephine was hidden and listened. She thought perhaps she might have a quiet word in an effort to smooth some feathers. As she listened to Josephine's utterances she frowned, cocking her head to hear a little better.

"O good Iago, what shall I do to win my lord again? Good friend, go to him; for, by this light of heaven, I know not how I lost him. Here I kneel. If e're my will did trespass 'gainst his love, either in discourse of thought or actual deed, or that mine eyes, mine ears or any sense delighted them in any other form. Or that I do not yet, and ever did, and ever will, though he do shake me off to beggarly divorcement, love him dearly, comfort forswear me!"

Ingrid tiptoed away as she heard Josephine continue speaking.

"Pearl," she said, addressing the other woman insistently, "that's *not* mumbo jumbo Josephine's speaking."

"Well, it sure sounds like it to me," Pearl answered, snottily.

"No, it's not," Ingrid continued, her heart beating overtime. "If I'm not very much mistaken, it's Shakespeare. What Josephine's quoting is Shakespeare. In fact, I think it's from Othello. And that's a speech by Desdemona."

"Desde who?" Pearl asked, nonplussed.

"Desdemona. She's Othello's wife. Oh my god, I'm stunned."

"Well I just wish she'd stop. It's just so annoying hearing her going on like that all day long. You can stay here if you wish but I've had enough."

And with that, Pearl said goodbye and marched out of the library.

Ingrid could still hear Josephine talking to herself and was in two minds about whether to interrupt her. She decided against it and tiptoed away unseen.

Arriving home, she texted Josephine to ask for an interview.

Can we meet tomorrow? Need to get your story. Any time will suit me.

Ingrid waited two hours for a reply but when it came she almost jumped for joy.

Yes. 10:30. I'm ready. Thank you. J

Ingrid spent the rest of her evening just *thinking*. She decided against making a list of questions as she had done with the other residents. She wanted a relaxed, spontaneous conversation with Josephine, which she hoped might produce the unexpected revelations she believed lay just below the surface of Josephine's life. She went to bed wishing ten-thirty wasn't still hours and hours away.

Chapter Three

On her way to meet with Josephine the next day, Ingrid stopped at a local bakery and bought them each tea and doughnuts.

"I haven't had one of these in so long," Josephine gushed, as she took a bite of the frosted jelly pastry.

They were sitting in a shaded, secluded spot on the grounds within admiring distance of Jack's horticultural handiwork.

Ingrid smiled seeing Josephine enjoy such a simple treat. Strawberry jam dripped down her chin, while the white frosting stuck to her fingers like glue.

"You know," Josephine continued, between bites, "when I was a child I never knew such delicious things existed. I mean, you got an ice cream a couple of times during the summer if you were lucky…but doughnuts… never."

"You were poor?"

"I didn't think we were, child. I always got fed. Shoes on my feet. My own room. I couldn't complain. And the place we lived was nice, too."

"Where was that? Where'd you grow up?"

"California. Little town outside Burbank called Westville. Of course, Burbank wasn't like it is today. Lots of green fields. Depots. Saloons," Josephine said, with a laugh.

"Any siblings?"

"No. Just me, Mama and Daddy."

"Happy child, were you?"

"No complaints. Lots of friends. We had fun from morning to night."

"What did your folks do?"

Josephine smiled and shook her head.

"Daddy was a grave digger. That's what the man did all day long. Hard, tough work, but he never complained. Did what he had to do to support the family. The good thing was, he was never out of work," Josephine chuckled and clapped her hands. "No, siree. The man was never out of work.

"I'd visit him sometimes, in the graveyards. Of course, I didn't appreciate the meaning of death or even being respectful. So, I'd dance around the headstones, singing silly songs, yelling their names like they could hear me. And that man let me do it. Probably helped to get him through his day."

Ingrid, too, giggled at the image.

"And your mother?" she asked. "What was she like?"

"Strict," Josephine replied, nodding and raising her eyebrows. "Made me mind. Oh yes, that was Mama. And she had a lot on her plate, too. Took care of everyone, or tried to. And she had a full time job as well."

"Doing what?"

"Seamstress. Oh my, child, I gotta tell you she was something else with a needle and thread. Could make a silk purse out of a sow's ear that woman. Really. And fast, too. I'd sit and watch her sometimes and get dizzy from my eyes trying to keep up with all those stitches.

"I think that's where I got my love of movies and the theater from. She was in high demand from one of those big film studios back then. They'd be calling her in a panic wanting her to fix some big star's costume. *Gone with the Wind*. You heard of that one?"

Ingrid nodded enthusiastically. "Of course, it's a classic."

"Well most of those dresses came right out of my mama's fingers. She was so proud to work on that film."

"You must've been so excited, as a child, to be around all that glamour."

"'Cept it wasn't glamorous for her, just hard work. She never got much recognition for what she did. And the pay wasn't that great, either."

"Josephine, can we talk about just you for a while?"

"All right."

"Yesterday I was in the library with Pearl and I overheard you talking to yourself. What was that all about?"

Josephine frowned.

"Nothing. It was nothing."

"Pearl thought it was mumbo jumbo, but I know differently. I recognize Shakespeare when I hear it."

Josephine stared blankly at Ingrid as if to say, *Why are you making all this fuss over an old woman's mumbling?*

Instead, she said, "We all have our heroes. He just happens to be mine. I learned it in school and remembered it. That's all there is to it, child. Okay?"

Ingrid shrugged, but she knew there was more to Josephine's evasion than she let on.

"Sure, but if I'm to include your story in the documentary I need to know the *full* story. You understand that, right?"

"All in good time, child. All in good time."

The rest of their session focused on Josephine's teenage years with some of those recollections being wrenching and heartbreaking memories, so much so that Ingrid called a halt to their talk for the day.

They sat for a while in silence. Ingrid stroked her new friend's hand, wondering all the while how Josephine would ever get through this. But even in her sadness Ingrid sensed Josephine possessed an incredible inner strength.

Indeed, here she was, some seventy years later, remarkably self assured, willing to look back on a life that gave her and made her…what? Ingrid did not yet know but she guessed there must have been monumental moments that brought Josephine from that point to this.

Finally, she gently led them both back to the main building and settled Josephine in her room to rest.

"You take care now. Okay? If you need anything just call or text me."

"Ingrid," Josephine answered, a sweet smile creasing her still handsome face, "I want you to come back tomorrow. I *need* you to come back tomorrow. I had hardships, yes, but I knew the world still held promise for me. I'd like to tell you about that if you'll listen."

"I will, Josephine. I will," Ingrid responded, with a tight hug. "You get some rest now and I'll see you in the morning."

Ingrid spent a long time that night thinking about how hard to push Josephine for her recollections. After all, her main purpose was to make a realistic documentary, warts and all, that told the truth. She knew before hand there would be moments in which the residents would become emotional and upset, joyous and introspective. Those feelings and experiences would be the very essence of the film and Ingrid needed to extract and harvest them to be successful.

At the same time, she hadn't reckoned on meeting someone like Josephine who obviously had a huge story to tell. Depending on what Josephine eventually told her, Ingrid seriously thought of switching gears and making this documentary only about Josephine. The other residents' stories would certainly not be lost or untold; a follow-up film could bring the project full circle.

Ingrid again brought tea and doughnuts the following morning. This time the pair sat in the comfort of Josephine's room, which was cozier than Ingrid had imagined. There was a bathroom, a comfortable looking bed, a good sized dresser, pictures on the wall and a host of knick-knacks on every shelf. In one corner sat a beautiful flat-screen television. Even the views from the large picture window were glorious.

"You're spoiling me too much," Josephine said between bites, as powdered sugar clung to her cheeks like soft, white whiskers.

"They're a bribe," Ingrid teased, as she, too, enjoyed a sweet treat.

After finishing their mid-morning snacks Josephine asked Ingrid to go to one of the drawers in her dresser and get her a clean handkerchief.

"You'll have to rummage around some I'm afraid. I'm not the neatest person when it comes to arranging my things."

Ingrid obliged but felt uncomfortable searching through someone else's personal items. The top drawer contained no handkerchiefs. The second drawer down was a mess but she thought she saw them under a pile of underwear. As she turned over the clothes her hand fell on an envelope. It was hard for Ingrid not to see who it was addressed to – Ms. Josephine Benson at her Westville, California home.

Ingrid moved the clothes out of the way and looked more closely at the envelope. To her astonishment the return address was *Academy of Motion*

Picture, Arts and Sciences. The envelope was clearly postmarked January 16th, 1950.

Ingrid now faced a dilemma; she was more than intrigued by the envelope but felt conflicted about how to proceed. Also, Josephine had specifically asked her to go to these drawers. Did she mean for Ingrid to find the envelope?

It was one of those moments in life when a split decision needs to be made. Without another thought for the consequences, Ingrid took hold of the envelope, turned and waved it in front of Josephine. She raised her eyebrows and waited.

With a look of great surprise, Josephine said, "Oh, no child, you found it." Covering her eyes with her hands, she mumbled, "Now I'll have to tell you everything."

Chapter Four

Ingrid gently embraced Josephine while leading her to an easy chair. She kneeled in front of her, holding her hands in one of hers while still grasping the envelope in the other.

"Josephine, you don't have to tell me anything you don't want to," Ingrid smiled, reassuringly. "But I have to admit I am very curious. I mean, *Academy of Motion Picture, Arts and Sciences*...c'mon, I know what that means."

"Open it," Josephine ordered, her head held high and proud.

"Really, you don't have to do this," Ingrid reiterated.

"Dear child, I said open it...so, open it. Go ahead."

Carefully, Ingrid reached into the already opened envelope and pulled out a card embossed with gold lettering. Her hand trembled a little and her heart beat faster as she brought the words into view.

Dear Ms. Benson,

It is my distinct honor to inform you that you have been nominated for an Academy Award in the category of Best Actress in a Supporting Role for your performance as Desdemona in the 1949 film Othello.

The Academy congratulates you for your outstanding performance. Along with the other four nominees, I hope you will be able to attend the ceremony at the RKO Pantages Theater on Thursday, March 23rd.

I offer my personal congratulations on your nomination and look forward to meeting you at the ceremony.

Very sincerely,
Charles Brackett, President

"Oh, my god!" Ingrid screamed. "Are you kidding me, Josephine? You were nominated for an Oscar!"

Josephine used a dignified grin to confirm the news.

"Pretty cool, eh, for an old broad?"

"Wait a minute," Ingrid said, looking at the envelope again. "This is dated January 1950. How old were you, for goodness sake?"

"If I've got my math correct…I was twenty."

"Twenty!" Ingrid yelled again. "You were nominated for an Oscar at twenty?"

"I was."

"For playing Desdemona? Now I'm beginning to understand the whole talking to yourself in the library scenario."

"A guiltless death I die. Farewell. Commend me to my kind lord. O, farewell!"

Josephine chuckled to herself before pulling a hand across her throat and grimacing.

"Desdemona's dying scene?" Ingrid offered.

"The very same," Josephine confirmed. "Quite good, wasn't I?"

Ingrid nodded enthusiastically, still trying to come to terms with Josephine's revelation.

"I'm going to need some time to process all of this; to get my head around it. I'm just so stunned. Does anyone here know?"

"Of course not, child. It all happened a long time ago. Nobody knows my name. Nobody cares anymore about what happened all those years ago."

There was sadness in Josephine's voice that almost cut Ingrid in half.

"Yes, Josephine," Ingrid insisted, "people will. This is exactly what I'm talking about. It's the whole reason I'm making this documentary. I need to bring these stories to life. Whether you like it or not, you are part of history."

"But it was just a movie, child," Josephine responded, modestly. "At the time I didn't think I'd done anything special."

"Josephine," Ingrid said, plainly, "you were nominated for an Academy Award. An *Academy Award* for goodness sake! You've done something very few people can even dream about. And let me tell you something else; to be nominated your performance must've been spectacular. I mean, oh, my god, I'm in the presence of an Oscar nominee."

"I do not know. I am sure I am none such."

"Okay, you can stop with the Desdemona charade now," Ingrid answered, grinning. "And before we go any further with this, tonight I'm going to track down a copy of the movie and see just what it was you were up to. Jesus, this is so exciting!"

"Zach," Ingrid yelled down the phone, "you are not going to believe any of the shit I'm about to tell you!"

Zach Jeffreys lifted another forkful of Chinese sweet and sour to his mouth as he prepared to listen to his crazy friend's latest wild idea.

"Ingrid, hi to you, too." He chewed and swallowed before giving her his undivided attention. "What? What is it I just can't wait to hear?"

"No, really, Zach, this is completely cool shit. And I'm going to need you sooner that I thought."

Zach wiped his mouth and settled back on the couch. He was so used to Ingrid calling him at all hours with half-baked proposals and hopeful projects that he knew would never see the light of day.

But he'd known her since they were in film school together, where he studied the art of cinematography, and realized that her passion for becoming a filmmaker would eventually lead to a spectacular career.

He was not in the least surprised when she won the Murray Film Institute Award, but he was taken aback when Ingrid asked him to be her cinematographer on the documentary project.

"You know me, Zach. You understand exactly what it is I'm always aiming for. You're the only one I trust to take the shots and turn them into a masterpiece. Honestly, I can't do this without you. I don't *want* to do this without you. And, besides, the prize came with fifty grand, which I'm more than willing to share."

His response was simple and heartfelt.

"Count me in, of course, but keep your money. I'm doing this because I believe in you, Ingrid. So, yeah, let's go make a movie."

And so for the next half-hour Ingrid brought Zach up to speed on her visits to the nursing home in general and her meetings with Josephine in particular.

"So, I need you to work your magic and find this 1949 movie of Othello. Doesn't matter what time you send it over. Just, please, find it for me."

"On it already," Zach responded, as he began the search. "Hopefully it'll get to you in the next half-hour."

"Great! Then I'll call you. I know it's short notice but I'd like you there with me tomorrow, Zach. Can you manage?"

"Just tell me when and where."

"Will do. Now, go to work and find me that movie."

As good as his word, Zach forwarded *Othello* within the hour. Ingrid made popcorn, grabbed her note pad and began streaming.

The black and white film opened with the cast superimposed upon a panoramic shot of old Venice. The accompanying music was suitably dramatic and mournful.

Ingrid's quick eyes scanned the list of characters and actors. Sure enough, third from the top, she read *Desdemona............Josephine Benson*. Although she had always taken Josephine at her word, Ingrid was gratified to see the official confirmation. Still awed, she stopped the movie for several seconds to read over and over again – *Desdemona............ Josephine Benson*. The moment was profound and almost magical.

The first scene in which Desdemona appeared brought her face to face with her father. It was full of conflict and Ingrid marveled how this raw twenty year old handled what must have been monumental pressure. Her delivery, poise and command of such difficult lines reminded her of someone of the stature of a young Meryl Streep. The performance was that impressive.

She stopped the film again, this time to study Josephine's face and body movements. Her astonishing beauty took Ingrid's breath away. High cheek bones seemed to frame her wide, dark eyes. Her mouth, sensual and alluring, also struck a completely innocent chord with its youthful smile and childlike diffidence. Her black hair hung in long ringlets around her slim shoulders like a crinkled scarf.

Ingrid moved on, this time paying particular attention to Josephine's vast array of facial expressions. For one so young, she thought, she seemed to effortlessly cover a vast landscape of emotions with just a meaningful look or a poignant gaze.

In all of her scenes with her co-star, Stewart Harding, Josephine not only held her own but managed to match his command and presence by significantly stamping her own demeanor and style on the film with every line she uttered.

As the movie neared its conclusion, Ingrid wondered how Josephine handled Desdemona's dying scene. After all, she was only twenty and possibly unfamiliar with tragedy. But then Ingrid recalled Josephine mentioning some hardships she'd suffered as a teenager. Perhaps those memories were all she needed to pull it off.

The scene moved forward with Othello angrily flinging Desdemona onto a low bed. As she tries to get up among terrifying appeals for mercy, he kneels beside her, puts both hands around her throat and begins to strangle her. Her head is over the side of the bed, with her flailing hands trying desperately to grip Othello's muscular arms.

Ingrid's eyes were wide open as she held her breath watching Josephine gurgle and struggle to stay alive.

Finally, she delivers her last line: *A guiltless death I die. Farewell. Commend me to my kind lord. O, farewell!*

Instantly, Ingrid recognized the line. It was the same one Josephine quoted to her earlier in the day, word for word, perfectly, and delivered as if seventy years hadn't passed at all. Ingrid just shook her head in disbelief. It was the performance of a lifetime and now she understood just why Josephine had been nominated for an Oscar.

Chapter Five

For nearly seventy years, Josephine Benson had kept her remarkable achievement mostly to herself. Now, in a flash, it came to light in the most extraordinary way: a total stranger had unearthed in a second her secret of a lifetime.

After Ingrid left, Josephine sat silently in her room with only her galloping thoughts for company. Finally, she lay on her bed, closed her eyes and tried to think what she would tell Ingrid the next day. For her age, her memory was good, but as she tracked back through the years there were gaps she found hard to fill.

Nonetheless, her mind was clear about the major events. She smiled and chuckled as she remembered some, while others brought tears to her eyes. People, long since gone, now danced before her, taking her quickly back through times she'd actually lived but which now seemed somehow unreal or unbelievable.

She walked again down the path of her disappointments, imagining what she could have done to change anything. The same applied to her successes, finding herself wondering why she, Josephine Benson, had deserved any of the good things that happened to her.

In the end, when she grew tired of recalling her past, she thought on balance she'd lived an interesting life. She felt proud and satisfied of her ninety years on earth. Now the question was, would Ingrid Strauss feel the same way?

For her part, Ingrid watched *Othello* twice more before succumbing to tiredness and sleep. Each time she noticed different aspects of Josephine's performance which only enhanced her already esteemed view of this young woman's acting ability.

She was awake by six o'clock and immediately called Zach.

"Get yourself going, buddy," she crackled down the phone. "We need this amazing woman on film ASAP. I'll pick you up at nine. Be ready."

Zach not only didn't grumble, he actually welcomed Ingrid's insistent demand. Being with her usually meant uncertainty, spontaneity and excitement. If she was enthusiastic about something then it was not only good but potentially spectacular. He showered, ate, grabbed his gear and was ready by nine.

On the way to the nursing home Ingrid talked non-stop filling Zach in on her discovery of Josephine's Oscar nomination.

"Can you imagine, Zach, being twenty and nominated for an Academy Award? It's just mind blowing."

"Ingrid, I watched the movie, too," Zach admitted. "She deserved it. From my point of view the cinematographer did one heck of a job. The angles, the close-ups and the way each scene was staged…just great. But none of it would have mattered if she hadn't been as magnificent as she was. You're right…just mind blowing and I can't wait to meet her."

"I'm seriously thinking of splitting the documentary into two parts," Ingrid admitted. "The first would be the other residents telling their stories, which believe me, are amazing in their own rights. And then the other part would be solely devoted to telling Josephine's story. What d'you think?"

"I think you need to decide that for yourself. But it does seem that way you'd get the best of both worlds," Zach advised. "Whatever you decide it'll be an amazing documentary and I'm just happy to be along for the ride."

"Zach, seriously, you're never just going to be along for the ride. You work magic behind the camera, so shut the hell up about being a hanger-on," Ingrid admonished, with a huge grin.

"Your humble servant," Zach retorted, bowing his head, prayer-like from the passenger seat.

"I wish," Ingrid answered, laughing. "Oh, look, we're here."

Ingrid helped Zach unload his equipment before they made their way inside the nursing home. They found Sylvia in the lobby and Ingrid introduced her to Zach.

"Can we talk for a second?" Ingrid enquired. "There've been some changes I'd like to make."

"Sure. Let's go to my office."

With the door closed, Ingrid began explaining to Sylvia what she had in mind.

"Do you know anything about Josephine's past?" she pointedly asked Sylvia.

Taken slightly aback, Sylvia said, "Well, yes, some of it. Why, what do you mean?"

"Do you know she was once nominated for an Academy Award?" Ingrid replied, raising her eyebrows and opening her hands.

"What?" Sylvia answered, incredulously. "You mean, an Oscar?"

"Yes, an Oscar."

"Oh, I think she must be pulling your leg, Ingrid. She's quite the joker is our Josephine. The residents come up with all sorts of crazy stories sometimes."

Zach quickly pulled out his phone, brought up the movie and handed the device to Sylvia.

"Take a look, Sylvia," he said, politely. "Don't think this is a joke."

Sylvia studied the scene for a few seconds before handing back the phone.

"Hard to tell if it's her or not."

"Then look at this," Zach offered, as he pulled up the character/actor list.

Sylvia read – *Desdemona............Josephine Benson* over and over again just as Ingrid had done.

"I'm floored," she exclaimed, looking bemused at both of them. "Right here in our home we have an Oscar nominee?"

"You do. Amazing, eh? And to think it happened seventy years ago. Now," continued Ingrid, "in the light of that discovery I'm thinking of changing the format of the documentary. I'd like to split it up into two parts. The first would consist of some of the other residents telling their astonishing stories, and then part two would be devoted to Josephine."

"Would you give the others a fair hearing? They've been so looking forward to having their day in the sun."

"Of course. That's what the project is all about – documenting lives that seem to have been lost or forgotten. But, because of her age, I'd like to concentrate on Josephine first. I'd like to get her story in the can as soon as possible."

"Yes, that makes sense," Sylvia said, with a smile. "Don't want to lose this now."

"Exactly. And the other thing I'd like to do is keep this between ourselves. The less people who know about this the better. I want the documentary to be a surprise and speak for itself."

"Gotcha. My lips are sealed."

"Sylvia, you're the best and, again, I can't thank you enough for all your help."

Zach took a quick look around some of the available rooms for taping Josephine's segment, finally settling on a section of a small, window-filled lounge. After setting up the lights, boom and camera, he found a comfortable chair for Josephine and decorated the area on both sides of it with vases of fresh flowers. He checked his equipment one last time and told Ingrid he was ready whenever she wanted to start.

"There you are," Ingrid said to Josephine, after knocking and opening her door. "We're all set to go. But first, oh my goodness, Josephine, I watched *Othello* last night...three times, actually. You were more than amazing and absolutely deserved your nomination. I can't wait to hear the full story. Are you feeling okay about all of this?"

Josephine, dressed in a colorful floral blouse, patted the bed beside her.

"Sit yourself down, child and tell me what I'm supposed to be doing."

Ingrid perched on the side of the bed and gently held Josephine's hand.

"First and foremost, I need you to relax and just be yourself. If you have trouble remembering just keep on going. Zach, my camera guy, can fix that later. When you need a break let me know.

"Now, I'll be sitting opposite you but I won't be on screen. I'll be asking questions, prompting and getting as many details out of you as I can. Then later, Zach will edit my part completely out so it will seem like you're just having a long, intimate conversation with the viewer. Sound all right?"

Josephine took a while to respond but when she did her answer was full of reason.

"When I was in that film, before I was to shoot a scene, I would always think of my mother."

"Your mother?" Ingrid asked.

"Yes. Working on those films as she did being a seamstress, she got to see a lot of actors and actresses perform. She would often come home and over dinner tell Daddy and me about what she'd seen and heard.

"And the one thing that stuck in my silly ol' head was how she knew a good one from a bad one."

"How?" Ingrid pressed, intrigued.

"She said she could always tell by how the good ones prepared. They knew their lines backwards and forwards, even the ones of their fellow actors. They knew where to stand, follow the director's orders and were always, always on time.

"And that's what I did, over and over again. Young as I was, I followed those rules and I guess it paid off. So last night, child, I did the same thing. I prepared myself for today. Well almost," she chuckled, "because I kept falling asleep and forgetting where I was. But I've remembered a lot of what happened so I guess I'm about as ready as I'll ever be."

"One other thing," Ingrid cautioned. "I'd appreciate it if you'd keep your story to yourself for now. I want the documentary, when it comes out, to be fresh and extraordinary. Can you do that?"

Josephine smiled again.

"Oh, nobody listens to my ranting anyway, but I will keep my big mouth shut."

"You're a treasure," Ingrid told her, guiding her to the door. "C'mon, let's go make a movie."

Chapter Six

For Josephine, this moment caused a myriad of emotions to bubble to the surface. Walking with Ingrid she felt scared and defensive, but also liberated and happy. For the first time in a long time, Josephine knew she was about to release a lifetime of feelings, both good and bad but long since repressed.

"Zach," Ingrid said, ushering Josephine through the door to the set, "I'm honored to introduce my new best friend, Ms. Josephine Benson."

Zach put down his light meter, wiped his hand on his shirt and hurried over.

"Ms. Benson, I'm Zach Jeffreys and I'm truly humbled to meet you."

They shook hands as Josephine studied this stranger for a few seconds, taking in his short, dark hair, neatly trimmed beard and features that made her raise her eyebrows.

"My, my, Ingrid, if only I was a few years younger. So pleased to meet you, young man."

"Oh, don't tell him that," Ingrid mocked. "He already thinks he's God's gift to women."

They all laughed as Zach led Josephine to her appointed seat.

"This is nice," she said, looking around and settling in. "I feel comfortable already. Thank you, Zach." She winked and turned to Ingrid. "Now, where do you want me to start?"

"Just as soon as Zach tells us he's ready to roll I would like you to introduce yourself and begin with your earliest memories and just carry on from there. If you get stuck, don't worry. I'll jump in with a question or you can stop and take a break. Do you need anything before we start?"

"No, child, thank you. As Stewart always told me before our scenes together… *Now is not the time to panic, dear heart. Remember the audience. That's who you're doing this for.*"

"All right," Zach said, standing behind the camera. "All you have to do now is look straight ahead and begin talking. After three. One, two, three…"

"My name is Josephine Benson and I'm ninety-one years young," she began, with a broad smile and a firm, calm voice. "My earliest memory is when I was about four, sitting on my daddy's lap and he bouncing me up and down like a yo-yo. I must've loved it because I don't recall ever screaming or hollering at him to stop.

"I was raised in a small town in California called Westville, just outside Burbank. That's important because of what my mama did to help feed the family. We were poor but we always got by. Lots of people were kind and gave us things. That helped my mama and daddy. I enjoyed the life I had because I always had hopes and dreams.

"My parents taught me love and forgiveness, because they were always loving and forgiving. Those lessons have served me well, too. They tried to do their best for me with what they had. And they always reminded me that I didn't need to be perfect.

"School, when I grew up, was a one-room place with only the bare essentials to help us with our lessons. I remember my teacher was Miss Howe. My, I thought she was the loveliest thing I'd ever seen. She helped me a lot, passing on clothes she'd gathered. They were cute but I didn't pay too much attention to my appearance. I'd go change and she'd say, *Josephine, you are such a pretty little thing. You're also smart and kind.* Those comments stuck with me and made me who I am, even today, at ninety. I think that little girl did pretty good.

"But she never let us get away with anything and, believe me, we tried real hard.

I was a good student but I recall always being tired, having a hard time keeping my eyes open on account of the illness. Something to do with my lungs and poor blood. Doctors thought I'd caught something bad from the muddy creek we used to swim in every summer.

"Anyway, they took me to the hospital in Burbank and I think I spent maybe a month or more in there 'til they said I was cured. It was about that time, I was maybe eight, when I got real interested in the movies on account of my mother…"

"Josie! Josie!" Mrs. Benson called to her daughter. "Supper's on the table. Time to eat."

Josephine washed her hands as her father poured water from a big steel kettle into the stone sink. He carried her to the table in his muscular arms, a tradition she always enjoyed.

"Have some exciting news to tell you," Mrs. Benson said, her eyes dancing with joy. "But first, honey, you should tell us how your day was at the school house."

Josephine put down her fork and finished chewing. She remembered being told many times it wasn't polite to talk with your mouth full.

"It were good, Mama…"

"It *was* good," Mrs. Benson interrupted. "Remember those verbs you've been learning."

Josephine nodded respectfully.

"Sorry, Mama. It was good. Miss Howe taught us some real neat ways to add hard numbers together. I think I know how now. Then she let us go outside. I played hopscotch with Earl and Hannah May. We had a real good time."

"Good. That's good, honey. What about you, Daddy?" she asked, turning towards her husband.

"Same job, different day," Mr. Benson replied, dourly. "We dug three new ones and filled in two more. Not much else to say."

"'Cept you're doing important work for people," Mrs. Benson answered, as sweetly as possible. "Folk die and folk need to be buried. You're doing God's work."

Mr. Benson nodded as he helped himself to another spoonful of rabbit stew.

"Mama," Josephine squeaked, "what's your news?"

"Oh, my, let me tell you it is exciting! Got to work today on one of those big new movies. It's called *Gone with the Wind*. Must be costing lots of money because all the dresses I've been sewing and mending are just so rich and beautiful. And I heard today that Clark Gable is the big star. My, he's such a handsome man if you don't mind my saying so, Daddy?"

With delicious rabbit stew gravy dripping down his chin, Mr. Benson shook his head as if he didn't give a damn.

"Is it a love story, Mama?"

"I don't know, child, but Miss Vivien Leigh is in it, too, so I'm guessing it might be."

"Oh, I hope so, Mama. Them love stories are…"

"*Those* love stories," Mrs. Benson corrected again.

"…sorry, Mama. Those love stories are so nice and friendly. Can I come visit with you sometime?"

"I won't make any promises but I'll try my best."

"Thank you, Mama."

Two weeks later Josephine's mother gave her daughter the surprise of her life.

"Tomorrow morning, child, you put on your Sunday best because I'm taking you to the studio. They gave me permission and said they'd even have a special treat in store for you."

Excitement and expectation for children produces vastly different reactions. For Josephine, the prospect of being taken to a big movie studio made her imagination run wild. She constantly watched the barnyard clock by her bed as the swishing tails of two cartoon goats moved around its face indicating each slowly passing hour.

Her mind jumped all over the place as she wondered what the surprise her mother had promised could possibly be. Perhaps it might be watching her sew or mend a pretty dress. Maybe she'd be allowed to play with some of the animals she always saw in the films. She didn't really know but she hoped for many things…many wonderful things.

For this special occasion, the head of wardrobe for the studio, whose husband happened to own a '31 Packard, offered a ride to and from the studio. Usually, Mrs. Benson walked a mile to the nearest bus stop, so this was, indeed, a treat for her, too.

When morning finally came, at an early six o'clock, Josephine made her bed before laying out her good church clothes. She wanted to look her best, to make her mama proud.

"Now, don't you just look like the prettiest picture I ever did see," Mrs. Benson exclaimed, running her eyes over Josephine from head to foot. "Isn't she a sight for sore eyes, Daddy?" she continued, glancing at her husband.

"Growing up fast and good," Mr. Benson, added. "You deserve one of my biggest hugs ever," he said, opening up his huge arms.

Josephine loved feeling her father's strong hands around her back. They made her seem safe and unafraid.

"All right," cautioned her mother, "you remember those rules I told you. Now, we'd best be getting outside. Mr. Hoyle will be here any moment."

Within minutes Mr. Hoyle arrived in his shiny, cherry red '31 Packard. Josephine had never seen such a sight in her life. To her, the car was like a huge, magic castle, with its high sides, silver running boards, monster trunk, white-walled tires and gleaming silver everywhere. She stood gazing at it for the longest time until Mr. Hoyle came around and pointed out the sparkling silver hood ornament.

"I see you've noticed the Goddess of Speed," he said, proudly.

"It looks like a girl flying through the air," Josephine offered. "What is she holding, Mr. Hoyle?"

"A silver tire. That's why she's called the Goddess of Speed, because this darlin' can move very fast."

Josephine saw herself flying through the air, too, before her mother ushered her into the top-down back seats.

"Mama, this is a *big* automobile," Josephine squealed, as she sank into the lush leather seat. "I feel like a real princess in my shiny carriage."

"Then you just enjoy it, honey-child, 'cause this won't happen very often."

Josephine pulled herself up and stared back at the people who stared as the car passed them by. She began smiling and waving, thinking she was the queen of heaven and the Goddess of Speed.

She grasped her mother's hand and squeezed, saying, "Thank you, Mama. This is the best day of my life."

"Oh, we're not finished yet with your surprises," Mrs. Benson offered, nodding. "We've got a few more treats up our sleeves for you, girl."

Josephine could barely take it all in. Her heart jumped and her eyes couldn't possibly get any wider. *More surprises! More surprises!* Her mind raced again, imagining what could be any better than this.

When they arrived at the studio Mr. Hoyle acted like the perfect gentleman, helping the ladies down from the car.

"And when you're ready to return home it will be my pleasure to drive you," he said, bowing.

Mrs. Benson and Josephine shook his hand.

"Why, Mr. Hoyle," Mrs. Benson offered, "I think you're the kindest man I've ever met...except for my husband," she added, with a smile. "What do you say to Mr. Hoyle, Josephine?"

Remembering her manners, Josephine whispered, still in awe of the experience, "Thank you kindly, Mr. Hoyle. Just wait 'til I tell all the kids at the school house what I got to do. They ain't never going to believe me!"

"*They're not* going to believe me," corrected Mrs. Benson.

"Sorry, Mama. *They're not* going to believe me," Josephine repeated.

Mr. Hoyle laughed, secretly impressed with the way Mrs. Benson reminded her daughter to use proper grammar.

"And you two are most welcome," Mr. Hoyle said, before bowing again and walking back to his car.

Mrs. Benson held Josephine's hand as she led them through the big double wrought iron gates. They were met just inside by a security guard who waved them through without a second thought.

"Good morning, Mrs. Benson," he said. "See you've got yourself an assistant today."

"Indeed I do, Mr. Watson. My daughter, Josephine."

"How d'you do, young lady?"

Josephine nodded, scared out of her wits to see a man in uniform.

"Let me give you one of our special badges," Mr. Watson continued, with a smile. "Only very important people get one of these."

He bent down and pinned a gold star with the letters VIP onto Josephine's dress.

"Now you're all set to go," he said, enthusiastically. "You both have a wonderful day."

Mrs. Benson led Josephine through a maze of stage sets making Josephine's eyes bulge even wider. To her, the sets looked like different, wonderful scenes from wonderland, with their strange, colorful buildings rising before her like something she'd only seen in a dream.

A street, complete with stores and street lamps; a castle flying so many red, white and blue flags; the inside of a grand mansion and, best of all, models of a scarecrow, a lion and what appeared to be a person made out of tin. It was almost too much for Josephine to comprehend.

Mrs. Benson, noticing her daughter's astonishment, smiled.

"Pretty amazing, eh, honey-child? I told you there'd be surprises."

"Oh Mama, I can't believe it!" Josephine gushed. "You must be very special to work here, Mama."

Chuckling, Mrs. Benson answered, "No, baby, I'm just lucky. Now, c'mon, I'll show you where I work."

There were five seamstress' stations scattered around a large airy room full of light. The other four women were busy sewing and altering clothes when Mrs. Benson and Josephine walked in. They stopped working immediately, rushing over to greet their colleague and her daughter.

"My, my," Loretta Pearson exclaimed, as she set eyes on Josephine. "Ain't you just the prettiest thing I ever saw?"

The hug she gave Josephine was warm but crushing. Josephine could barely breathe but she whispered a thank you all the same.

The other ladies also gathered around, sprinkling the air with compliments and good wishes. After things settled down, Mrs. Benson took Josephine to her own station and began showing her daughter all the tools of her trade. To Josephine, everything her mother demonstrated seemed very complicated. She was amazed how her mother could possibly remember it all.

Mrs. Benson took some scraps of discarded material, sat Josephine down at her sewing machine and talked her through the process.

"This is how you hem. This is how you make a buttonhole. This is how you fix a tear."

The list went on and on. Mrs. Benson noticed Josephine's eyes were becoming glassed over and decided enough was enough. Now was the time for another surprise.

"Honey child, your mother's got a real big treat for you. One I've been working on for quite a while."

Mrs. Benson went to one of the storage cupboards and pulled out a large, white box. It was decorated with a huge, red bow.

"This is for you, sweetness, and I hope you like it."

Josephine stood back admiring a box that was almost as big as her.

"It's not my birthday, is it, Mama?"

Mrs. Benson laughed.

"No, it's not. This is just something I wanted to do for you to let you know how special you are and how much I love you. Now, open it up."

Josephine carefully removed the bow and took off the lid. Inside was a mass of pink and blue tissue paper. She carefully rummaged around, removing the paper until she found another, smaller box.

Before taking out this box she glanced at her mother, who nodded that she should open it.

"It won't bite, honey," she assured, smiling. "Go on, open it."

Josephine lifted the lid and stared into the box for the longest time.

"Well, aren't you going to take it out?" her mother asked, encouragingly.

Josephine carefully removed a midnight blue dress that she soon saw was covered with silver sequins. She held it up before her, stunned that anything so beautiful was hers.

Finally, she gasped, "Oh, Mama! Oh, Mama, it's so pretty." And as tears flowed down her soft cheeks, she cried, "Is it mine? Is it really mine?"

"Sure is, honey-child," her mother answered, as she, too, began to cry. "Now come with me. We got to have you put that beautiful dress on. C'mon."

The dress was long and flowing, making Josephine seem much older than her eight years. Looking in the dressing room mirror, she also *felt* older, like a real grown-up.

Before Josephine hardly caught her breath, her mother whisked her off to the make-up department, where her friend, Sally, stood waiting to do her magic.

"My, my," Sally exclaimed, "you look like a million dollars already! All I need to do is fix your hair a little and add a teeny-weeny something to your face."

Sally placed a white shawl around Josephine's shoulders and went to work. In a short time she transformed an eight year old girl into a starlet to rival any on the set.

"So, what d'you think, baby?" she asked a startled Josephine.

The astonished child could barely speak. She did, indeed, look like a million dollars. She couldn't believe the person staring back at her was really her…really little Josephine Benson. It was amazing.

Presently, there was a hustle and bustle in the make-up room as an entourage entered surrounding a young, pig-tailed girl, maybe fifteen years of age. She wore a blue gingham pinafore dress with an off-white, short-sleeved blouse, which gave the impression she had just come in from the country. She made herself comfortable before a large mirror and waited to be attended to.

Josephine stepped back, scared of all the commotion this apparently important person had caused. But the young lady, out of the corner of her eye, saw Josephine retreating and yelled for her to stop.

"Yes, you," the girl continued, as Josephine, startled, halted in her tracks. "You don't have to leave just because I'm here. C'mon, sit down next to me. My name's Judy. Judy Garland. What's yours?"

Josephine could hardly move let alone sit down. She looked at someone who was fresh-faced, poised and so beautiful. She stood frozen to the spot until Judy left her seat and led her to the chair next to hers.

"There," Judy said, warmly. "Now, tell me who you are?"

"Josephine Benson," she whispered, still afraid. "My mama works here as a seamstress."

"Oh, I think I know her!" Judy exclaimed. "She makes the most fabulous clothes for all of us in the movies. She even made this," Judy commented, pointing to her outfit. "And I know she made yours, too," Judy continued, "because you look so beautiful."

"Thank you," Josephine replied, shyly. "Are you in the movies?" she quietly asked, still in awe.

"Yes, I am. In fact, I'm making a movie right now. It's called *The Wizard of Oz*. So much fun. Did you walk through the sets as you came in?"

Josephine nodded.

"And did you happen to see a scarecrow, a lion and a tin man?"

Josephine nodded again.

"They're all in the movie. When I'm done here I'll take you and show you around if you like?"

Josephine could hardly believe what she heard. *A real movie? Me, on a real movie set?*

"Yes, I'd like that very much if it's not too much trouble for you? I know you must be real busy."

"Oh, I get to take all the breaks I want," Judy answered, confidently. "I'll even introduce you to my dog, Toto."

By the time Josephine and her mother returned home they were both exhausted from having done and seen so much.

Despite her tiredness, Josephine could not stop thinking or talking about every magical thing that happened to her that day.

"Daddy, it was just the best day of my life! Mama showed me where she works and what she does. And all her friends told me how beautiful I am."

"Which you are, sweetie-pie," interrupted her father, proudly. "Which you are."

Josephine blushed but secretly loved the comment.

"And then I met this girl, Judy...Judy..."

"...Garland," said her mother, helping her out.

"Yes, Judy Garland. Thank you, Mama. She's a real film star and she's making a movie called *The Wizard of Oz*. She was so kind and showed me all over the beautiful sets. There's a farmhouse, where she lives. A beautiful village called Munchkin land, full of bright, colored flowers, cute little houses and a bridge over a river. And, oh, a yellow brick road that she and her friends take to meet a wizard, I think.

"There's a forest with apple trees that talk. And a witch's castle... and...and," Josephine continued, taking a breath, "an Emerald City with big green doors.

"Her friends are a scarecrow, a lion and a tin man. And, oh, I almost forgot, she has a dog called Toto. He's so cute and kept giving me kisses all the time."

Josephine took another breath before saying, "Judy told me a secret I'm not supposed to tell anyone, but I think it's all right if I tell you. She said she wears sparkly, ruby slippers in the movie. I guess they're magic."

"My, my," Mr. Benson said, raising his eyebrows. "Sounds like you've had one very happy day."

"Oh, and I forgot...Judy said she'd take me to the big party they'll be having when the movie comes out. That's if it's all right with you, Mama?"

"Oh, yes, honey-child, it most definitely is all right with me. In fact, I've got a sneaking suspicion your daddy and me will be there, too."

Josephine didn't understand what *sneaking suspicion* meant, but she was overjoyed that her parents would be there with her.

"And now, sweetness," said her mother, with a frown, "I think it's time someone went off to bed."

Dutifully, Josephine kissed her father, hugged and thanked her mother for the longest time, and went quickly off to bed to hopefully dream of witches, Toto, Judy Garland, ruby slippers and, of course, the mysterious yellow brick road.

Chapter Seven

Josephine didn't realize it but from that point on her life would never be the same. Her excitement from her day at the studio did not wane for a second. In fact, after meeting Judy Garland and seeing all the amazing, beautiful sets, Josephine Benson, at the tender age of eight knew what she wanted to do; what she wanted to be.

Returning to school, Josephine regaled her friends and her teacher, Miss Howe, with such colorful and charming stories about her experience that Miss Howe decided there and then to start an after school activity for the kids to write and perform their own play.

Josephine and her friends came up with a story involving a good genie who grants each neighborhood kid one wish. For the fifteen students in the schoolhouse this was a moment that mattered in their lives; a moment when they could reach beyond themselves to create and become something bigger, something more meaningful, exciting and exclusively their own.

Each child created his or her own character, while the oldest boy played the genie. Mrs. Benson offered to make all the costumes, the result of which stunned the students and Miss Howe. On the day of the performance Mrs. Benson even brought in some of her friends from the make-up department, making the characters believable, exquisite and unforgettable beyond words.

Of all the performances that evening, Josephine's stood out like a shining star. She remembered her lines perfectly, delivering them with confidence, clarity and emotion.

Afterwards, one member of the audience drew her aside, telling her exactly how well she'd done.

"Oh, you were just amazing, Josephine. I can't believe you've never acted before. Now I'm jealous. How can I ever hope to be as good as you? Your future is set. You, young lady, are going to be a star."

Josephine could hardly believe her ears. She knew it wasn't true, but she secretly loved hearing all the lovely, kind words Judy Garland had just said to her. *Judy Garland thinks I'm going to be a star! Oh, my!*

For Josephine, the next six years were filled with excitement, hard work and horizons almost beyond her wildest dreams.

As good as her word, Judy Garland invited Josephine and her parents to the premiere of *The Wizard of Oz*. For a ten year old, to be at such a magical event, with so many famous people, was not only surreal but life changing. If Josephine knew before she wanted to become an actress, then the premiere and all that entailed cemented her ambition. As she was later fond of saying, "Shakespeare said it all when he wrote, *'the be-all and end-all'*."

Mrs. Benson made sure Josephine's feet remained firmly planted on the ground. Her school work always took precedence over her burgeoning acting aspirations and, to her credit, Josephine continued to take school not only seriously but enthusiastically.

For the remainder of her time under Miss Howe's care Josephine flourished in an atmosphere that provided not only her, but all the students, with an encouraging mix of hard work, commitment and fun.

Plays and skits now became a regular part of the school's curriculum. Miss Howe saw how much these activities spilled over into other areas of the kids' education, improving beyond measure their writing, math and social skills. It was a program she would continue long after the initial class had left.

As much as Josephine loved and respected her classmates she knew at the age of fourteen it was time to move on. Fortunately, Mrs. Benson heard of a new, progressive academy not far from their home outside Burbank and managed, with a few pulled strings, to secure an interview for her daughter.

"Mama," she recounted later, "I was so scared. Three people asked me all sorts of questions, and I don't know if I did well or not. Then, they brought in someone from the film studio and he told me to act out this part he gave me on a piece of paper.

"I think I did okay because when I finished everyone stood and clapped me. Then they wanted to know if I had anything I'd like to perform. I think I must've surprised them when I did my favorite scene from *Romeo and Juliet*, 'cause someone said, 'You know Shakespeare, young lady?'

"I was still shaking when I left, but they all clapped me again and said I'd hear back real soon."

"Well, sweetness," Mrs. Benson answered, "as long as you did your best."

"And it sounds like you did," Mr. Benson added, confidently. "Whatever happens, child, we're so very proud of you."

The good news came quicker than anyone expected. A letter arrived three days later addressed to Josephine herself. This in itself thrilled her beyond measure since she'd received very little mail her whole life.

Dear Miss Benson,

We are pleased to inform you that a place has been reserved for you in our academy beginning in September. The members of the board were very impressed with you audition and feel you will be a real asset to our institution.

The letter went on to describe the terms of the offer, indicating that a full scholarship had already been purchased in her name. She was asked to accept or decline the offer within one week.

Josephine didn't understand most of the contents of the letter but she knew she wanted to go to the academy as much as she needed to breathe.

"What's a 'scholarship'?" she asked her mother, still unsure if it was a good or bad thing.

"Simply means you get to go there for free, which means a lot to your daddy and me."

"So, we don't have to pay anything at all," Josephine continued to ask, still bemused.

"That's right, honey. Seems someone else has taken care of that for us."

"But I don't know anybody rich enough to do that, Mama."

"Well, somebody knows you and cares enough about you to send you to that fine school for free."

It wasn't until years later that Josephine discovered her benefactor was none other than Judy Garland herself.

In September, Josephine Benson, spit and polished, in a new dress created by her mother, entered Burbank Performing Arts Academy for the first time. To say she was scared and shaking from head to foot would have been a massive understatement. It was worse than that; much, much worse. Josephine was literally speechless and in a torpor for most of her first day. So bad were her symptoms that she spent most of her time with a nurse who tried valiantly to help a fourteen year old girl out of a self-imposed coma.

At home that evening, Josephine vowed never to return. Her parents quietly listened until she'd finished her irrational ranting. Mrs. Benson finally put up her hand.

"Sweetness," she began, sharply, "that is quite enough. Me and your daddy don't want to hear any more of this foolish talk. It's all right you were scared. It's fine you were so nervous you couldn't speak. But let me tell you one thing that is not fine…you saying you are not going there anymore just because of those feelings.

"This, child, is an opportunity of a lifetime. Someone has given you the chance to follow your dreams. And you want to quit…just because you're scared! No, no, no. That is definitely not going to happen."

Josephine listened to the chastisement with a stone face. She well knew her mother spoke the truth. The problem was not with not wishing to return, the problem was coming face to face with kids who were probably better than her. For Josephine, this prospect was overwhelming.

At her grade school she was always the star, whether performing or writing the plays. But here, in an environment where everyone seemed to be talented, precocious and self-motivated, Josephine thought she could never, ever, measure up. She imagined herself as only being a failure, with her dream of becoming an actress as elusive as catching the wind.

"Tell us why you're so afraid, honey-child?" her father gently asked. "There isn't anything in this world you can't fix if you put your mind to it."

Josephine took a deep breath and began pouring out her heart. The scene was painful, heart-wrenching and sad. Her tears streamed down her cheeks, pooling in her lap until her new dress was soaked. But after blurting out her explanations, after trying hard to make sense of her desperate feelings, she actually felt better.

"What you've done," began her mother, encouragingly, "is to give yourself plenty of reasons why not, but not enough reasons why. Now, tell us all the reasons why you should and must go back to that school."

Josephine sniffed back more tears as she began thinking and turning a jumble of reasons over in her mind.

Finally, looking straight at her parents, she answered, "Because when you have dreams you should do the best you can to make them come true...no matter what."

"Even if it scares you half to death?" queried her mother.

"Especially if it does that, Mama. You've always told me the road is hard, not easy. But that doesn't mean you should just give up. I'm sorry, Mama, I kinda forgot all that good advice."

"But now you've remembered it," cut in Mr. Benson. "So, no harm done, child."

Josephine went to bed that night with a fresh outlook, making a promise to herself to no longer be scared but to just enjoy her new school as much as possible.

When she returned the next day she found a surprise waiting for her. As she entered the classroom her classmates gathered around her, offering huge hugs and beautiful words of encouragement. To say Josephine instantly became a different, more confident, student would be as inaccurate as saying the Mona Lisa is just a pretty painting.

Her first year skipped by remarkably swiftly despite the country's increasing involvement in the war. The students were largely protected from too much knowledge of the conflict by a curriculum that left them almost breathless, with little time to think of anything else but learning their craft.

At home, the war did raise its ugly head because both of Josephine's parents became involved in the ongoing efforts to support their country and the troops who were fighting.

Mrs. Benson joined a group of her colleagues at the studio making uniforms and parachutes for the troops on the front lines. Josephine's father, too old to be conscripted as a fighter, worked hard all day in a munitions factory, turning out the hardware he hoped would help win the war.

To their credit they seldom discussed with Josephine what they contributed towards the war effort. It wasn't that they particularly wanted to protect her from knowing too much about the war; it was more about just getting on with the jobs they knew they had to do with as little fanfare as possible.

Josephine, meanwhile, had her hands full with acting, writing and trying to master her regular educational subjects. She loved them all, even her math classes, which she found frustrating and challenging at times, but nevertheless interesting and worthwhile.

She excelled at English, adoring all the assigned books as well as improving her grammar and reading skills. The stories she wrote earned high praise for their creativeness, style and structure. She seemed to know instinctively how to pace a story so that the reader would always be kept guessing. She began writing plays so well that by her second year many of them were performed, on stage, by her peers.

As Josephine turned fifteen and the war dragged on, she unfortunately was destined to discover that not all casualties of war occurred on the battlefield.

One afternoon, in the summer of 1944, Mrs. Benson, hurrying to complete another uniform at her station, accidentally cut her hand on a pair of sharp scissors. At first, and through the next day, she thought nothing of it. It was only when it began to throb and swell that she realized she might have a more serious problem to deal with. And by the next afternoon, Mrs. Benson found herself in hospital as a very, very sick woman.

Chapter Eight

Ingrid Strauss stopped her interview, telling Zach to take five and to please get them all some tea. Then she sat close to Josephine, holding her hand and gently rubbing her shoulder.

Shortly after Josephine began reminiscing about her mother's illness, she started shaking her head and weeping softly. Ingrid immediately sensed this was a pivotal moment in her story, indeed one that may well cause her friend to call a halt to the whole project.

"Josephine, listen to me," she whispered closely, "you can skip this part if you like. I know how difficult reliving these hard times is for you. You don't need the stress. You don't need to put yourself through this ordeal. And you certainly don't need me asking you all these personal questions. If you want to cancel the whole thing I will fully understand. You are now more important to me than any documentary."

Josephine took a long time just staring at the floor, considering Ingrid's kind words. In her mind's eye she could still clearly see her mother as she was then, barely conscious, her face red and bloated, with her eyes just staring blankly at the ceiling. Even now, Josephine thought she could save her.

Ingrid's soft voice brought her back to reality.

"Josephine, we're going to stop for a while. I'm going to take you back to your room. You just need to rest, have some tea and be somewhere safe and comforting."

Ingrid helped the older woman up, guiding her down the hallway and eventually settling her in her favorite easy chair. Zach appeared, setting down two mugs of tea, before Ingrid drew a finger across her throat. He quickly retreated and began packing up his things for the day.

"I'll stay with you as long as you need me to," Ingrid vowed, after handing Josephine her tea. "I'm so sorry this has upset you. That was never my intention."

Josephine looked at her and smiled weakly, before taking Ingrid's hand in her own.

"It's so long ago now and yet it seems just like yesterday. I want to tell you. I do. It's a part of me, however painful. Please, dear, go tell your friend I want to go back. Tell him not to leave. This is really important for the story and for me."

Ingrid frowned. She was reluctant to put any undue pressure on a ninety year old woman. Yet, she saw in Josephine's eyes a determined, fierce look that told her she was made of steel. Ingrid decided not to argue the point, hurrying off to stop Zach from packing and leaving for the day.

Back behind the camera, Ingrid led off the interview with a softball question designed to ease Josephine back into the fray. But Josephine would have nothing of it.

"I left off talking about my mother's illness. We should begin again there," she insisted, sitting back, composed and ready.

Ingrid nodded before asking one of the most difficult questions she would ask in the whole documentary.

"Josephine, you were fifteen years old when your mother was admitted to hospital. When did you first realize she might die?"

Calmly, Josephine replied, "Well, I never did. My mother *dying*? The thought never entered my head. At the time, I hoped she'd only be in there a little while. My father kept telling me not to worry, that Mama would soon be home again.

"But two days crept into three. And before I knew it she'd been in a week, getting worse and worse every day. My father sheltered me from a lot of the drama, insisting I still go to school each day. But every night I saw her, she looked so ill, so bad."

Ingrid shifted uncomfortably, balling up her hands, feeling tense and intrusive. But she also understood her job here was to help Josephine tell her story in the most honest way she could.

"Did she recognize you? Could she still talk?"

"I think she did right up until the end, least that's what I kept telling myself. I'd try and hide my eyes from all the swelling, all the bloating that almost changed her from the beautiful woman I'd always known.

"So, I'd lay down on the side of the bed with her, cuddle with her and tell her about my day. Sometimes she'd look at me and smile, but, no, she didn't ever speak to me again. I like to think she heard every word I said, every word my daddy said, but I just don't know."

"Were you with her when she passed, Josephine?" Ingrid asked, again feeling like an intruder.

"Of course. Daddy brought me to the hospital, warning me first. It was really late. Really quiet. Apart from one nurse, it was just Daddy and me. He sat on one side of the bed, me on the other. We both held her hands, whispering to her, trying hard not to let her see us crying.

"We must've been there for a couple of hours before Daddy leaned in to kiss her and said he couldn't feel her breath on his face. He called for the nurse and…and…that was it. She died right before our eyes. Peacefully. It was so peaceful.

"I remember jumping onto the bed, hugging her for all I was worth, never wanting to let go. In the end, they had to pull me off." Josephine shook her head, still in disbelief. "Worst time of my life – then or since."

"How about your daddy, Josephine?"

"He took me home. He was very strong and brave until we got inside. Then he sort of collapsed into a chair and wept hard until morning. I stayed with him all night but I could never stop his weeping. From that point on he was a broken man, like half of him had died as well. He never recovered. He was never the same again. It was all so sad."

Ingrid choked up too, remembering someone close who she had lost, thinking time really heals nothing.

"But Mama's funeral was an upbeat occasion," Josephine eventually continued, bringing Ingrid out of her funk. "Lots of music; lots of laughter; lost of really nice people saying wonderful things about her.

"I didn't quite understand how we could have such a grand send-off for Mama because we hardly had two cents to rub together. But there was food and, of course, plenty of drink for the adults. She would've loved it. I know I kept thinking that. She would've loved it.

"It meant a lot to Daddy and me that lots of folk from the studio came and paid their respects. Made us feel like she was held in real high regard. Even Judy came, which surprised people but not me. That was the type of giving person she was. She even made a little speech and spent most of her time comforting me, making sure I was going to be okay.

"Years later, I learned it was her who'd paid for Mama's funeral. I returned the favor twenty-five years afterwards, when I helped pay for hers because she was almost broke."

Ingrid noticed the time had slipped by and, even though Josephine still seemed strong and talkative, decided now would be the moment to stop. They had covered a great deal of territory and information which Ingrid needed to pore over at length that evening. But the basic structure of the documentary was taking shape. She was elated with how things had progressed in such a short time.

She escorted Josephine to the dining room where they had tea together, talking about anything except her new friend's past. They were now relaxed in each other's company, laughing as though they'd known each other for years.

When Ingrid finally left for the night, the hugs they gave felt more like the embraces of close family members. Their relationship was now a credit to them both.

The day had been an emotional rollercoaster for Ingrid, so she could hardly imagine what traumatic feelings had streamed through Josephine's mind. *The woman's ninety, for goodness sake. What the hell are you doing? What are you putting her through? And for what? A documentary. Your stupid documentary!*

Ingrid pushed her half-eaten frozen dinner aside and gulped down the rest of her wine. Self-doubt had never been a problem for her. If anything, Ingrid had always suffered from an excess of confidence, usually convinced her actions, whatever they might be, were right and justified beyond reason. But, now? Now, she wasn't so sure.

The questions kept popping into her head. Am I doing this for me or for her? Can Josephine survive the emotional pressure I'm putting her through by remembering her past? How might her life change when the documentary is finished? The list went on and on. Just when she seriously thought of calling Zach and telling him she was abandoning the project, her phone rang.

"Ingrid, dear, I'm sorry to call so late," a tired-sounding Josephine began.

This is it, Ingrid immediately surmised. *She's about to make my decision for me.*

"Josephine! No, of course it's not too late. I told you, you can call anytime, day or night. What's up?"

"I've been thinking about the day…"

Here we go.

"…and what I've been remembering." There was a long pause on the line.

Oh, oh. It's over.

"So much," Josephine continued. "I've recalled so much I thought I'd buried a long time ago."

"Josephine," Ingrid cut in, softly, "you don't have to explain a thing to me. I completely understand. I know how hard this has been for you. I'll come and say goodbye tomorrow, and then I won't darken your room again. I'm so sorry this has caused you so much pain. Honestly, that was never my intention. My intention was just to tell your incredible story to the world."

The line went silent again.

"Josephine? Josephine, are you still there?"

Finally, Ingrid heard a chuckle from the other end.

"Honey-child, you think I want to quit just because I'm a little upset? No. No. No. And no again! You really thought that?"

This time, Ingrid took a while to respond. What she heard was both a relief and confirmation. Her project wasn't dead after all.

"Oh, Josephine, it just tore me apart what you were going through. But to hear you say you want to continue…well…there are no words, really."

"My mama told me I should never quit just because something's real hard. So, you and your young man should be here bright and early tomorrow morning so we can get some more work done. Now, I'm kinda tired, so goodnight and don't be late."

Ingrid poured herself another glass of wine, really relaxing for the first time in a long time. She was now able to sit back and take stock of where they were in Josephine's amazing story.

When she first began thinking about making a documentary about older people's lives, she thought the cumulative effect of interviewing them might produce, at most, a few, really interesting stories. *How wrong was that!*

Instead, she'd unintentionally stumbled upon a goldmine in Josephine Benson. *Academy Award nominee! Befriended by Judy Garland! A fan of Shakespeare! Performing Arts School! The loss of her mother!* And by this time, she was still only fifteen years of age. Amazing.

But what interested Ingrid now, what she ached to learn from Josephine, was what happened next. How on earth did she make it from fifteen to ninety? And how on earth did she end up in a nursing home being bothered by a documentary film maker?

Ingrid suddenly realized she might be becoming too obsessed with uncovering more revealing details about Josephine's life. Her job, as a film maker, was to simply tell a story wherever it may lead, not to go out of her way to sensationalize it. Ingrid suddenly realized that direction was where she may well be headed. She called Zach for a reality check.

"Zach," she fired down the phone, "I need your help."

"Again?" he joked, before asking about the problem.

"How d'you think it's going so far?"

"Well, pretty amazing, actually. You don't?"

"I'm worried."

"Not like you, Ing. Are you getting concerned Josephine's not going to make it much further?"

"Oh, God, no, Zach! The woman's as strong as a horse. No, it's me. I'm not sure I'm being objective enough."

Zach snorted down the phone.

"Hmm. Definitely not like you. Think you're getting too close?"

"I'm beginning to wonder if I'm consciously looking for more and more sensational stuff instead of just letting her story unfold. Am I hoping for too much from her now, Zach? Am I getting too far ahead of myself and Josephine?"

"You know, Ing, when you're behind the camera a lot like I am, you get an early sense of a person. Are they holding back? Are they telling the truth? What is it they're really trying to say?

"Josephine soon struck me as a straight shooter. She's not into bull-shitting you, in fact, quite the opposite. She simply wants to tell you her story as she remembers it. The questions you're asking don't seem to me to be leading her where she doesn't want to go. You're just coaxing her to recall things as best she can.

"Of course you need to pursue those areas most pivotal in her life otherwise you're wasting your time. But she's telling you what really happened in, quite frankly, an astonishingly down-to-earth way. So, no, your not being subjective. You're doing just fine. And, by the way, I can't wait to find out what happened next to her. Jeez, Ing, she's only up to, what, fifteen and I'm already blown away."

Ingrid didn't immediately reply, letting Zach's good sense and counsel sink into her brain. Then she smiled and nodded.

"What would I do without you, Zach man? Always there to give me a good boot up the ass. Thanks, buddy. Thanks a lot. Oh, be back at the nursing home by nine tomorrow, will you? Apparently, Josephine can't wait to get started again. Me, too. See, ya, bro. Bye."

Chapter Nine

After Mrs. Benson's passing, the Performing Arts School became Josephine's sanctuary and savior. Still fragile, but determined to carry on as best she could, Josephine found an abundance of love and purpose from her teachers and fellow students.

Help was always on hand for those days that were less than kind for her. But it was reassuring and solidly tangible help, not pitiful or merely sympathetic. Josephine soon came to realize no one would feel sorry for her just to feel sorry for her. The school became her family as well as her refuge, which resulted in a once scared and almost lost fifteen year old becoming strong and independent in her own right.

As much as her mother's death devastated her, Josephine slowly discovered an unexpected benefit; without her mother always behind her, always there to prop her up, Josephine actually began to find her own voice. Tentatively at first, but within six months she found a confidence and an unswerving determination which both amazed and electrified her.

As well as at school, the results of these new feelings manifested themselves most significantly at home. Mr. Benson could not, nor ever would, fully recover from his loss. More and more, Josephine found herself the parent rather than the child in their house. And it was a role she seemed willing to accept. The changes didn't happen overnight, but slowly, each day, the responsibilities gradually built until Mr. Benson relied so much on her and not the other way round.

Josephine cooked and cleaned while simultaneously working hard at school and continuing with her writing and performing duties. The latter activities were not chores but a positive form of therapy and rejuvenation. They kept her sane, grounded and always moving forward.

Meanwhile, Mr. Benson struggled to come to terms with his wife's sudden passing. A shell of his former self, he often became overwhelmed with grief, sitting in his room, sometimes for hours, crying and mumbling at the picture of her he found hard to put down.

Josephine tried everything she knew to comfort and relieve his despair. Sometimes she felt he was improving, going for days, even weeks, without breaking down. But eventually his darkness returned and she found herself back at square one. For one so young, it was at times all-consuming.

And yet, in the midst of this maelstrom, Josephine continued to discover positive strengths from within. And those strengths always emanated from the lessons learned at her mother's feet.

Now, after being forced to grow up fast, she began to feel almost like a different person. Mostly, she found an awakening of her confidence, which enabled her to think there really were no limits to what she might achieve.

As she entered her final year at school, a now seventeen year old Josephine began seeing her future in terms of how far she could go with an acting career. With her home life stabilizing somewhat and her father now seemingly better managing his grief, Josephine funneled most of her energy into all the school's productions.

Such was the quality of the plays, musicals and reviews being performed that the school began attracting the notice of professional groups and even some minor studios.

After one successful performance, a director with a local company specifically sought out Josephine.

"What is your name, young lady?" he asked, as he studied her features.

"Josephine Benson, sir," she replied, full-voiced and confident.

"Yours was an impressive performance tonight. How long have you been acting?"

Josephine smiled, as she answered, "Probably for most of my life. That's the way it seems, anyhow, sir."

"Tell me what you like about it?"

Josephine took a few seconds before replying, "Two things," she said, again with confidence. "I love being able to portray people who are totally different from me. Different feelings. Different mannerisms. And certainly different personalities."

"And the other?" he asked.

"Oh, that's easy," she grinned. "It's so much fun!"

The director studied her for a few seconds before asking, "Do you know Shakespeare's *'Antony and Cleopatra'?*"

Josephine's eyes lit up.

"We've studied it here and performed some scenes. I like her because she seems to be so complicated and driven."

"It's our next youth production. I think you'd make a credible Cleopatra. Would you be interested in auditioning?"

Josephine was momentarily stunned and speechless. *Me, in a real play? Oh, wow!*

"Yes, sir, I would. It would be an honor to try out. Thank you."

"I'll send the school all the details," the director concluded, as he whistled out the door, leaving Josephine still speechless.

Two weeks later Josephine found herself cast as Cleopatra, Queen of Egypt, in her first professional production. Dizzying was how she would describe it later, with forms to sign, lines to learn and daily rehearsals to attend.

Her experience with the school stood her in good stead. She'd learned discipline, timing and positive interaction with other actors, as well as confidence in her own ability to project and deliver a solid performance. The director seemed immediately impressed, so much so that he allowed Josephine some input into how Cleopatra should be portrayed.

For Josephine, it was important to stay true to Shakespeare's ideal, but she suggested a softening of some of her characteristics. Instead of lustful, Josephine offered a flirty rendition, with which she felt more comfortable. Instead of domineering, she played her with a subtle touch of over confidence. And instead of petulance and scheming, she fashioned a Cleopatra with more mood swings and changes in manner.

The director, however, still kept a tight rein on Josephine in rehearsals.

"Sweetness, that will not work in this scene," he insisted. "Listen to your lines. Would she really behave like that? I don't think so, and so, she's not. I want you to be more direct, more confrontational. She is the Queen of Egypt for god's sake!"

Josephine took the director's comments to heart, sometimes feeling she was letting him down for not truly understanding her role. She continually told herself this was a learning experience, again recalling her mother's advice to be open and accepting of new challenges and different points of view.

The mechanics of the play were a revelation, too. Sets needed to be navigated; blocking, positioning and movement had to be precise; entering and leaving a scene needed to be smooth, if sometimes dramatic, and just physically working with other, more seasoned actors, had to be perfected and enjoyed.

But at the end of rehearsals the majority feeling of the cast, director and crew was one of triumph and joy. Josephine, as one of the leads, felt nothing but love and respect from everyone. She was elated by the atmosphere and couldn't wait for opening night.

Josephine's positive attitude and general happiness began to transfer to her father. Never a gregarious man, he began taking more interest in his daughter's obvious natural abilities, asking questions about her daily life, the play and, more importantly, her future.

He came to realize how derelict he'd become in his role of father and supporter. In the past, when Mrs. Benson was alive, he mostly deferred to her whilst loving Josephine in the best way he could.

But now it was his turn to step up. He took on extra jobs to give Josephine a better life. He attended some of her rehearsals, sometimes applauding loudly in an empty theater, and sometimes crying, taken aback by his daughter's moving performance. To say he was proud almost beyond words was a massive understatement.

"Your mother, honey child," he told her one evening, while they sat on the porch, "would be over the moon with you. Oh, my, yes! Look at you, how you've grown, what you've done, what your about to do. Oh, yes, over the moon she would have been.

"I'm so sorry she's not here to see what a wonderful young lady you've turned into. But I want you to know that when you step out onto that stage she will be right there with you…every step of the way. And that's the truth, honey child."

"I know, Daddy. I know," Josephine answered, softly, holding his hand. "There ain't…sorry…there isn't a day goes by that I don't miss her so much. And I know that's the same for you, Daddy.

"She taught me so many good things. How to rightly behave. How to treat other people. And how I should never be afraid. I couldn't have done all this without her. She's here," she continued, touching her heart, "every single minute I breathe.

"And you, too, Daddy. Working so hard to help me all the time. I cry sometimes knowing just what you're doing to sacrifice for me. When I'm on that stage, Daddy, I want you to know you are always in my heart. I love you so much, Daddy."

Josephine folded herself onto her father's lap, arms tightly around his neck and tears softly rolling down her cheeks. This was a moment that mattered for both of them; an affirmation that what they shared was special, almost beyond words.

On opening night, Josephine was justifiably nervous but full of confidence, too. She always prided herself on knowing her lines inside out, which naturally left her the space to perform and project without the constant worry of missing cues or timing.

She glanced out through a slit in the curtain to see an audience much bigger than she expected.

"There must be three or four hundred people out there," she gasped at the actor playing Antony. Screwing up her face, she continued, "Please, James, don't let me mess up. Please."

James grinned while engulfing her in his enormous arms.

"Jo, listen to me. You've got this. You know the part backwards and forwards. Rehearsals have been great. Just go out there and do what you do best – act your ass off!"

Fortunately for Josephine, Cleopatra emerged very early in Act One, giving her no time to think about the audience or her nerves. And as befits a queen, Josephine charged ahead with her lines, performing them crisply and with appropriate authority. Immediately, she felt comfortable, smiling knowingly at James as they bounced the scene off one another.

When not on stage, Josephine looked on from the wings, drinking in the atmosphere and wonderment of being a part of her first professional production. And all the while she thought...*if only Mama could see me now.*

Throughout the evening the director offered Josephine subtle tips and continued encouragement, even though he clearly understood the performance he had on his hands. Even the audience, for long periods, sat mesmerized by a Cleopatra unlike any they'd seen before.

Of course, this adulation occurred before her final scene, a scene in which many an actress had, for one reason or another, failed to deliver a realistic and believable ending of Cleopatra's death. It was a moment full of possible pitfalls and crushing disappointment.

But Josephine, even at her youthful age, knew instinctively how to play the moment, with a regal air, lacking in pathos, yet full of appropriate sense and feeling. When asked later how she managed to conjure up such a profound yet down to earth performance, she explained that Cleopatra had to die a queen just as she knew her mother did.

The play ran for four nights and a matinee to near sold out audiences, which the company had never before experienced.

At the last night's wrap party the mood was justifiably ecstatic, joyful and overwhelming. The director addressed the cast and crew with high praise, pride and humility. The moment touched all of them as never before.

Amid the throng, just before Josephine was about to leave with her father, an imposing figure pushed his way through to her. Josephine at once seemed mortified by this stranger, staring at him as if he were unreal; an apparition.

He shook her hand, paying his respects, before speaking calmly but with authority.

"Miss Benson, I'm Stanley Masters and I wonder if you could spare me a few minutes of your time?"

Josephine still stared, hardly believing her eyes. She well knew who Stanley Masters was since he had directed many of her favorite films. *True*

Happiness; Lost but Not Forgotten; Memories and the one she loved the most, *Cara's Story*. And now this legendary director was standing in front of her asking permission to speak. The moment was truly unreal.

She managed a reverent response.

"Oh, yes, Mr. Masters, I do know who you are, and it's a real honor to meet you, sir."

"No, young lady, the honor is mine. I just wanted to tell you how much I enjoyed your performance. I have honestly never seen a Cleopatra played so well or movingly as you did tonight. May I ask how old you are?"

"I'll be eighteen on my next birthday, sir," she shyly answered, bowing her head. Out of the corner of her eye she saw her father still waiting to take her home. "Oh, and sir, this is my father."

"Mr. Benson, it's a pleasure," he said, shaking his hand. "I have to tell you your daughter is quite remarkable considering her youth." Turning back to Josephine, he continued, "I would like to give you my card. Please make an appointment with my office so we can talk about an upcoming project of mine. I think you might be perfect for one of the roles."

Josephine took the card, mesmerized as if it was made of gold.

"Sir, yes sir. But are you sure you've got the right person? I haven't had any parts in any films yet."

Masters laughed while respectfully patting her arm.

"Well, I pride myself on noticing extraordinary talent, young lady. You certainly fall into that category. So, yes, I am sure I have the right person in you. Now, if you will excuse me, I must be off. Please make that call. You won't regret it. Mr. Benson," he said, acknowledging Josephine's father, "very pleased to meet you, too."

When Masters had left, Josephine threw herself into her father's arms.

"Oh, Daddy. Oh, Daddy, what do you think he meant by saying all those nice things about me?"

Mr. Benson held his daughter at arm's length, smiling reassuringly.

"Honey child, I'm not sure but I think he may want you to be in one of those fancy films of his. I think he wants to turn you into one of those big movie stars."

Chapter Ten

"Stanley Masters! Stanley Masters!" Ingrid cried out in disbelief, interrupting the filming and startling Josephine. "Oh, my god, Josephine, I'd completely forgotten he directed you in *Othello*. The man's a legend and *you* got to work with him!

"I mean, he's right up there with Capra, Welles, Wilder and Hitchcock. Just hearing you say his name blows my mind."

"I don't know anything about that, child. All I can tell you is, they don't make them like him anymore. He was always a gentleman with everyone; cast, crew, producers and writers. Never once did I see or hear him lose his temper. And still he managed to get the best out of all of us. I was so sad when he passed over – heart attack, I heard, some time in the late Seventies."

Ingrid shook her head, gesturing to Zach with her outstretched hands as if to say… *Can you believe this woman worked with Stanley Masters?*

"All right, Josephine," she said, shrugging and smiling, "now I'm nearly over *that* shock, let's try and get you back on track. Are you okay? D'you need a break?"

"I am still very good to go on for a while," Josephine answered, her eyes lighting up with a cheeky smile, "if you can keep up?"

Ingrid poked out her tongue and grinned, too.

"So, where were we?"

"I just told you how my daddy thought I was going to be one of those big movie stars. And I did, also."

"Now, Josephine," Ingrid began, reverting to her interviewing tone as Zach rolled his camera, "after Stanley Masters gave you his card and asked you to call his office, what happened?"

"I left it for a few days because I was so nervous I could hardly speak. But eventually I called. They were very friendly, setting up an appointment and telling me Mr. Masters would send a car to pick me up.

"My, oh my, I felt like that eight year old princess again when I rode in that big car to go to Mama's studio. This time it was more modest but I still felt excited and special. My daddy insisted he came with me, which I was glad about. I could never have gone to such a place on my own."

"It was a meeting with Stanley himself, I assume," offered Ingrid. "Did he tell you what his project was?"

Josephine raised her eyebrows.

"Not only Stanley but a lot of other people, too. I'd never been in such a big room like that before. And everyone was looking at me. My daddy saw how frightened I was and held my hand the whole time.

"But Stanley couldn't have been nicer. He told me not to worry, to just look at him, which I managed to do. Then he began talking about his next film called *Othello* and how he thought I might have a role.

"Of course, I'd have to audition and do something called a screen test but that if I was as good as he saw me as Cleopatra I would probably get a role of some kind."

"When did he mention you playing Desdemona?"

"Oh, not for quite a while," Josephine replied, with a chuckle. "Guess he was still hedging his bets."

"Were you still at school at this time?"

"Yes, but I only had two months left. Stanley said he would begin the auditions and test as soon as I graduated. I couldn't wait," Josephine said, with a sparkle in her eyes. "And he was as good as his word. Two weeks out of school and I was at his studio performing," she continued, glancing at the wall clock. "Oh dear, sweetheart, I'm afraid you're going to have to excuse me for a while," she said, slowly rising. "It's karaoke time in fifteen minutes."

"Wait. What? Karaoke?" Ingrid answered, almost disbelieving.

"That's right, dear, every Thursday afternoon. And I have to go and change. Why don't you and your young man join us. We have a ball."

Thursday afternoon karaoke in the large activities room was the highlight of the week for most of the residents. Scheduled to last two hours, it often ran far beyond that because of the sheer number of hams eager to perform.

The nursing home staff, too, always enjoyed the event, going above and beyond to make sure the atmosphere was authentic and fun.

The deluxe karaoke machine had been purchased through a staff fundraiser, while Sylvia Richards, the administrator, emceed the proceedings with all the flash and hype of a Las Vegas night club. To further encourage the audience and performers, a glass of wine, a beer or a soft drink was set at each place.

As soon as Ingrid set foot in the room she felt the palpable buzz of excitement and joy emanating from the crowd. The residents were happy, talkative and, above all, laughing. Her spirits were immediately lifted as she and Zach took their seats in the back. The moment was totally unexpected and exhilarating.

"Ladies and gentlemen," Sylvia began, exuberantly, "and special guests," she continued, glancing at Ingrid and Zach, "welcome to the moment you've all been waiting for…Thursday afternoon karaoke!"

Cheers and applause greeted Sylvia's remarks.

"As usual, we have a large number of would-be Sinatras, Dolly Partons and who knows who else signed up for our show, so I will detain you no longer. Without further ado, let's have a very warm welcome for our first performer, Betty Harper."

Confidently, Betty stepped onto the small stage, winked at the audience and signaled for the music to begin. Dressed as Madonna, complete with a pointy bra over her blouse, she offered a hilarious rendition of *Material Girl*. Pouting and suggestive, Betty immediately won over the crowd, which responded with whoops of delight. Just the way to start the afternoon.

Ingrid and Zach shook their heads, clapping and laughing along with everyone else.

"This is so fantastic," Ingrid said over the noise. "And she's only the first."

"We've got to get some of this in the documentary," Zach answered, still laughing. "Maybe next week, if Sylvia agrees."

Ingrid nodded before the next performer took to the stage.

This time it was Jack, the nursing home's unofficial gardener. Again, there was no hint of nerves, which wasn't surprising since he was a retired school teacher. Jack was nattily attired in a dark suit, white shirt and red tie. He looked dashing and suave.

"Time, my friends, for a little of Ol' Blue Eyes," he smirked, smoothing down his hair. "And no rushing the stage when I'm done," he joked.

His friends were already with him, clapping and hooting for all they were worth.

He cued the music and the early strains of *New York, New York* filled the room. Again, Ingrid was totally amazed by the performance. Jack strutted and played to his audience almost as well as Frank himself. His voice, although raspy and out of tune, still did the song justice. In the end, the whole room joined in and anyone not knowing the time of year would have thought it was New Year's Eve.

Sylvia called for an encore which Jack, feigning the right amount of humility, duly obliged. Zach and Ingrid were on their feet, hooting and howling with the others. Both had never experienced anything like it before.

After several more folks sang their songs and an intermission, Ingrid was surprised to see Pearl Lister, Josephine's nemesis, preparing to perform. Ingrid remembered her from the scene in the library where she seemed prim, proper and rigid. It would be interesting to see how she might handle singing in front of so many people.

Sylvia calmed the audience before quietly introducing Pearl. True to form, Pearl looked demure, controlled and almost passionless. That is, until the music started and she began singing Julie Andrews' *My Favorite Things*. Ingrid could barely believe her eyes and ears. What a transformation! Her timing and diction were crisp. Her subtle movements impressive. And, above all, she seemed to be having so much fun. Just enjoying her was therapeutic in itself. *Honestly,* Ingrid thought, *can this get any better?*

Pearl played to the crowd while they responded by repeatedly singing the refrains over and over again. In the end Pearl signaled *enough* by pretending to faint through sheer exhaustion. Jack helped her off the stage and back to her seat as the applause rang around the room.

"Now," Sylvia said, "we come to our final performer." She glanced towards Josephine who was already standing and ready to go. "I know this lady is a favorite of you all and so, without further ado, I give you the amazing Miss Josephine Benson."

Josephine, resplendent in a full length cream dress and a shocking pink head scarf, took the microphone from Sylvia and waited for the cheers to die down. Ingrid found herself holding her breath, wondering what this ninety year old woman would do.

"In honor of a dear, distant, friend," she began, brightly, "I give you the great Eartha Kitt's *Just an Old Fashioned Girl*."

"Oh, my god!" Ingrid mouthed to Zach. "She knew *Eartha Kitt*."

"I have no idea who that is," Zach whispered in reply, with a shrug.

Ingrid frowned before quietly answering, "Dumbass. I'll tell you later."

Zach shrugged again as they turned to the stage to listen to Josephine, who had dispensed with the karaoke machine.

She stood silently for a few seconds, eyes closed, as if collecting memories from long ago to guide her through. But when she began not a sound was heard except her mesmerizing voice, which purred and rang with the strange diction that was Eartha Kitt through and through. All her movements were reminiscent of the late singer, right down to the raised eyebrows and suggestive smiles. Hers was not just a great performance; it was a moment that left everyone watching stunned and just grateful to be there.

While Josephine gracefully accepted the accolades, Ingrid noticed something about her performance which strongly suggested she had done this many times before. She was polished and confident as well as exuding an almost star-like quality. Ingrid could clearly see Josephine perhaps fifty years ago belting out tunes in some nightclub somewhere. She made a mental note to ask her friend later about her supposition.

With the performances complete it was time for everyone to talk, laugh and enjoy what remained of their drinks.

"So, what did you think of our little concert?" Sylvia asked Ingrid and Zach, with an expectant grin. "Not bad, eh?"

"It was so good, Sylvia, that Zach suggested we incorporate it in the documentary. I agree, if that's okay with you?"

"I'd be disappointed if you didn't. It'll be wonderful to show some of the positive things that go on in here. And I know for sure these folks would get such a kick out of seeing themselves performing in a movie, so to speak."

When Sylvia left to mingle, Ingrid sought out Josephine, determined to discover more about her singing history. She found her nursing a cup of tea, feet up, in an easy chair.

"Well, Josephine, you continue to amaze me," she crowed, pulling up a chair and sitting close. "Eartha Kitt? Really, now."

"What, child? You think I made that all up? Really, now."

Ingrid grinned and shook her head.

"No, I totally believe you. What I want to learn is when and how?"

"I'm ninety-one, sweetness," Josephine answered, sipping her tea. "Lot of years to fill and I think I filled them pretty good."

She chuckled and continued sipping her tea.

"Oh, no, Miss Smartass," Ingrid countered. "You're not getting off that lightly. This is all about your *whole* life. You need to spill the beans about you and Eartha Kitt."

"All in good time, honey child. All in good time. But right now I need to take a nap. That singing up there sure took it out of me."

She closed her eyes and lay back in her seat. Ingrid took the cue, leaned in and kissed Josephine softly on the cheek.

"Yeah, you've certainly earned a nap, Miss Benson. I'll see you bright and early tomorrow."

Josephine waved goodbye before suddenly opening her eyes and calling after Ingrid.

"I will tell you this, sweetness. That Oscar nomination was only the start. Oh, yes, indeed. There's a whole lot more for sure and if you're a real good girl I might tell you about it one day."

She closed her eyes again while Ingrid could only begin to wonder what on earth to make of it all.

Chapter Eleven

"I want you to block everything out," Stanley Masters began, as Josephine stood before him and his assistants, "and just read as naturally as you can. You can begin in your own time."

Josephine Benson, just eighteen years of age, looked around the room and was instantly terrified. Cameras, lights and so many people surrounded her while waiting for her to start her screen test. The words on the paper seemed a blur as she tried her best to focus. She felt isolated until she saw her daddy gently nodding and holding his hand across his heart as if telling her this was her moment to shine. Josephine nodded back, even managing a faint smile.

"How now, my lord? I have been talking with a suitor here. A man that languishes in your displeasure."

Stanley stepped forward, playing the part of Othello.

"Who is't you mean?"

"Why, your lieutenant, Cassio. Good my lord, if I have any grace or power to move you, his present reconciliation take; for if he be not one that truly loves you, that errs in ignorance, and not in cunning, I have no judgment in an honest face. I prithee call him back."

"Went he hence now?"

"Yes, faith; so humbled that he hath left part of his grief with me to suffer with him. Good love, call him back."

"Not now, sweet Desdemona; some other time."

"But shall't be shortly?"

"The sooner, sweet, for you."

"Shall't be tonight at supper?"

"No, not tonight."

"Tomorrow dinner then?"

"I shall not dine at home. I meet the captain at the citadel."

Stanley stopped speaking his part and stood directly in front of Josephine.

"With this next speech of Desdemona's, I want to hear from you a very convincing tone and your movements should be strident, too. Remember, you are trying your best to persuade Othello to take back or reinstate Cassio to his good graces. I need to hear your strong belief that your opinion is the right one for Othello to accept."

Josephine tried hard to absorb Stanley's directions as her mind still fought the fear and apprehension she felt just being in the same room with him. She took a few seconds to calm herself before nodding that she was ready to proceed.

"Why then, tomorrow night, or Tuesday morn, or Tuesday noon or night, or Wednesday morn. I prithee name the time, but let it not exceed three days."

She ended the line emphatically, even gesturing with her finger in Stanley's direction. He nodded and smiled.

"Yes! Exactly that. Good. Good. Carry on."

"I' faith, he's penitent; and yet his trespass, in our common reason save that, they say, the wars must make examples out of their best is not almost a fault t' incur a private check. When shall he come? Tell me, Othello. I wonder in my soul what you could ask me that I should deny or stand so mamm'ring on. What? Michael Cassio, that came a-wooing with you, and so many a time, when I have spoke of you dispraisingly, hath ta'en your part – to have so much to do to bring him in? Trust me, I could do much –"

"Prithee no more. Let him come when he will! I will deny thee nothing."

Again, Stanley stepped in front of Josephine.

"With this next speech, you need to show your ability to convince Othello that you are not testing him in any way, merely that he should do what is right and just. Okay?"

Josephine nodded, this time more confident she would be able to deliver the lines as he wished.

"Why, this is not a boon. 'Tis as I should entreat you wear your gloves, or feed on nourishing dishes, or keep you warm, or sue to you to do a peculiar profit to your own person. Nay, when I have a suit wherein I mean to touch your love indeed, it shall be full of poise and difficult in weight, and fearful to be granted."

"I will deny thee nothing! Whereon I do beseech thee grant me this, to leave me but a little to myself."

"Shall I deny you? No. Farewell, my lord."

"Farewell, my Desdemona. I'll come to thee straight," Stanley said, finishing the scene, before nodding exuberantly. "Good! Good!" he enthused, stepping closer and giving Josephine a celebratory hug. "I have to tell you, Miss Benson, you did everything I wanted and more. Now, I want you to go with this young lady and our photographer will take some studio shots of you. Head and shoulders...that sort of thing. Nothing to be alarmed about. Now, off you go and thank you again for your time and performance. I will be in touch."

It would be the last Josephine heard from Stanley Masters for nearly a month. As the days dragged on she assumed the worst; that she failed her test and had been passed over for another, more experienced actress.

Her father consoled her as best he could, but at times like these it was her mother Josephine missed the most. She kept busy, trying hard not to think about the audition or what she might have done better. Slowly, as she played the scene over and over in her mind, Josephine decided her performance for Stanley was not only good but worthy of all she was, all that she had learned.

At times like these, her mother's voice came through to her loud and clear. *You hold that head of yours high and proud, sweetness. As long as you did the best you could there is nothing to blame yourself for. If they don't want* *you, then that's down to them and their poor judgment.* Josephine could hear her mother laughing at her last comment.

In an effort to take her mind off her disappointment, Josephine began looking in earnest for work. It was tiring and demoralizing since no one seemed in a huge hurry to hire someone whose only experience was high school and local theater. But then one morning, close to four weeks after finishing her audition, the mailman brought her a letter. Opening it, she saw it was from Stanley Masters himself.

"Daddy! Daddy!" she cried out. "Mr. Masters wants me to be in his new film. Look! Look!" she almost screamed, as she handed her father the letter.

"Oh my! Oh my, sweetness. I guess you really did it. You, in a film… can hardly believe it. Come here and give your ol' daddy a hug."

They sat close rereading the letter as Mr. Benson purred out his pride in his daughter's accomplishment.

"Seems like I've got to go to his office and sign some papers," Josephine said. "And he's going to send another car, too. You'll come with me, won't you, Daddy?"

"Sure. Sure, baby. And I'll make sure I take a real good look over those papers. I'm not letting you get into anything bad, d'you hear?"

"Thank you, Daddy. Thank you. I love you so much."

"Your mama would have been so proud of you, too. We gonna go out tonight and celebrate a little. Not every day a daddy gets to take a real movie star to dinner!"

As big as she was, Josephine climb onto her daddy's lap, threw her arms around his neck and hugged him for the longest time. It was a moment they would both remember for all of their lives.

Josephine, totally unprepared for the reception she received at the studio, almost ran from the building before Stanley Masters could reach her. It was only the huge bouquet in his arms that stopped her. He gestured for her to stop walking away and make her way over to him.

"Miss Benson," he began, leaning in and smiling, "we are all so glad you could come today. Please, you and your father come over here and sit. I have some exciting news that I think you'll want to hear sitting down."

Josephine, awed but curious, took a seat and waited as Stanley brought in one of the leading men of the day, Conrad Taylor. Josephine stared without blinking as Stanley ushered Conrad towards her.

"Miss Benson, I'd like you to meet your new co-star, Conrad Taylor. And Conrad, this is your new co-star, who is going to be one of the greatest Desdemonas ever, Josephine Benson."

Conrad, dark, handsome and grinning with a million dollar smile, extended his hand.

"So very pleased to finally meet you, Josephine. I can't wait to get started."

Josephine stared at both men for what seemed like an age before looking at Stanley.

"You mean, I got the part? I'm playing Desdemona? But, Mr. Masters, I thought she was a white girl?" Josephine asked, confused.

"In this film I'm turning things on their head," Stanley confirmed. "There's absolutely no reason you cannot play her."

"You mean it? You really, really mean it?"

"Oh, it was never in doubt," Stanley told her. "The only hold up was trying to sign up this guy," he continued, with a laugh. "But as soon as he saw your test he couldn't wait to play Othello."

"That's right," Conrad confirmed. "I couldn't believe it when Stanley told me you've never been in a movie. My word, at eighteen you have the talent of a seasoned actress. And I know you'll make an amazing Desdemona."

Josephine could hardly believe her ears. This was *the* Conrad Taylor not only speaking to her but also telling her what a great actress she was. The emotion of the moment quickly caught up to her as she burst into tears. The two men, completely understanding her reaction, let the tears play themselves out until she recovered. They waited with reassuring grins.

"Daddy. Daddy, did you hear all that, Daddy?" Josephine almost wailed to her father. "I'm going to be playing Desdemona. Me, Desdemona. I can hardly believe what I'm hearing."

Mr. Benson stepped forward, embracing his daughter in his massive arms.

"Sweet child, it ain't nothing but what you deserve. Let me tell you that. These fine men have made the right decision. I know that for a fact, too."

Stanley interrupted them to give out some more good news.

"We're going to have you both go down to our legal department now and sign some papers. You read them carefully, now. I want you to be satisfied and happy with what I'm offering. But I will tell you we'll be paying you one hundred dollars a week for as long as we're making the film. How does that sound?"

Oh good Lord! One hundred dollars a week. Josephine could only imagine how much money that was. She was used to scrimping and living on just a few dollars *a month*. Now someone was going to pay her one hundred dollars. It all seemed too good to be true.

But it wasn't. The contract she was offered, which her father carefully looked over, did indeed specify one hundred dollars a week. In addition, there would be a car to take her to and from her home, as well as all meals and numerous incidentals she hadn't even thought about. Her father gave his consent and Josephine signed her first movie contract. It was another moment that mattered and one she would remember all her life.

Shooting started on the movie in the summer of 1948. Josephine had turned nineteen earlier that year and the studio threw her a small party as a kind gesture to welcome her into their family. Attending were her father, a few friends, Stanley Masters, her new co-star Conrad Taylor and one surprise guest.

"Well, now, just look at you," a glassy-eyed Judy Garland began, as she sauntered through the door. "My little child is all grown up. My, oh my."

Josephine, startled at Judy's presence, ran over and hugged the now famous movie queen. Overwhelmed that such a star would even remember her from so long ago, she found herself tongue-tied and teary-eyed.

"Oh, it's okay, sweetie," Judy's voice comforted her. "Come over here with me so we can spend some quiet time together. C'mon."

Judy led them to a small alcove where she drew up two chairs.

"So, I hear you've got yourself quite a part in Stanley's new film."

Josephine nodded, still self-conscious.

"And Conrad's co-starring. That's going to be some challenge. He'll expect a lot from you. But," Judy continued, "if Stanley's put his faith in you then you're half-way there. Stanley doesn't make mistakes…simple as that."

Josephine listened carefully as Judy imparted more advice. She began to feel more at ease, more confident about the weeks and months to come.

"By the way," Judy said, grabbing Josephine's hand, "I've seen your test." Nodding and smiling, she continued, "Quite frankly, my dear, I was blown away. Now I'm looking over *my* shoulder."

They both laughed before Judy became serious.

Leaning in, she whispered, "Don't let them eat you alive, sweetie. This business – and it is a business – will chew you up and spit you out if you allow it to. Even though you're young, be sure to always try and stick up for yourself. Remember, and this is so very important, you and only you own yourself and your integrity. Do what *you* think is right. Otherwise you might end up like me…full of booze and pills. That's all, sweetie. That's all."

Josephine seemed stunned by Judy's admissions, but as she looked at her more closely she saw how her friend's features had changed since their first meeting. Judy's face, always angelic to Josephine, now appeared fatter and puffier than she remembered. Her eyes, once sparkling with youth and promise, showed wear and tear, tiredness and almost resignation. The images shocked Josephine so much she averted her gaze.

"I know. I know," Judy conceded. "But I'm okay, sweetie. I can take care of myself. But you…you're just starting out, so I need you to listen and learn. Sure, take the roles, have fun but also be aware of what might be around the next corner. That's all I'm saying…be aware. Now, enough of me being a downer. Today is all about you. So, let's go grab ourselves something to drink and have some laughs. C'mon. C'mon."

Chapter Twelve

After a weekend break Ingrid was anxious to get Josephine before Zach's camera and have her relate the nitty-gritty details of actually making *Othello*.

By this time, Josephine was elated to be basically telling the story of her life. She found it emotionally fulfilling and fun. The process of remembering, hard as it sometimes became, gave her enormous pleasure even when the details were seemingly trivial or unimportant. Events and moments long since forgotten provided her with an inner glow, suggesting that perhaps her life had meaning after all. And to be relating it to a wider audience...well that was such an added bonus.

"Josephine," Ingrid said, as they sat in their normal interview positions, "this next portion of the documentary is all about you making *Othello*. I want the audience to get a real sense of what you went through, what it meant to you and, more importantly, how you think it turned out both personally and for the project in general.

"I know I can't wait to hear your story because it's not only amazing but historical as well. So, my dear, whenever you're ready, I'll begin with my first question."

Josephine relaxing, made herself comfortable for what she knew was going to be a long session. She smiled and nodded approvingly at Ingrid, ready, as always, to proceed.

With a twinkle in her eyes, she answered, "I did a lot of thinking back over the weekend, sweetheart. My, oh my, I sometimes have to pinch myself that it all really happened. But it surely did," she chuckled. "It surely did."

"All right," Ingrid jumped in. "Let's start." She glanced at Zach who gave her the thumbs up. "Now, Josephine, we're at the point where you're about to begin work on the movie. Can you describe your first day on the set?"

"Just sheer hard work," she replied, laughing. "I was given the script and a coach. She stayed with me every day for about three weeks going over and over my lines until I was word perfect. Exhausting, let me tell you. I was exhausted. I mean, Stanley really meant for me to earn my hundred dollars a week. Oh, yes!

"But on the bright side, I was so ready. Stanley worked methodically, planning out every scene, making sure we understood exactly the effect he wanted. Conrad helped me a lot, giving me tips to sharpen my performance, making sure I was comfortable and just being there for me when I needed it."

"And when the filming actually started," Ingrid asked, "how was that? I mean, this was your first film, Stanley had invested a lot of faith in you, so I imagine the pressure was enormous."

"Well, you know what," Josephine replied, pointedly, "Stanley, learning my lines and working with the other actors were not my biggest problems. Oh, my word, no! My biggest problem was the actual filming process. It was a lot different in those days. And I wasn't prepared at all."

"How so?" Ingrid asked.

"For one thing, everything seemed so large. Bulky cameras. Huge bright lights. Technical people all over the place fixing this and fixing that. It quite overwhelmed me for a while.

"But the hardest of those things to cope with were the bright lights. You see, Stanley decided to film it in Technicolor, which was quite a new thing back then. And to make sure the colors came out right they had to use these very big, bright lights to keep the reds, greens and the rest true and realistic. I'm telling you, making a movie back then wasn't the easiest thing in the world.

"Anyhow, the bright lights really got to me. They gave me headaches, affected my eyesight and made me very dehydrated. My lord, they even had one person on set whose only job was to keep me drinking lots of water between takes. And if they saw I was getting weak and weary, Stanley would order a halt for an hour or so. I tell you, making a film back then wasn't all glamour and excitement. Most of it was just sheer hard work, grit and determination to get you through each day."

"Josephine, could you tell us how Stanley directed you and, also, how was it working with such a famous star as Conrad Taylor when you were so young and this being your first film?"

Josephine took her time answering. She seemed to be replaying the events in her mind, nodding occasionally and gently smiling.

"Stanley, I remember clearly, told it like it was. But he also wanted us to be pleased with our performances so he asked for lots of input. For instance, say, after a scene where Conrad and I were at odds, Stanley would want to know how we felt it played. Did we feel emotionally attached or thought we were convincing enough? If we said we thought we could do better, he would say, *Just as I thought, sweethearts. Just as I thought. You want to do it again, don't you?* I liked that very much about Stanley. He actually cared what we mere actors thought.

"Conrad, as I've told you, helped me a lot. It was almost as if he saw me as his little sister. Very protective. Generous in our scenes together. Always professional but an awful lot of fun. He loved playing practical jokes on me. And I usually fell for them. One time he told me he had a brand new way for me to get home. Naturally, I figured there was a shiny, fancy motor car waiting, just like the one Mama and I rode in that time.

"So, he blindfolds me and leads me out to the parking lot. When he took the blindfold off there was this polished gold chariot awaiting me, which he'd managed to borrow from the set of one of those Roman epics someone was making. It was so bright in the sun it almost blinded you.

"However," Josephine paused, giggling, "instead of it being driven by a couple of black Arabian stallions, there were only two poor, pathetic donkeys hitched up to it. We laughed so hard...my, oh my! But that was Conrad...always ready with a joke or a prank. And, I might tell you, we went for a ride around the parking lot and caused quite a stir. Oh, yes!"

"The film itself?" Ingrid asked. "How long did it take to complete?"

Josephine thought for a moment.

"I guess we finished our parts in about four or five months. I remember it seemed like such a long time to produce a two hour film. But then it took Stanley quite a while to edit it and do all the technical things he had to do."

"So, it was released in nineteen forty-nine then?"

"Yes. I believe it was around May or June of that year. I had turned twenty earlier so it was kind of like a birthday present to me."

"What did you think when you saw it for the first time?"

Coyly, Josephine answered, "I thought I was pretty darn good. My daddy was there. At the end of the movie he stood right up in front of everyone, clapping and hooting for all he was worth. *That's my girl,* I recall him yelling. *That's what I'm talking about!* The embarrassment almost made me hide under my seat."

"Was it strange seeing you up on the screen?" Ingrid asked. "Could you really believe it was truly you up there?"

"Oh, I have to admit, child, it took me by surprise. But after some few minutes I kind of got used to it, almost like watching someone else. And let me tell you one thing, I thought that actress, whoever she was, couldn't have played the part any better," Josephine laughed. "But, yes, I was proud and humbled at the same time."

"One of the most difficult parts in the play is obviously the scene where Othello kills you," Ingrid offered. "It is brutal and tragic at the same time. How did you and Conrad approach that and what were Stanley's directions to you both?"

"There's a very interesting back story to that whole scene which I only found out about after we shot it," Josephine confided. "Stanley was adamant it had to be real, violent and uncompromising. At that moment, his vision was that Othello was jealous, hateful, bordering on crazy and capable of anything.

"Without my knowing, he took Conrad aside and told him to pick a fight with me, Josephine, before we shot the scene. So he did. I remember it so clearly because Conrad had never acted that way towards me. But that morning, while I was in makeup, he stormed in, told everyone to leave and proceeded to verbally lash me until I was sobbing.

"It stunned me. I couldn't believe what I was hearing. He told me I was being selfish, stealing the scenes from him, making him look second rate. When I tried to tell him no, that I truly wasn't doing any of those things, he became more enraged, getting right into my face and saying what a jealous little harlot I was.

"Of course, it was magnificent acting on his part. Totally took me in. Totally convinced me he hated my guts. When he finally left I just sobbed and sobbed. And before I knew it Stanley summoned me to the set to shoot Desdemona's death scene, so I had to pull myself together and get on with it.

"As Conrad and I began, I saw he was still mad at me, so much so that I was genuinely scared he might do me actual physical harm, which, of course, was all part of their plan. Desdemona in that scene should be bemused and eventually terrified. I truly was," Josephine chuckled. "But we got through it in just one take and Stanley couldn't have been happier. He marveled at our intensity, passion and different emotions.

"I, of course, still shook from head to foot, puzzled over Conrad's strange behavior towards me. That's when they told me their plan. Took a while to sink in, but profound apologies and a huge bouquet of flowers convinced me they were telling the truth. I actually punched him on the shoulder for doing what he did to me, but the end result was stunning. We made that scene so real and believable, which was what Stanley was hoping for all along."

Ingrid beamed as she listened to Josephine's incredible recollection.

Shaking her head in amazement, she said, "And I can attest to the fact that the ruse worked. Othello strangling you terrified me. It made me shiver and I wondered how you two managed to pull it off.

"Now," Ingrid continued, getting back to the documentary, "tell me about the film's release and how it was received."

Josephine took her time before nodding slowly and smiling.

"The film came out around July or August, I think. Oh, Stanley set up this real fancy premiere, with press folk and photographers. He also invited lots of stars he knew and, God bless them, most of them showed up. My daddy came with me, looking smart in a new suit I bought him with some of the money I'd earned. I also got myself a real pretty dress so I could look my best for the night. Judy was there, too, to support me and Daddy. That was so nice of her to bother.

"We received some lovely reviews after the film finished. People rushed up telling me how great I was and that I was sure to get an Oscar nomination. Well, that was the first time I'd ever thought about something so grand. Me, an Oscar nomination? That just seemed like a wild dream to someone so young and raw like me. But that's what people were saying.

"Oh, what a wonderful evening that was! And afterwards, they took us to one of L.A.'s fanciest restaurants for a huge party. I tell you, I felt like the belle of the ball. And my daddy stood tall and proud beside me, loving every minute and acting like the true gentleman he was.

"We talked some about Mama, how she would have loved it, too. That talk made me sad, but I knew she was right there with us, sharing the moment and laughing, too. And I knew I owed that poor woman so much. Wouldn't have achieved most of what I did if it hadn't been for the values, strength and discipline she instilled in me right from when I was an itty-bitty child."

"And how did you deal with this new fame suddenly being thrust upon you?" Ingrid asked. "I mean, you had led quite a sheltered life up until then."

"Oh, it certainly wasn't easy let me tell you that, child. Good job my daddy was around to help me keep my feet firmly planted. The next day, after the party, he sat me down for some honest talk. And he didn't mince his words, either.

'Sweetness,' he began, 'I know you're thinking you are on top of the world right now. And that's all fine and good. You deserve everything you've gotten so far. Worked hard. Done what people asked of you and more. So, yes, you've earned everything you got.

'But it's probably not going to last forever. And I want you to think about those times. They paid you some pretty good money right along. Take my advice. Try and save as much as you can for when times get difficult.

'You might go on to be a real big movie star or it may all end tomorrow. No one knows in this life. I know Stanley wants you to go out and promote the film, and he'll be paying you real handsome for doing that. He may even want you in some more of his films.

'But right now all of this is new to you so you have to plan for the worse. I'm not saying you're not going to make it because I know you'll do your best. All I'm saying is be prepared. Sock as much as your money away as you can. Don't worry 'bout me. I still got my grave digging job and that suits me fine.

It's a steady paycheck that gives us most of what we need. I'm not going to be around forever so you got to look to yourself. D'you understand me, child?'

"Naturally, I told him I did. But I was already twenty years old, co-starring in my first film, confident and so sure I was going to be the next …well…Judy Garland. But what he said made a lot of sense. Oh, I knew that, too. And, my daddy was still my daddy. I'd best behave as I knew how or I'd have him after my hide.

"So, with Stanley still paying me fifty dollars a week to do a lot of promoting work and promising me other roles in his films, I settled down having a real nice life. The studio taught me how to behave and speak when being interviewed. I learned poise, self-control and how to express myself without sounding brash or selfish. And I took those lessons to heart. They served me well in the years to come. Oh, yes they did."

Ingrid listened carefully while making a mental note that she, too, would be well served to follow some of that advice. After all, in her business ego could give rise to overly self-importance or worse, ignorance. Yes, she had won the prestigious Murray prize, but that was just the beginning. Now she needed to prove herself all over again.

Focusing once more on Josephine, she asked, "As exciting as those times were for you, how on earth did you handle the next momentous event in your life? I mean, an Academy Award nomination for Best Supporting Actress? Surely that must have been something you only dreamed about?"

Josephine nodded and smiled in agreement, opening her hands before her as if to say, *You got that right, sister!*

But what she actually said was, "Oh, my, I just can't wait to tell you all about that."

Chapter Thirteen

Before Josephine could continue with her extraordinary story, Ingrid decided to give her a week's break. In doing so, it would also give her a chance to document some of the other residents' stories. After all, Ingrid's initial project was to tell as many interesting lives as she could. Discovering Josephine's remarkable life history sidelined her somewhat from that goal, but it would also be disrespectful to ignore some of the other important tales from a variety of folks in the nursing home.

Ingrid had already decided to split the documentary into two parts. Part one would be a compendium of recollections from five or six residents, while part two would solely focus on Josephine. Since there was a lot of ground to cover, Ingrid resolved this was the best way to construct a meaningful documentary of those involved.

During her initial talks with a lot of the residents shortly after she began the project, Ingrid narrowed down her list of potential story tellers to six, not including Josephine. There were three men and three women, all of whom had something special to say. After discovering Josephine's amazing history, Ingrid couldn't wait to get started on some of the others.

"Jack," she said warmly, welcoming the home's resident gardener into the hot seat, "we're so looking forward to hearing from you. This is Zach, our expert camera guy. He'll position you in a minute exactly where he wants you. But, before that, can you tell me a little more about your story?"

Affably, Jack smiled and began speaking a mile-a-minute.

"I was a teacher for a good many years, ending up as the principal at a junior high school. Loved the kids. Still see some of them to this day. One in particular, as a matter of fact. We kinda have a strong bond, a connection if you like. I was the football coach, too, and he was one of my best players. Like a son to me, he was."

"And you helped him in some meaningful way?" Ingrid asked.

"I did. You see…"

"Okay, Jack, this is beginning to sound very interesting, so how about Zach gets you settled and we'll start?"

Zach positioned Jack, adjusted his camera and lights, then signaled for Ingrid to begin the interview.

Before starting, Ingrid told Jack she'd insert the appropriate introduction to the audience later, but for now she would lead off with questions that zeroed in on his particular recollection.

"You were a teacher and football coach," she began. "That career must've given you so much pleasure and reward."

"Oh, certainly," Jack eagerly confirmed. "Some of the best years of my life."

"You must have affected so many lives in so many positive ways," Ingrid suggested.

"Hope so," Jack agreed. "But I'm not sure the kids always saw it that way," he continued, with a laugh.

"Have any of those connections with the kids stayed with you? I mean, do you still see any of them?"

"As a matter of fact, I do," Jack replied, nodding enthusiastically. "And it all started way back in nineteen eighty-four. Kid on the team, Scott, was sixteen at the time, talented, fit and just happy to have finally made varsity.

"After his first season he began complaining of feeling run down and tired all the time. We just put it down to a long, hard season. But by Christmas he was worse. Turns out his kidneys were playing up."

Jack twisted a little before taking a breath.

"As the months went on he deteriorated very quickly, so much so that he soon ended up on a dialysis machine. That helped a lot and for about a year he did okay. But late in his senior year, when he'd just turned eighteen, he was diagnosed with end-stage renal disease.

"Everyone at school was devastated. Such a great kid," Jack continued, shaking his head. "Obviously, I'd had a lot of contact with him and his family. As I said, he was like a son to me.

"In those days, transplants were usually limited to relatives and close friends. Most of his kin were tested but no one came close to a match. I figured I was a close friend so I volunteered. I was, what, forty-four or five and healthy as a horse. My tests came back good with my blood group and tissue type being compatible. So, I immediately said, let's do it."

"You gave the boy one of your kidneys?" Ingrid asked, visibly stunned.

"Yes, I did and I'd do the same today. It was a no-brainer, really. Our surgeries went smoothly and I was back at work in six weeks. Scott took a little longer, but he pulled through nicely. Couldn't play football again but at least he had his life back."

"How selfless of you," Ingrid said, still awed by Jack's revelation. "And you two have kept in touch?"

"We meet every chance we get. If you're here next week you'll see him. He has a great family. Lovely, peach of a wife and two smart kids. They all give back to the community without even thinking about it."

"And his health?"

"Beautiful. No problems as long as he takes his meds. No reason he won't live longer than me," Jack laughed.

"And, finally, would you say that was one of the highlights of your life?" Ingrid asked.

"No," Jack answered, seriously. "It wasn't one of the highlights. It was *the* highlight. No question. What else can ever beat helping to save someone's life?"

Ingrid smiled and nodded.

"Wow, Jack! That's all I can say. We're done here, but, oh my, what a story. What a story. And who could have possible known?"

The next resident Ingrid sat down with was Betty Harper, who had thrilled everyone on karaoke afternoon with her rendition of Madonna's *Material Girl*. Her appearance this time had none of the flamboyance of that occasion. Instead, she seemed slightly apprehensive of the camera, lights and Ingrid.

"Mrs. Harper," Ingrid began, respectfully, "we spoke briefly a few weeks ago when I first came here. I was very impressed and interested with what you told me. So, I'd really like to include your story in our documentary if you agree?"

Betty clearly remembered talking with Ingrid but she didn't feel, then or now, that any of her reminiscences were that big of a deal.

"If that's what you think, dear, but I've led an ordinary life. Got married to a lovely man. Had three good children. And here I am now, in my golden years, enjoying the time I have left. But," Betty continued, "if you think any of that's worth sharing, then I'm certainly game to try."

Ingrid smiled sweetly, almost sad that Betty didn't realize or understand what a difference she had made to the world in her own, small way.

"Actually," Ingrid said, encouragingly, "what you've done in your life is truly amazing. Not only is it worth telling but your story is one example of why we're here."

Taken aback, Betty just answered, "Really? All right, if you think that, then I'm happy to give you what I can."

"Now," Ingrid began, reassuringly, "I know all this paraphernalia may be disconcerting, but just relax as much as possible and imagine you and I are having a friendly conversation. Expand on my questions as little or as much as you like. Okay?"

Betty nodded, adjusted her position and waited to begin.

"In your long life there have obviously been moments, events, family and people of which you are particularly proud. What would you say are some you cherish above all others?"

"Oh, that's easy," Betty answered, swiftly. "My marriage and my children."

"And how long were you married?"

"Well, Albert and I met when I was just nineteen and he was a year older. That was in nineteen fifty-six. We had fifty-seven wonderful years together." Betty shook her head as she remembered. "But it was sudden for him, so I was so grateful he didn't have to suffer."

"What was his occupation?" Ingrid asked.

"He sold real estate. Very good at it, he was, too. Gave us a comfortable life. The kids and I never wanted for anything."

"Tell me about your children? Three, I think you said?"

"Yes, three. Oh, my, what blessings they all brought us. Marion, the oldest, David and Grace. All very different in their own ways but all of them bound by the family motto…"

"Which is?"

"…which is…to be of value."

Ingrid raised her eyebrows in surprise, wondering how that ethos transferred from parents to children.

"So, what do each of them do? Their careers, I mean," Ingrid asked.

"Marion is Chief of Anesthesiology at nearby Archibald Medical Center. David, would you believe, is an international concert pianist. And Grace, bless her heart, is the director of an A.S.P.C.A. facility."

Despite being taken aback by Betty's revelation, Ingrid remained professional while trying hard to think of an appropriate and relevant question.

"Could you tell me a little about their upbringings? How did you and your husband managed to cope with what I imagine was the challenges of such diversity within your children?"

"Good old plain and simple nurturing, of course," Betty replied, as if the question was so easy to answer. "We realized early on that each one was different from the other in their likes and dislikes. But we always treated them in the same way. Their interests may not have been ours but we acted as if they were. For instance, when David, at a very early age, began showing an interest in music, particularly classical music, we encourage him as much as we could. Not necessarily our cup of tea but we knew he deserved his chance.

"Now with Marion, she knew in fourth grade she wanted to be a doctor. There was no dissuading her; that was her aim. So we did everything in our power to make sure that happened. And part of the nurturing of the kids was also to hold them to very high standards. We were tough, perhaps too tough sometimes. With all three, schoolwork always came first. Homework had to be done…and not just done but done right… before they could do anything else.

"But along with the demands we made we also taught them kindness, responsibility, courage and how to have fun. That was so important… making time for them just to be kids.

"With Grace, that was never a problem. From the time she could walk and talk she related to dogs, cats and any animals, really, with such crazy enthusiasm. And sometimes that was dangerous, but she didn't care. Spiders, squirrels, snakes, you name it and Gracie was right there, saving them from goodness knows what. Honestly, it was heartwarming just to sit and watch her. And years later she has the perfect job."

Ingrid sat almost mesmerized as Betty talked. Who could've known this elderly woman, now confined to a nursing home, had made such a contribution to society? Ingrid was thrilled. Her documentary would be all the richer for Betty's story.

"Tell me," she respectfully interrupted, "was it all they thought it would be? I mean, did your children, down the years, have any regrets for the paths they took and you let them walk?"

Betty grinned broadly.

"No, not at all. They tell me to this day how much they've enjoyed and continue to enjoy their lives. And most days they thank their dad and me for all we did despite being demanding and pushy parents."

"Could you update their current lives? What are they doing now?"

"Well, David doesn't play concerts anymore. All that travelling finally wore him down. I mean, the poor man was in Boston one day, with the London Philharmonic the next and then flying off to Australia to perform there. He did that for over thirty years, so I guess he's earned a break.

"He teaches a lot now instead, which he finds so rewarding. Oh, and when he comes here to see me, he plays for us all," Betty said, proudly. "Now, Marion still puts in sixty hours a week, as well as mentoring and running all sorts of hospital programs. She has a great family; loving husband and two amazing kids. And she seems to be as hard on them as we were on her," she said, with a laugh. "Saving lives is all she ever wanted to do and she's still doing that, bless her.

"Gracie, who's now, what, fifty-eight, I think, has spent her whole life caring, in one way or another, for any and all animals that come her way. How many she's saved or rescued I can't imagine. But I do know all of them would have had a worse life or no life at all, without her care and dedication. She truly is a saint."

After a few more questions and answers, Ingrid concluded the interview with her own, personal, comment.

"Thank you, Mrs. Harper, for sharing your remarkable story with us. The way you raised your children, the values you instilled in them and the sacrifices you and your husband obviously made is a real testament to the love you have for them. Through your example they certainly have made a huge difference in the world for over forty years."

Betty was stunned to hear Ingrid refer to her life in those terms. That a relative stranger would think she and her husband had done something extraordinary and, through their children, had contributed in some meaningful way to making the world a better place, thrilled her beyond measure.

Over lunch, Ingrid and Zach discussed the morning's interviews, with both of them expressing amazement at what they'd heard.

"This place is a freaking goldmine," Zach said, with real astonishment. "I had no idea about any of this stuff. I mean, first Josephine and now these two. Your grandmother deserves a medal for pointing you in the right direction."

"I know what you're saying, Zach," Ingrid agreed. "Honestly, when I started thinking about this project I imagined I might get a couple of good stories at most. But these folk have blown me away. And that's why I think more and more this documentary, when it's finished, will be so important in shining a light on an otherwise hidden part of our society. These stories, these people's lives, need to be told. We can't afford to lose them."

Zach nodded and smiled before his face took on a serious look.

"Ingrid, listen to me. I still don't think you fully realize what you've stumbled upon here. I've worked on quite a few documentaries. Most of them tell a good story but by their very nature they don't always manage to fully explore the human side. And they can't because usually they're made up of old photographs or newspaper cuttings.

"What you've got here are the actual people telling their actual stories in real time, along with all the emotions that go along with that. I'm telling you, this project, if you don't mess it up," he continued, with a laugh, "can take you who knows where."

This time is was Ingrid's turn to be stunned. For someone of Zach's reputation to give out such unsolicited praise and advice, was humbling, meaningful and terrifying at the same time.

"Oh, great," she answered, grinning. "Now you're just scaring the shit out of me!"

"It is what it is and you've done it all by yourself. But this is only the start. Once we've completed the editing and added some other stuff I have in mind, you might have a masterpiece on your hands. Don't say I didn't warn you."

Getting up to leave, Ingrid said, "Now you're really scaring the shit out of me!"

The schedule for the afternoon was to complete three more interviews, including one with two family members of residents with Alzheimer's or dementia. Again, Ingrid looked forward to them with eager anticipation and hopeful expectancy. As the weeks passed Ingrid became increasingly happier with her contribution to the process, particularly with her interviewing techniques. Being with Josephine taught her so much about which questions to ask and, more importantly, which not. Now, as she prepared to sit down with two more residents and the family members, Ingrid felt confident she could do compassionate justice to anyone's story.

"I understand," Ingrid began, as she faced Charles Austin, "that you were a chief of police for many years." She left the statement hanging for him to respond and expand.

"Yes, ma'am, I was. Twenty-three good years and twenty-one years before that working my way up."

"And you've been retired how long?"

"Just going on seventeen now."

"But you haven't been idle, I understand?" Ingrid suggested.

Charles laughed.

"I wish, but my wife, God rest her, didn't let that happen."

"What did she do?"

"Well, at family gatherings or whenever we had friends over, I'd inevitably launch into a story or two about something that happened on the job. And it got to the point where folk actually looked forward to hearing them.

"So, one day my wife said, Chuck, instead of giving these stories away for free, you should write a book. You can imagine my reaction," he said, a wide grin spanning his tanned face. "Ever writing a book was the farthest from my mind.

"Then after a few months into retirement she mentioned the idea again. I told her I didn't think I had that kind of ability. But she was adamant, saying I'd done a lot of writing over the years, which was true. And the reports on cases and incidents were very detailed, covering so many different scenarios. So, one day I sat down and gave it a shot."

"You began a book?" Ingrid asked.

"Yup. I ran my mind through a lot of the old cases, brought several of them together, changed the names and places and, hey presto, I was off to the races."

"Did you manage to finish it?"

"Took me two years, but I got it done. But let me tell you, anyone who says writing a book is easy is not telling the truth. All it is, mainly, is a lot of hard graft. But it also surprised me," he admitted.

"How so?"

"Because, although you have an idea of how you want the story to go, a lot of stuff happens in the book as a result of, say, a new character or a paragraph you never saw coming. You really get to surprise yourself sometimes, which is a good thing because if you can surprise yourself then it's a damn good bet you're going to surprise the reader, too."

"Did it ever get published?" Ingrid inquired, fascinated by the unfolding details.

"Sure did, by me," he replied, with a laugh. "Cost me eight hundred bucks, but it was all worth it when I held that first copy in my hand." Shaking his head, Charles said, "Me, an author, whoever would have thunk it?"

"Now, that was some time ago," Ingrid mused. "Did you carry on?"

"Now I have four," Charles revealed, proudly. "And surprisingly, a small, loyal following. Got some great reviews and, better still, a royalty check every year from the publisher."

Again, Ingrid was amazed by another remarkable and surprising story by someone supposedly forgotten by mainstream society. Here, in this nursing home, was a man who'd written *four* books. It was a tale she could hardly wait to tell.

"Are you still at it? Do you have another one in the pipeline?"

"Halfway through the next one as we speak. It's a sequel to the second one I wrote. Lots of people wanted more of that story so…here I am, six months later, slogging away."

They both laughed.

"Oh, c'mon, Mr. Austin," Ingrid chided, playfully. "I'm really not buying it's a slog for you any more. Out of the blue, you found a new passion. That's obvious. And to still have the urge to be creative…well, what can I say? You are one amazing human being and I thank you for sharing your fascinating story. Thank you."

The next interview Ingrid wanted to conduct was with someone of whom she was slightly apprehensive. That Pearl Lister had even agreed to an interview seemed in itself amazing. After all, Pearl was the person who always gave Josephine a hard time for one thing or another, but mostly for always mumbling to herself or alluding to one or other famous people she'd known. Pearl never believed any of it.

But here she was, sitting opposite Ingrid, seemingly ready and willing to open up about some very interesting parts of her past. In a previous conversation, she casually mentioned not everyone liked, or needed, to boast of their connections to someone of note or notoriety, but that didn't necessarily mean they had none. Indeed, she felt she herself had a family history comparable to many and, in most instances, more extraordinary and touching.

Ingrid, after long hours of persuasion and cajoling, finally convinced Pearl to sit down with her and record her story. And, so, it was with nervousness and excitement that the two women now sat ready before Zach's cameras and lights.

"Ms. Lister, what was the catalyst that began your journey of discovery about some of your ancestors?"

Pearl, prim and proper as always, in her trademark tweed suit, shifted uneasily in her chair before addressing Ingrid as a teacher might talk to a wayward pupil.

"Well, my mother's death, of course. That left me essentially an orphan," she said, with the hint of a grin, "even at my advanced age. And since my parents never really told me much about our relatives and I had time on my hands, I decided then was the moment to see what I could find out on my own."

"How did you begin? *Ancestry dot com?*"

"Yes. I knew nothing, so that's where I started. Later, I had a lot of help from some nice people in England, Ireland and Italy. Anyway, I was immediately hooked. It started with an old family heirloom which had been handed down from generation to generation. A tattered leather sewing kit with the initials MGS stitched on top. I'd seen it growing up whenever I rummage through the attic, but my mother never gave me any clear answers when I asked about it.

"A family heirloom was all she told me, and when my time came I should treasure it. Inside, there were crude, thick needles, lots of different colored thread on what looked like hand-made wooden spools and a piece of red fabric, silk, I think, on which someone had begun to embroider the initial P."

"So, perhaps a wife had started sewing something for her child?" Ingrid surmised.

"Yes, or her husband," suggested Pearl. "But it took me a long time to assume that and, more importantly, who the initials MGS belonged to."

"So," Ingrid said, excitedly, "you found out. What exactly did you discover?"

"Well," replied a still calm Pearl, "let me guide you through what I found. My father, James Lister, was the only child of Henry and Grace Lister. Grace emigrated to the United States from Ireland, landing at Ellis Island in nineteen hundred one. She was an O'Neill from County Cork.

"Her father, John O'Neill, had married a Mary Shelley in eighteen eighty-four. He was a hardworking potato farmer, but fell on difficult times and decided to bring his family over here for a new beginning.

"Now, the woman he married, Mary Shelley, happened to be one of the daughters of Percy Florence Shelley and his wife, the former Jane Gibson St. John. They were married in eighteen forty-eight and produced two daughters, Mary and Claire."

"Wait. Wait," Ingrid insisted, holding up her hand. "Are you going to tell me what I think you're going to tell me?"

"I don't know. Am I?" Pearl replied, with a definite twinkle in her eyes.

"That you're related in some way to Mary Shelley and Percy Bysshe Shelley?"

"Oh, I'm not just related to them," Pearl answered, proudly. "In fact, I'm their great, great, great granddaughter." She left the statement for Ingrid to grasp.

"*The* Mary Shelley?" Ingrid asked, incredulously. "The one who wrote *Frankenstein*?"

"The very same," Pearl smirked. "Pretty neat, eh?"

"And Shelley, the great English poet? Pearl, you'd better not be kidding me."

"Not at all. I'll let you see all the evidence later, if you like. But first, I'd like to show you this."

Pearl reached into her bag and took out a package carefully wrapped in brown paper.

"Open it," she almost ordered Ingrid.

Gingerly, Ingrid untied the ribbon and removed the paper.

"Oh, no! Oh, my! Is this…?"

"Yes, what you're holding in your hand is Mary Shelley's sewing kit, which is now about two hundred years old."

Ingrid carefully turned the priceless object over in her hands, noticing the initials MGS stitched on the outside.

"They stand for Mary Godwin Shelley," Pearl informed her. "Godwin was her family name."

Ingrid stared aghast, almost unable to comprehend what she held so close to her.

"Open it up," Pearl again commanded.

Very tentatively, Ingrid opened the precious kit.

"Do you see the piece of fabric?" asked Pearl.

Ingrid nodded.

"Carefully unfold it. What d'you see?"

"Oh, my god, it's the piece of silk you said she must've been working on. The 'P' is exquisite. So beautiful."

"I'd like to think she was embroidering it for her husband and that when he tragically died she couldn't bring herself to finish whatever it was she was making."

"Wait. Shelley, the poet, died tragically? Your great, great, great grandfather met an untimely end?"

"He did," Pearl confirmed. "As I understand it, they were living on the coast of Italy, near Pisa. He couldn't swim but loved the sea. One day, he and a friend set out for a twenty mile boat ride late in the day. A storm blew up and they never arrived at their destination. His body washed up on the shore three days later. He was not yet thirty. They cremated him right there on the beach. And with that, one of England's most famous poets was gone forever."

"Pearl," Ingrid stammered, stunned, "I had no idea. This is such an amazing story."

"And you're the first person I've told it to."

"Oh, Pearl, this will enhance the documentary beyond measure. I am so very, very grateful to you for sharing this with us. I promise you it will receive the recognition it deserves."

"I just didn't want such a piece of history being lost," Pearl answered, modestly. "And I trust you to make that happen."

The last interview of the day was with Mary Shapiro and Frank Monroe.

"Thank you so much for being willing to sit down and talk on camera," Ingrid began. "I understand this may be difficult for you."

"No. No," Mary answered, pleasantly. "We both feel it's important for my mom's and Frank's father's stories to be documented. So, thank you for shining a light."

During the next two hours Mary and Frank shared their experiences of caring for a parent with Alzheimer's. Their words were touching, heartfelt, meaningful, sad but also upbeat.

"My mom no longer knows who I am," Mary confided, "but I still know who she is inside. We talk about things that happened in the past and sometimes, for a second or two, I see a flicker of recognition. So I do know my old mom is in there somewhere. She always seems happy even if I don't understand where that comes from."

"That's absolutely right," Frank agreed. "They are still in there somewhere. Sometimes my father makes gestures or tries to touch me in the same ways he did when I was a kid. He remembers those things, but not who I am. That's the hardest part for both of us. And, he still has his stubborn streak. If he doesn't want to do something, he won't."

As the interview wound down, Ingrid asked both Mary and Frank if they only had five minutes of lucidity with their parents what would they say to them?

Almost simultaneously, they both answered, "That we love you so much and thank you for everything."

And with those precious words Ingrid finished the interview and cried.

Chapter Fourteen

Although she didn't know it at the time, January 16th, 1950 would be the day that changed Josephine's life forever.

After *Othello's* release in the late summer of the previous year, she was kept busy with promotional work, caring for her father and meeting often with Stanley Masters in preparation for other roles he had in mind for her. In addition, Josephine secured several well-paying advertising spots on the radio and in a few magazines. She promoted everything from toothpaste to motor cars which made her giggle until the serious checks arrived. Needless to say, her bank account now held a tidy sum for someone her age.

As she tended to household chores on that January morning, her father handed her an official-looking letter. The back of the envelope was embossed in gold lettering with the magical words *Academy of Motion Picture, Arts and Sciences.*

Josephine stopped her dusting, wiped her now shaking hands and carefully opened the envelope. She read the contents to herself and then aloud to her father.

"Dear Ms. Benson, it is my distinct honor to inform you that you have been nominated for an Academy Award in the category of Best Actress in a Supporting Role for your performance as Desdemona in the 1949 film Othello. The Academy congratulates you for your outstanding performance. Along with the other four nominees, I hope you will be able to attend the ceremony at the RKO Pantages Theater on Thursday,

March 23rd 1950. I offer my personal congratulations on your nomination and look forward to meeting you at the ceremony. And it's signed, very sincerely, Charles Brackett, President."

Mr. Benson remained speechless for a few seconds before hurrying to embrace his beaming daughter. He lifted her, spun her around and hugged her almost to death before letting go.

"Yes! Yes! Yes!" he yelled, fist-bumping the air while grinning like a spoiled child with goodies. "You did it! You did it! You did it! Oh, my word, this is one glorious, special day. Yes, yes, yes, indeed!"

Josephine remained speechless, her mind in a fog as it tried hard to comprehend what she now knew…that she was, indeed, a true Academy Award nominee. She glanced at the words again, shaking her head and eventually smiling her famous smile.

"Daddy, I can hardly believe this," she whispered. "Me, little ol' me, getting recognized like some of those real life actresses. I sure hope they haven't made some kind of mistake."

"No mistake, child. No mistake," her father insisted, continuing his impassioned encouragement. "Ain't nothing but what you deserve. You *made* that film, baby. Would have been nothing without you in it."

They sat for awhile, side by side, holding hands and just staring at the letter.

Finally, Mr. Benson began to say, "Baby, your…"
"I know, Daddy. I know," Josephine interrupted. "She would have been so proud of me. I know that. I owe her so much, Daddy. You and she have always done your best for me. I'm so sad inside that she's not here with us."

"But she *is*, sweetness, she *is*. She's in your heart every minute of every day. With you when you're sleeping and helping to guide you whenever you need that extra little push. Don't ever think she's not watching over you, because that's what she's doing…watching over her baby girl."

Josephine dried her eyes before studying the nomination letter again. To herself she thought, *You know, Josephine Benson, you aren't so bad after all. Academy Award nominee at twenty. No, sir, that's really not bad at all.*

The time between the arrival of the letter and the actual ceremony was filled with so many moments Josephine found almost overwhelming. Stanley Masters arrived at her house later in the day carrying a huge bouquet and an invitation to one of Los Angeles finest fashion houses.

"I've arranged everything for you," he enthused. "Pick out what you want and they'll do the rest. And I know whatever you choose you're going to look spectacular."

Stanley also told Josephine he would like to throw a party for her whenever she felt able to attend, and that on Oscar night she and her father would be driven to the theater in a sparkling limousine.

Judy reached out to her, too, as well as a couple of the other nominees in her category. To hear from these legends thrilled and humbled Josephine more than she could say.

It would be an evening to remember forever for Josephine and her father; an evening when all of her dreams came together in one huge extraordinary moment. Sleeping very little the night before, she tossed and turned continuously thinking about the possibility of actually winning which, in reality, she didn't imagine she would.

Stanley, strangely enough, hadn't dwelled on the possibility either. In fact, as she thought about it, apart from their early congratulations, no one from the studio ever mentioned her winning the award.

Josephine heard that the winners were expected to say a few gracious words to the audience. She hoped Stanley or one or other of the writers might assist with her speech. But that kind of help never materialized. Instead, and as a safety net, she and her father spent many afternoons working on something appropriate for her to say should she win.

In the end, they decided to keep the speech short and to the point. It was four sentences long including the list of names of those she wanted to acknowledge for helping her along the way. And she intended for the final person she would thank to be her mother.

Josephine awoke on the morning of March 23rd tired but calm. She bustled around with odds and ends until two colleagues of her mother showed up around eleven to fix her hair and make-up. That they would do this for her filled Josephine with happiness. It meant her mother was a real part of the celebration as well as still being remembered and loved by some of those at the studio.

"We got to pretty you up, girl," Aleisha told her, leading her to the mirror. "Not that you need that much by the way, but you gotta look extra special tonight. Mildred, here, will do your hair, then I'll do the rest."

Josephine settled in her chair as Mildred began working on her hair.

"I'm thinking, sweetness," Mildred began, "that we pull some of this over to the side, like so, and then the rest we can sort of drape around your cheek like this. Yes? What d'you think?"

"I love it!" crowed Josephine, secretly thinking she looked gorgeous already. "Let's do that."

Mildred worked for an hour, teasing, cutting and using all the tricks of her trade. When she finished Josephine was stunned at the result.

"Look what you've done to me," she beamed, turning this way and that. "Oh, Mildred, thank you. Thank you so much!"

"Ain't nothing but what you deserve, young lady. We doing this for you and your precious mother. She's been guiding my hands like you wouldn't believe."

They both laughed but, in truth, the statement was correct.

"Now," Aleisha said, taking over, "make-up time. Ta-da! You close those pretty eyes of yours and leave the rest to me."

For the next forty-five minutes Aleisha did what she did best – make a pretty face even prettier. Guided by Josephine's already striking features, Aleisha enhanced rather than transformed her look, making her more sophisticated, grown-up and appropriate for the grand occasion.

When Mr. Benson walked in he literally stopped in his tracks, amazed by what he saw of his little girl now becoming a woman.

"I'd like to hug you, sweet child of mine, but I know I'd just mess up all the good work these two lovely ladies have done. My word, it's magic you've got in your hands," he said to Mildred and Aleisha. "What a gift you've given us."

The two women took the compliments in stride, nodding and grinning.

"This isn't anything your dear wife wouldn't have done, d'you hear?" Aleisha answered. "We're just sorry she's not here. But, let me tell you, she sure did some good things of her own in times gone by. Oh, yes!"

By three o'clock, Mildred and Aleisha began helping Josephine get dressed. True to his word, Stanley Masters arranged for one of the best fashion houses in Los Angeles to measure and make Josephine's gown. Now she was ready to actually wear it for the first time.

The dress, cream colored and off the shoulder, had a flared skirt reaching to the ground. It looked spectacular against Josephine's dark skin. The women spent a long time making sure every aspect of her appearance shone through. When they finished, Josephine felt like Cinderella going to the ball.

"Now that's what a star looks like," cooed Aleisha. "I mean, you gonna be the best dressed one there, girl."

"No doubt 'bout that," agreed Mildred, flaring out the skirt. "Eyes gonna be raised when they see you arrive."

They fetched Mr. Benson, who just stared and stared for the longest time. Tears filled his eyes as he struggled to find the right words to say.

In the end, he carefully hugged his daughter, nodding and whispering, "You so fine, baby. You so fine."

"You, too, Mr. Benson," Mildred said, admiringly. "You, too."

Laughing, he bowed to the compliment.

"My very first tuxedo, ladies. And probably my last."

This time they all laughed as he thanked them profusely for everything they'd done for Josephine.

"It was our pleasure," Aleisha replied. "Now, girl, you go get 'em, d'you hear? Bring us back that Oscar."

Josephine, still awed by her transformation, diffidently told them she would do her best.

"But I should win," she purred, holding out her hands, "just for what you've done for me. Thank you. Thank you. Thank you."

The limousine Stanley sent for them arrived promptly at five. It was a gleaming black Packard, similar, Josephine thought, to the one that had taken her and her mother to the studio when she was eight or nine.

The Pantages Theater seemed magical as Josephine stepped from the car. It was ablaze with lights, with a spotlight trained on the new arrivals. Josephine squinted, holding onto her father's arm as a throng of photographers chronicled her every step. Already it seemed overwhelming and they hadn't even made it inside.

Escorts were on hand to guide them to a private area where Charles Brackett, the president of the Academy, was on hand to say a few words to all the nominees. He was gracious, congratulated Josephine on her fine accomplishment then moved on to the next person.

They were seated in the seventh row with an excellent view of the stage. Josephine recognized many of the famous stars in attendance, whispering to her father about this one and that. Two of the other nominees in her category, Celeste Holm and Ethel Waters actually came up to her, introducing themselves and wishing her luck. The moment seemed surreal to Josephine, who had only read about such stars in the variety magazines she avidly purchased.

Minutes before the ceremony started, the orchestra filed into the pit beneath the stage and began playing some of the well known songs. Shortly afterwards, the curtains parted and Charles Brackett strode in to officially open the proceedings. Josephine could hardly concentrate on his words because mostly what she heard was the beating of her heart.

Brackett then introduced the host for the evening, actor Paul Douglas. Josephine thought he gave a very funny speech, especially when he told the audience the Academy had always wanted a Douglas to host the show, but unfortunately Kirk wasn't available.

As he spoke, Josephine could not take her eyes from the set behind him. It consisted, in the center, of one huge, sparkling Oscar and, on either side, all the Oscars to be presented that evening. As the lights played upon them, Josephine imagined them to be golden lamps, with each signaling her name. She couldn't wait to hold one. She couldn't wait to hold a golden lamp in her hand.

After some of the less well-known awards were handed out, Paul Douglas introduced Ray Milland as presenter in the Best Supporting Actress category. As he read the names, Josephine stared straight ahead, hardly breathing, gripping her father's hand and anxiously waiting for Mr. Milland to open the precious envelope. The moment seemed to last forever.

"And the Oscar for Best Actress in a Supporting Role goes to…Mercedes McCambridge for All the King's Men."

As the audience clapped and waited for the actress to make her way to the stage, Josephine smiled while bowing her head and trying to come to terms with the sudden loss.

Rubbing her hand, her father bent in close, whispering, "It's all right, baby. Really, it's okay. Just you being here among all these famous people… well, that's enough of an acknowledgment for me."

Josephine nodded that she understood but deep inside her heart there was a hurt she knew she'd never get over.

Chapter Fifteen

Ingrid still saw the hurt on Josephine's face and in her eyes as her friend described the moment the Oscar went to someone else.

"It must seem just like yesterday," she surmised, with a resigned smile of sympathy. "How on earth did you get through the rest of the evening?"

"Honestly, I think I was in a fog. I mean, I accepted I didn't win but at the same time I started to think less of myself. But folks were gracious and supportive. Lots of them gave me hugs, including Mercedes. She told me she felt lucky to win since this was her first role, just like me. And she kindly told me as a member of the Academy she had actually voted for me. That made me feel so much better coming from her."

"And in the days afterwards," Ingrid asked, "how did you cope?"

Josephine sighed as a wry smile creased her face.

"Locked myself away. Didn't want to see anyone. Daddy was great, giving me time to work things out by myself. After all, I was twenty-one, so I guess he felt I should be able to handle such a disappointment.

"And he was right. I came back stronger in my mind and more determined than ever to become the actress I knew I was. So, I went to the studio, showed my face around and met with Stanley. He'd already told me about some other roles he wanted me for. I thought the best way to deal with the loss was to go back to work."

"Did he or anyone else mention the Awards?" Ingrid asked, curious to learn of people's reaction to Josephine returning to the studio.

"Oh, he wanted to know how I was; how I was holding up, but nobody directly came right out and said they were sorry I didn't win." Josephine took a breath before continuing. "I found that very strange indeed."

Ingrid immediately sensed there might be another part to the story so she pressed Josephine for more details.

"I have to ask," she began, cautiously, "whether you felt there was any…any…bias to you not winning the Oscar? I mean, here you were, barely twenty-one, in your first film role and an African American to boot. Did you feel any of those…those…personifications worked against you?"

"Never crossed my mind," Josephine firmly answered. "As you say, I was only twenty-one and very new to the business. I just assumed the voters preferred Mercedes' performance to mine. I was fine with that, too. I saw her film. She was excellent."

"But?" Ingrid pointedly asked.

"But after a few days around the studio I began to hear some disturbing rumors."

"Rumors? About what?"

Josephine looked down, taking more than a few seconds to answer.

"Well," she began, seriously, "some of the people I really liked and trusted hinted at first, then later told me outright, that it was never intended for me to get the Oscar."

Ingrid frowned, totally confused by what Josephine intimated.

"Wait. Wait. Are you saying…?"

"Yes, dear, that's exactly what I'm saying." Shaking her head, she admitted, "They wouldn't let me win. They couldn't. I was a black woman and it didn't fit in with their…their ideals, I suppose."

"Oh, Josephine," Ingrid sighed, "you're sure that's what happened?"

"Now I am, but back then I was just like you, not believing a word of it. In fact, I tried putting it out of my head. I went about my business but the whole idea kept nagging at me.

"When I told Daddy, he said he wouldn't be surprised but not from any of the people I knew and respected. He told me to speak with Stanley, that he might know something. So, that's what I did."

"And," Ingrid questioned, "what did Stanley Masters tell you?"

"Just to go and see him and bring up something like this was so awkward for me, as you can imagine. But I summoned up the courage and spoke to him. Just him and me. I told him what I'd heard, that people said I was never going to be allowed to win on account of the color of my skin.

"When Hattie McDaniel won in nineteen forty, she was the first black person to do so. People told me that didn't go down so well with some members of the Academy. So, I told Stanley I just needed to hear the truth...was I never going to win?"

Ingrid signed to Zach to cut the camera before comforting a visibly upset Josephine. They sat close, holding hands, with Ingrid whispering consoling, sympathetic words. Eventually, Josephine calmed down enough to continue with the interview.

"And what did Stanley eventually tell you?" Ingrid asked, as delicately as possible.

"Well, I gave him a lot of credit for behaving like the gentleman I knew him to be. He told me that, yes, he did know before hand I wasn't going to win. He fought for me as best he could but he was just one voice among many, more important people."

Ingrid frowned.

"He already knew and he still let you go on believing you might win?"

"I know, dear. I know. Sounds dishonest, doesn't it? But then Stanley told me his side. He said he did what he did because he wanted me to experience everything about being nominated. That's why the dress he paid for, the party he threw and the limousine he sent for Daddy and me.

"He told me he needed me to feel like a winner because of my performance in his film. He voted for me simply because he felt my acting was the best."

"How did his telling you all that affect you? Weren't you upset with him for leading you on when he knew you couldn't win?"

"I remember sitting in silence as his explanation washed over me like some big wave. But then I realized he'd done the best he could for me. And his answer was to give me one of the greatest moments of my life. He could have done nothing but instead he made a young girl feel on top of the world if only for a while.

"So, no, I didn't hate him or anything, but after that everything changed for me." Josephine clasped her hands and briefly glanced away from Ingrid. "The information Stanley gave me made me sick to my stomach, knowing whatever I did, however good I was, would never be enough. I was a black woman in a white industry. I needed to come to terms with that."

Ingrid, visibly shaken by what she'd heard, tried hard to refocus on her job; she needed only to concentrate on helping Josephine tell her story, for better or worse, rather than becoming too emotionally involved.

"So, here you are, barely twenty-one, facing an awful truth but with a more than promising acting career ahead of you. I know you've said Stanley already had other roles in mind for you, but this was a crossroad, wasn't it?"

"More like a fork in the road, child," Josephine answered, pointedly. "I had choices, I surely did. None of them good, by the way," she continued with a chuckle. "But it was one of those moments in your life when you need to make a decision that's right for you. Not someone else. Not even your family. Just for you. Only for you."

Ingrid leaned forward, eager to learn more, knowing she needed to push Josephine to reveal the reasons behind the decision she made.

"You really had no one else but your father to talk to about your feelings did you? I know he was a proud man who loved you beyond measure, so how did he react and what advice, if any, did he give you?"

Josephine straightened her back, staring firmly at Ingrid.

"Well, I certainly wasn't prepared for the things he said to me."

"How so?"

"What he told me opened up whole new areas of his life I had no idea about. But he was honest and blunt, feeling I should know the kind of life he'd had."

"Which was?"

"Which was filled with injustice and more just because of the color of his skin. He told me stories that made me cry. It was hard to hear; hard to realize someone I love had gone through such horrors.

"Which is why his advice to me was to forget about the Oscar and just do the best I could with my acting for as long as I could. He told me there was always going to be someone or something out there ready to do me harm in one way or another."

"And how did you react to his advice?"

Josephine tossed back her head and laughed.

"I was twenty-one, confident and not ready to bow down to anyone. How do you think I reacted? I said, 'Daddy, no way! No how! I know my worth now and I'm not going to waste my time with people who don't value me just because I look different.'

"I remember him shaking his head, but then coming close and hugging me. Then he told me I had to do what I thought was right for me but to be prepared for all sorts of trouble up ahead. He would stand by me, support me and defend me in any way he could. In the end, he was crying, too. We were quite a pair, I don't mind telling you," Josephine recounted, smiling broadly.

"So," Ingrid asked, "what was the resolution? Here you were, an Oscar nominated actress with the world at her feet, supposedly, but with the realization you might never get a fair shake. I mean, what were your options? What were your choices?"

"Only two," Josephine replied, firmly. "Only two. Accept or move on. Daddy asked me not to rush into anything, so for a few days I mulled over what I should do. But, in truth, I'd already decided. In the end, I had to sit him down and tell him; tell him something I knew would break his heart."

"You decided to leave Hollywood, didn't you?" Ingrid stated, almost proudly.

"I did," Josephine confirmed. "That's what I decided and that's what I did. I left Hollywood for good."

"But...?"

"But my decision also included leaving my home, too."

"Wait...what? You left home, too?"

"It was time, but not easy. Daddy did his darndest to change my mind, but in the end he saw it was the right thing to do."

"So, you're planning to leave home and go...where?"

Josephine laughed.

"Only three thousand miles away."

"You went to New York?"

"Yes, I did."

"Why New York?"

"It was somewhere Judy thought I would do well. She absolutely loved the place."

"Judy Garland?"

"Yes. She'd reached out to me when she heard about the Oscar problem. Very supportive, although she didn't want me to give up acting. When I told her I'd made up my mind and nothing could change it, she suggested New York.

"That was a good sign for me because in one of my variety magazines there was an advertisement for singers to try out for The Count Basie Orchestra. I had a pretty good voice in those days," she laughed, "and Judy said she'd make some calls, which she did, bless her.

"The upshot was I was offered an audition which I took as another good sign. Of course, my daddy was almost beside himself with me going three thousand miles away, but having Judy help me with things eased his mind."

"And what was that like, having to leave your father after so many years together?"

"Not easy, I can tell you that, child. Heart wrenching for both of us but more so for him, I suspected. After all, it was a new adventure for me; a new beginning. But for him," Josephine continued, fighting back the tears, "he would be alone and lost for a while.

"And yet, not once did he try and persuade me not to go. That was the measure of the man, putting his own feelings aside and wishing me nothing but the best. I tell you, we spent a lot of time hugging and just chillin' out together before I eventually left. The night before I took him to dinner and gave him a present of a lock of my hair. My, my, you'd have thought I'd given him the world. And then early next morning, before he was up, I slipped away without saying goodbye. That would have been too hard for both of us. Two hours later I was on that train to New York."

Ingrid, in her mind's eye, saw Josephine silently leaving her house, boarding the bus to the station and finally settling into her seat on the train. She shook her head, imagining the kind of courage it took for a twenty-one year old back in nineteen-fifty to do that.

"And you had absolutely no regrets about leaving Hollywood and your acting career behind?"

This time, Josephine shook her head.

"Absolutely none. I couldn't see the system changing any time soon.

And, in fact, it didn't. Not for a long time. Then Sidney won his Best Actor Award in nineteen sixty-three, I think it was. Before that, only one black actress, Dorothy Dandridge, had even been nominated for Best Actress. That was in nineteen fifty-four for *Carmen Jones.*

"But things have definitely changed for the better in recent years. Whoopie, Jennifer Hudson, Octavia and Viola all won, as well as Lupita, who reminded me so much of myself. And Halle Berry, in two thousand two, finally got the big one for all of us. That was a moment I can tell you."

Ingrid felt it an appropriate moment to call a halt to filming for the day. She had so much footage to edit, so much to think about and so much to thank Josephine for.

"Let me walk you back," she offered. "And this time I'll make your tea. It's the least I can do for giving me so much to consider."

Chapter Sixteen

Loosely bounded by West 14th Street to the north, Broadway to the east, Houston Street to the south and the Hudson River to the west, Greenwich Village in the early 1950s was already an exciting gathering place for artists, poets, writers, jazz musicians and singers. Situated on the west side of Manhattan within Lower Manhattan, the Village exuded a creative atmosphere palpably felt by all who lived there.

When Josephine Benson arrived in the summer of nineteen fifty she immediately felt comfortable with everything and everyone she encountered. The Village bustled with life and a pulsating energy she found addictive and very familiar. It reminded her so much of the friendly climate of Stanley's studio.

Through Judy's friends, Josephine quickly settled into a small, but comfortable, first floor apartment on the corner of Morton and Bleecker Streets. From this location Josephine found herself close to the center of the Village and within walking distance of most of the attractions and hot spots it offered.

She spent her first few days wandering the streets, visiting cafes and night clubs and just enjoying being outdoors in Washington Square Park. But wherever she went she soon became immersed in the freedom the Village seemed to provide, whether it was the multi-talented street performers, the diverse singers she heard in the clubs or just the happy buzz of ordinary people on the streets. To say she fell in love with Greenwich Village would have been an enormous understatement.

Her appointment with Count Basie occurred three days after she arrived. Surprisingly, Josephine experienced few nerves, which made her feel even more confident about the interview. They met at the club where he was currently rehearsing and he welcomed her warmly. After some preliminary small talk the Count gave Josephine some bad news.

"It's my finances," he began, soberly. "Not doing too well right now. Having to disband the orchestra for a while but I'm trying to continue on with six to nine players depending on what I can afford that particular week.

"I do have the need for a singer but the pay's not going to be too good, I'm afraid. If you want to back out now I'd completely understand."

The news did come as a shock to Josephine, who thought the Count, from all the rave reviews she'd read, must be comfortably rich. He always seemed to be performing somewhere, including, sometimes, places abroad like France and Brazil.

She took a second to collect her thoughts but her decision never seemed in doubt.

"Mr. Basie," she began, firmly, "I…"

"Please," he interrupted, "call me Count. Everyone does and I like that."

Josephine nodded but deferred from using the title just yet.

"I came all the way from California just to sing with you. And that's what I intend to do if you think I'm good enough. I have saved some money of my own so right now I'm not desperate."

"Oh, I'd be able to pay you a little something, just not the big bucks I'd like to. So, if you're willing to work on those terms then I'd be grateful. Of course, when I get back on my feet I will make it up to you, have no fear."

"That's fine," Josephine answered. "I believe you will be a man of your word."

"All right then," the Count replied, smiling broadly, "I say let's have an audition."

He sat down at his piano, handed Josephine some sheet music and began to play the tune.

"Anytime you're ready just jump right in," he encouraged.

After quickly scanning the words, Josephine found the rhythm and started to sing. The first few bars were hesitant and sketchy but she soon got into her stride.

"Yes! Yes!" the Count shouted above the music. "You keep that going now. You got it, baby."

By the time she finished Josephine was exhausted, mostly from the Count's enthusiasm. She waved the sheet in front of her face like a fan before almost falling into a chair.

"That was sensational," he said, smiling broadly. "But it may have been a fluke. Let's try something a little harder."

This time Josephine found herself staring at the words to '*My Foolish Heart*'.

"This is a real standard," the Count told her. "Let me play the melody for you." His fingers softly glided over the keys as Josephine listened mesmerized to the strains as smooth as cream. "The song is about hesitant love and insecurity, chances and temptation. So, give me feeling. Make me believe you understand the possible rewards and consequences."

Josephine took a deep breath while trying hard to conjure up an appropriate mood and style. Her only references were her performances as Cleopatra and Desdemona, both of whom were sometimes sirens and sometimes pursued. Clearing her mind except for those images, she began to sing low and teasingly as the Count caressed the ivories.

Throughout the song he nodded and smiled as she became more comfortable with her performance. By the end she seemed lost in herself, closing her eyes, moving her hands and wishing the moment would go on and on.

"I don't need to hear any more," the Count told her.

Josephine frowned, afraid of his next words. She needn't have worried.

"You, young lady, if you accept, can begin singing with me as soon as we secure your Cabaret Card. And, I'll be paying you twenty-five dollars a week to start. What do you say?"

With eyes wide open, Josephine gave the Count her biggest smile.

"Really? You really mean I can sing with your band?"

"Yes, I do. But we've a lot of hard work to do. First, I'm gonna help you get your card. I know some people so that should not be too much of a problem."

"I don't understand," Josephine answered, frowning again. "I can't just rehearse and sing with you? I need some sort of card to be able to do that?"

The Count nodded.

"'Fraid so. Here in New York City all workers in our industry, including singers, have to get the card. Essentially, it's like a license. Can't sing without one. But don't you worry. We'll help you fill out the paperwork and in probably two weeks or so we should be good to go. In the meantime, that gives us plenty of time to practice."

"I promise you, Count, you won't regret hiring me," Josephine offered. "I realize I'm new to all this but I'll try my best every night not to let you down. I want to make you proud to have me in your band."

The Count came over, shaking her hand and giving her a gentle, fatherly hug.

"I know that, Josephine. I do. It's going to be great. Just you wait and see. Now, let's set up a schedule so we can get to work."

The next few weeks for Josephine flew by like hours were minutes and days just hours long. But she found the pace of her new life exciting as she began learning a whole different way of living, working and coming to terms with changes she could only have dreamed about a few months before.

One of the first things she did was sit down and write a long, expressive letter to her father, leaving nothing out, even her fears and apprehension for what lay ahead. To say she missed her father more than she could describe helped bring him closer in her mind's eye. She imagined him talking to her, advising her and always pushing her forward. In some ways, he had now replaced her mother as the dominant figure in her life, which seemed natural to her but hard to understand at times.

For so long her mother had been by her side, guiding her, teaching her and making sure she followed all of her standards. And for the most part, Josephine still maintained her mother's ideals even if she sometimes took a different path from the one she knew her mother might probably suggest.

But now, with her life caught up in a whirlwind, Josephine had to make many instant decisions. For those, it was her father's advice she followed, remembering some of his parting words to her. *Always try and do the right thing, for you and everyone else.* That's what he instilled in her and that's what she now tried so hard to practice.

Josephine found working for the Count to be an amazing experience. Including him, there were nine members along with two female singers. During rehearsals he told her she would join them as back-up singers for any of the special guests he could afford to contract. But he also told her each of them would be given plenty of opportunities to showcase their own talents and abilities every night, no matter what.

Around New York the Count and his band were very much in demand in small, intimate clubs. During rehearsals he schooled Josephine on the current jazz scene; what was popular and what was now considered passé. He mentioned more than once that before his financial troubles he and his orchestra often travelled to Europe, particularly to France, where he and the whole jazz scene were revered. He promised once his problems were behind him he would try and reform the orchestra and again travel the world. For Josephine, just the thought of experiencing different countries and cultures filled her with disbelief and expectant happiness.

It was during this time that Josephine met a saxophone player named Milton Sewell. He happened to live in an apartment above hers and the two bumped into each other one morning during a rainstorm. They were both after the same cab and, after some easy banter and laughs, decided to share the ride.

"Milton Sewell. It's a pleasure to meet you."

"Josephine Benson and likewise, Mr. Sewell."

"Milton, please. You live downstairs, I think. Seen you pass by a few times. Always going off somewhere."

Josephine giggled because what he said was true; she was always scampering off here, there and everywhere.

"It's just that I love New York and want to see all of it."

"So, where are you headed today in such a rush?" he asked.

Proudly, she answered, "Rehearsing with Count Basie. And you?"

"Well this is some coincidence," he said, a broad smile creasing his handsome face. "Me, too."

"Where to?" the cab driver asked impatiently.

"The Seabird Club," Milton informed him. "And, please, take your time."

The young pair laughed before settling down in the back of the cab.

"You a singer with the Count?" Milton wanted to know.

"Yes, I am. Just got myself hired. I'm practicing until I get my card. And you?"

"I play the saxophone. He heard me back when he was in Kansas. Told me when I turned twenty-one to look him up. So I did, and here we are."

While he spoke, Josephine studied his face. His skin, darker than hers, seemed to shine as the light touched his cheeks. His close cropped hair suited his broad features, while his eyes sparkled and danced with each word he uttered. Immediately, Josephine was smitten. She glanced away in embarrassment, hoping he hadn't seen her intense scrutiny of him. If he had, he didn't let on, which impressed her, making her feel more comfortable.

When they reached the club Milton held her door before paying the driver. He refused her offer to share the fare and escorted her inside.

The Count, already hard at work with the band, stopped the music and welcomed them in.

"Right on time," he enthused. "I like that. Come in. Come in. Get settled."

Milton unpacked his saxophone, taking his place with the band as if it was second nature. The other members warmly greeted him with high-fives and strong handshakes. The Count guided Josephine to the side and placed her in between his two established singers, Louise Michaels and Esther Harris. They introduced themselves, each giving Josephine gracious and welcoming hugs.

For the next two hours the band experimented with new tunes and songs, old standards and individual vocals. Soon, Josephine felt very much a part of the group, managing to hold her own with her solos, as well as supporting the other two singers.

The Count introduced something new he'd been working on – bebop. He explained he would use the genre sparingly and only so long as it made sense. He told everyone his music always needed to have feeling above everything else.

When the morning's session ended the group broke for lunch. Milton made sure Josephine wasn't left alone, bringing her food, drink and plenty of animated conversation. When the Count made his rounds he had something special to say to the pair of them.

"Great job! Great job! Loved your vocals, Josephine. Feels like you're going to fit right in. And Milt, you play as if you've been with us for years. How the both of you feeling about things so far?"

Josephine, still somewhat overawed by the Count's presence, hesitated to answer, so Milton quickly stepped in.

"Nothing better than to be here with you, Count," he replied, turning to Josephine. "Right?"

Shyly smiling and nodding, she agreed.

"This is just so much of a dream for me. Honestly, I have to pinch myself sometimes. Thank you again, Count, for giving me such a wonderful opportunity. I hope when we start performing I don't let you down."

The Count waved off her doubts saying, "Wouldn't have picked you, sweetheart, if I didn't think you could cut it. Now, let's get back to work."

Over the next two weeks the rehearsals picked up in intensity. Josephine and Milton travelled together every day, returned to their apartments together and began spending a great deal of their spare time in each other's company.

For Josephine, this was a whole new experience. Of course, she'd had lots of friends before but they were mostly in the context of a school situation. Now, on her own, this one-on-one friendship took on a completely different appearance.

Before, the only tried and trusted man she had known was her father. She looked upon him as her gold standard and the one person she could measure every one else against. His kindness and compassion; his good sense and reliability; his work ethic and moral judgment. These were the qualities she'd grown up with and these were the qualities that still guided her.

As she became more and more comfortable in Milton's company, Josephine often found herself comparing his actions with those of her father. What she experienced surprised her; Milton had all her father's good points and, as a bonus, was cute and funny, too.

For his part, Milton treated Josephine as he had been raised to treat not just women but everybody he met. To him, it was just natural to be kind, fair, considerate, and as good as he could be. His personality was not an act; he lived by his values each and every day no matter what situation he found himself in.

And the respect he always showed Josephine made her feel she could trust this man as she could trust her father. He would not take advantage of her and he would not use her in any way, shape or form.

Her strict upbringing never left her while she worked at Stanley's studio on *Othello* and it didn't leave her now. As their relationship naturally developed, Josephine found no difficulty in keeping her moral compass intact. But Milton made that decision easy for her since he never, even once, tried to compromise her ethics. Indeed, he realized he would have to earn her trust and for that he respected her even more.

And yet, despite Josephine's careful monitoring, the two of them over the next few months became as close as almost a couple could get. They rode to work together; they shared late night meals and snacks; they went to the movies and they always said goodnight chastely with kisses on the cheek. Their relationship was everything Josephine had ever dreamed about.

As fate would have it, Josephine's Cabaret Card was issued to her on the last day of rehearsals. The Count celebrated the event with a small party for her at the club.

"Just as well it came through," he beamed, "because tomorrow we pack up and head for the Café Society club for a three-week engagement. And you, sweetheart, are now a part of the band."

Chapter Seventeen

"I think I'm done for the day, dear," Josephine told Ingrid, after enthralling her with tales of Greenwich Village and Count Basie. "The hair salon's next and then bingo. Can't miss my bingo," she chuckled.

Ingrid and Zach warmly hugged her, with Zach this time escorting her down the hall to have her hair done. He returned shaking his head.

"My God, Ingrid, can you believe this woman? Oscar nomination and now singing with Count Basie. And there's gotta be much, much more. I mean, she's only reached twenty-one for goodness sake!"

Raising her eyebrows, Ingrid nodded in agreement.

"I know. She's a freaking goldmine. Who could've known? I can't wait to go over this stuff tonight and then continue on tomorrow. Who knows where she'll be taking us next?"

Bright and early next morning Josephine was ready to divulge more of her secrets.

"Love what they did with your hair," Ingrid began, smiling. "How'd the bingo go?"

"Made myself twenty dollars," Josephine replied, proudly. "But," she added, with a wicked sneer, "it's already spent. And if you come back to my room later I'll share some of it with you."

"Might just take you up on that," Ingrid answered, "especially if you keep surprising us."

Josephine nodded before stating matter-of-factly, "It's been quite a life, hasn't it?"

"All right," Ingrid said, bringing them back to the documentary, "Zach's ready, so let's pick up from yesterday. You are about ready to make your debut with Count Basie. What was that like, actually singing live with him?"

"Oh, he eased me into it. No solos the first couple of times, just backing up the other two girls. It was a lot of fun. He was so loved by everyone in the club. But then on night three he tossed one over to me."

"He let you sing on your own?"

Josephine nodded, eyes wide open.

"The one we practiced at my audition...*My Foolish Heart*. I managed to get through it, just, but I guess I did okay 'cause the crowd went wild. It was quite a moment for me, I can tell you that.

"People came up to me afterwards telling me how much they'd enjoyed the song. I can't even begin to tell you what that did for my confidence. But the next night I was back to being a back-up singer," Josephine said, laughing, "so I guess I knew my place."

"What about Milton?" Ingrid asked. "Was he still part of the band?"

"Very much so," Josephine agreed, but then grew quiet and strangely sad.

"What? Did something happen to Milton, Josephine?" Ingrid pushed.

"It was towards the end of nineteen fifty. The Korean War was in full swing. Our boys were being sent over there. There was a draft at that time and Milton got conscripted. He left just before Christmas that year."

"For basic training?"

"Yes. But by March of nineteen fifty-one he was in Korea with a gun instead of a saxophone."

Josephine sounded crestfallen at the memory. Ingrid signaled Zach to cut the camera for a moment.

"It's like it happened yesterday, isn't it?" she suggested, kindly. "We can move on from this if you'd prefer?"

But Josephine wouldn't hear of it.

"You need to hear the good and the bad. And I need to talk about this."

Zach turned on his camera as Ingrid proceeded with her questions.

"You had obviously become very attached to Milton and him to you. How did you manage to cope with his leaving?"

"We'd had a wonderful summer and fall together in the Count's band. Lots of engagements at clubs all over the city. At one point the Count managed to book Sarah Vaughan for two nights straight and Ella, too.

"Oh, I can tell you they were such unforgettable times. I mean, me singing with Sarah and Ella. And they were gracious and kind to all of us. So, I learned a lot that summer and fall, and Milton was with me all the way.

"And in case you're wondering," Josephine continued, with a laugh, "no, we didn't. We were close but not married. My upbringing kept my values and morals intact. The most we did was a chaste kiss goodnight most evenings. Not once, ever, did he pressure me into doing anything I was uncomfortable with. And for that I was truly grateful. I tell you, child, he was a man among men. Honest. True. Loyal. Just a blessing to know and be around.

"And let me tell you we'd grown very close since the time I joined the band. But it never entered our heads to be anything but tight friends until one day, maybe, we could get married. He respected me and I felt the same about him. Yes indeed, mutual respect was what we had and cherished. It was quite lovely, I can tell you."

"So," asked Ingrid, "how did you deal with his leaving for Korea? I mean, it must've seemed like a part of you was leaving, too?"

Josephine quickly nodded in agreement.

"Knowing he was the one for me, that I'd found someone to spend my life with and then to see him being marched off to war, well, it just ripped me apart inside. I didn't know anything about the war or Korea. I couldn't even pick the place out on a map. That's how ignorant I was. So, for him to be going and fighting people I'd never heard of…I could not get my head around that for a long time."

"Can you describe your last evening together? That moment must've been like a nightmare."

"No, the nightmares came afterwards, when he had gone. No, that last evening was so wonderful. Milton came to my apartment and cooked us the best meal I'd ever tasted. He brought flowers and a parting gift."

"Which was?"

"A locket with his picture inside," Josephine replied, proudly. "I still wear it every day," she continued, unclasping it and handing it to Ingrid.

"Oh, Josephine, he's very handsome. I can see why you were so smitten," she said, returning the precious gift.

"At the end of the evening...well, night, really...we shared our most passionate kiss ever. It went on and on." Shaking her head, she admitted, "I can still feel and taste him now all these years later. Yes, he's been with me every day since then."

"And how did life continue for you not seeing him each day and, also, not being with you in the band?"

"Difficult, but the Count and the others were my family now, so they supported me, making sure I wasn't lonely or too sad. And, of course, the clubs were now non-stop. After a few weeks with Milton gone I just concentrated on becoming a better singer so I might help the Count as much as possible.

"My daddy helped, too. He sent me lots of letters, trying hard to keep my spirits up. But mostly I worked all the time and wrote to Milton practically every day. I told him all about the clubs and the music, how much we all missed him and how much I just wanted him to come home.

"His letters arrived about every two months or so. They were upbeat but I think he protected me from knowing too much of what was going on out there. He was kind that way, always looking out for me.

"But I read in the papers a lot of the bad news about the war. Broke my heart to think of him suffering like that with his buddies. The conditions they put up with..." Josephine shook her head as if it was yesterday, "...just broke my heart."

"When did you see him again?" Ingrid asked, hoping her change of subject might make Josephine feel better.

"It was almost a year. Late nineteen fifty-one, around Thanksgiving. He sent me a wire as a surprise. The band was at the end of a long engagement at The Village Gate. The Count gave us the rest of the year off since we were all exhausted, so I was very excited to have the time to be with Milton.

"He was home for six weeks. My, oh, my, did we have fun. Did a lot of catching up. Talking. Walking..."

"Kissing, I hope?" jumped in Ingrid.

"Oh, yes, for sure," Josephine agreed, with a giggle. "And he came with a big surprise for me."

"Which was?"

"He took me out for a romantic dinner and proposed!"

"Milton asked you to marry him?"

"He did. Well, I was blown off my feet. Never expected that, but was I thrilled. Of course, he told me he would ask my daddy for his permission, but that on his next leave we would tie the knot."

"And what was your father's response when he heard?"

"Milton sent him a wire. Of course, I'd already told Daddy all about him so I don't think he was totally surprised. He wired back the same day with his okay and one piece of advice for Milton. *Just be sure to treat her right or else!* Milton wasn't sure if he was serious or not so I put him straight on that one! Then we both laughed.

"His next leave was set for sometime around July of Fifty-two so we planned the wedding for then. I tell you, we were the two happiest people in the world.

"And, on top of that, the Count told him there would always be a place in his band for him."

Ingrid beamed as Josephine related the story. She really felt as if her friend was actually marrying tomorrow.

"But you had to say goodbye again?"

"Yes, too soon. But knowing what was around the corner for us made the parting a lot easier. And the band got together again early in the New Year. No. No. That's not quite correct," Josephine suddenly remembered. "The Count's financial difficulties had eased a lot so he reformed his whole orchestra. I recall the moment clearly because I was sitting out my break in the show with James Baldwin, having my usual lemon and lime and listening to James enthrall us with some of his amazing, hilarious stories, when the Count pulled me aside to tell me the great news.

"'*Get ready, Jo,*' he began, '*to move on up to the big time! The Count's back in business! I'm re-creating the orchestra.*'

"Then he went on to tell me some of his plans which included several engagements abroad. Oh, my, was I thrilled to hear that news? I could see myself in France and Brazil already.

"He lined up some great musicians, too. I remember a few of them. Joe Newman on trumpet; Matt Gee, trombone and Floyd 'Candy' Johnson on tenor sax. They were something else, I can tell you. Just trying to keep up with them was hard for us girls but we managed. So much fun. So many laughs.

"Sometimes the Count also brought in Charlie, Dizzy and a very young Miles Davis. In all, there were sixteen players in the orchestra, with our first engagement at the Birdland Club. The Count had started to use a calmer, smoother sound to replace the bebop. A lot of the music was based on the new Brazilian style called the bossa nova. The audiences loved it."

For someone like Ingrid, who knew very little about jazz and its history, she found Josephine's recollections of those times not only fascinating but informative. She remained amazed by Josephine's clear memory of faces, facts and places.

"How on earth do you recall so vividly all those moments?" she asked, incredulously.

Josephine laughed but then turned serious.

"Because back then, that was my life. All those moments, all those incredible people were my life. I lived and worked with them twelve hours a day. They left indelible marks. I don't know if they were part of me but I was certainly so much a part of them.

"I mean, the early months of Fifty-two, even without Milton by my side, were really exciting. We began touring all over the United States. Then, in April, the Count took his orchestra on a three-week tour of France and Germany. What an experience! My eyes were wide open all the time.

"World War Two had been over for about seven years so a lot of the cities had been rebuilt. And the people were just so happy to see us. They crowded in the clubs, dancing the nights away and singing along with all the songs. My goodness, those people knew their jazz all right.

"On our down time we got to see so much. Paris, in particular for me, held me nearly spellbound. I'd been singing a new song *'April in Paris'* with the Count and it became a standard for me in the act. But to actually *be* in Paris and sing it…well, you can only imagine."

Ingrid could imagine it as she listened to Josephine describe the moments that mattered in her life.

"By now you must've been a polished performer," she suggested. "Did you have any ambition or thoughts to break out on your own?"

"None at all. How could I compete with Sarah or Ella? No, that never entered my head. I was completely happy singing back-up with the Count. It was a dream job. By June, I even got to see my daddy again. The Count took the orchestra to Los Angeles for a month of bookings. On my down time I spent a lot of time with Daddy.

"He was so proud of me. We sat for hours with me telling him all about my adventures, 'cause adventures were what they were. He showed me off to his friends," she continued, laughing, "like I was his prize ol' hen. We talked a lot about Milton. He told me he knew he was the right man for me. Daddy said Milton already seemed like a member of the family. He was so glad his little girl had found someone that good to share her life with.

"Before I had to leave again with the orchestra we made plans for my wedding. Daddy said he'd find extra work to pay for it but I told him I had that covered. Lots of people wanted to help, including Stanley and Mama's old friends at the studio. Stanley offered to buy me a dress and the reception would also be on him. After all that time he was still being good to me.

"So, I left Daddy feeling on top of the world. His little girl was getting married and he couldn't have been happier. Me, too. Now I just couldn't wait for Milton to come home."

Chapter Eighteen

On her way out of the facility after wrapping up Josephine's contribution for the day, Ingrid was stopped by Sylvia Richards, the Administrator, who asked her if she'd had a chance to interview Gwen Middleton and Clyde Weaver.

"Sorry. No," Ingrid answered, surprised by the question. "Why? Should I?"

"Well, if you're still looking for a couple of amazing stories, then you might want to give them a listen."

Always ready to hear and learn more, Ingrid readily agreed.

"Good," Sylvia continued. "If you've got a minute, they're both in the lounge. C'mon, I'll introduce you."

Gwen Middleton was confined to a wheelchair, the result of severe osteo-arthritis. She now had difficulty in even lifting her head a few inches.

Clyde Weaver, on the other hand, rose immediately to greet Sylvia and her guest, with ears that heard them arrive but without eyes to see them.

"Gwen, Clyde," Sylvia began, "this is Ingrid Strauss, who you know is making a documentary here."

"So pleased to meet you," Ingrid said, reaching out to grasp Gwen's almost frozen hand. Clyde offered his, also, as his head swiveled to learn exactly where the two were standing. At once, Ingrid realized he could not see them at all.

"I've been telling Ingrid she really should interview both of you for the documentary, but I haven't told her why. I'm going to leave the three of you to talk but, remember, you don't have to participate if you don't want to. I'll check back later."

"Please," Ingrid insisted, talking to Clyde, "let's sit and I'll let you know what I have in mind."

Clyde made himself comfortable as Ingrid drew up a chair between them. She took a moment to study both residents' faces, quickly noting Gwen had bright, bold eyes and a determined look about her, while Clyde had a kind, ready smile and plenty of frown lines.

"I've met some incredible folks here," Ingrid began, "people who have trusted me to tell their stories honestly and straightforwardly. This documentary is about them and you because I didn't feel they sometimes imagined their lives mattered anymore. I want to put on permanent record some of their accomplishments for future generations to study and understand what struggles sometimes constitute a life.

"I would love to hear both your stories, so if you could give me a small taste then I'm all ears."

She nodded towards Gwen and invited her to begin.

"To see me now you would find it hard to believe that I was once a world-class athlete," she offered. "My claim to fame is that I represented my country all over the world as a high-jumper. And, in nineteen sixty-four, I'm proud to say, I became an Olympian."

Before Gwen could continue Ingrid held up her hand.

"An Olympian?" Ingrid asked, incredulously. "You were in the Olympic Games?"

"I was," Gwen confirmed. "Tokyo..."

"All right," Ingrid politely interrupted, "that's enough for me. Yours is a story I've got to hear. Would you be prepared to talk to me in front of a camera?"

Gwen smiled and nodded.

"Of course."

"Great! You just let me or Sylvia know when that would be convenient for you. I'm thinking we'll need three or fours hours. Okay?"

Gwen nodded again before slumping back into her chair to listen to what Clyde had to say.

"Mr. Weaver," Ingrid started, earnestly, "your turn."

"First, my dear, I'm not deaf, only blind. You don't have to shout," he replied, with a grin.

Ingrid grimaced and apologized.

"Don't worry, dear, I get that all the time. Now, what do you want to know?"

"Simply, your story."

"Well, all right then," Clyde answered, gently. "When I was in my early forties I was elected mayor of a small town in New Jersey. At that time I still had my sight. I was re-elected four years later, so I guess I'd done an okay job.

"Early the next year...February, in fact, the town literally went up in flames."

"Mr. Weaver," Ingrid cut in, "was that connected in any way to your loss of sight?"

"Why, yes. Yes, it was."

Again, Ingrid held up her hand before realizing Clyde could not see her gesture.

Quickly, she said, "I'd like to stop you there, Mr. Weaver. Let's save the details for later if you'd permit me to interview you for the documentary?"

"Very fine, young lady. I'd like that very much."

"All right. I'll set up times for both of you and we'll go from there. I'm so excited to be able to include your stories in my film."

With Sylvia's help, Ingrid arranged for the interviews to take place two days later, with Gwen in the morning, followed by Clyde later that day.

After Zach set up his camera and lights, Ingrid wheeled Gwen into the room and made her comfortable.

"Any time you need a break just let us know," she informed her. "And any questions you don't want to answer well...we'll just move on. Okay?"

"Perfectly," Gwen assured her, raising her head as far as possible to look into Ingrid's face.

Ingrid smiled before asking her first question.

"I understand Tokyo holds special memories for you. Why on earth Tokyo?"

"Tokyo was where I officially became an Olympian," Gwen replied, proudly. "To be more specific, October, nineteen sixty-four."

"You mean, the Olympic games?"

"Exactly."

"You were in the Olympics?"

"Representing the United States…yes."

"Which sport?"

"Athletics. I was a high-jumper."

"And how old were you?" Ingrid asked.

"Twenty-five," Gwen answered, shaking her head.

"I have to ask – why high-jumping?"

"Well, if I could get out of this chair, you'd understand why," Gwen responded without a hint of regret. "I was a tall girl. Six one by the time of the Olympics. And I loved to leap over things. Always had done, right from a child. Wall, fence, you name it. If it was in front of me I'd just have to jump it.

"I had a gym coach in grade school who noticed my antics. He put in a word with the varsity coach, so by the time I entered eighth grade I was on the team. Pretty special, I can tell you."

"What sort of heights were you able to clear then?"

"At fourteen…about five feet one or two. Almost the height of a door," she giggled. "By the end of high school I was up to five seven."

"Did you go on to college?"

"Full scholarship to USC. Something I'd only dreamed about. We had a great team and some wonderful coaches, but I found college life hard."

"How so?"

"Well, in those days the Olympics were for amateur athletes only, except," Gwen continued, with a shrug, "for the East Germans and Russians. They had everything provided by the state. Not us. I studied, worked and trained. That was basically my life for four years. But it taught me to be self-sufficient and mentally strong.

"In my junior year I was so looking forward to going to Rome for the Sixty Olympics, but before the qualifying meet I tore a hamstring and that was that. My dream ended."

"But you got another shot, right?" Ingrid queried.

"Yes. By my senior year I'd recovered from the injury very well. In fact, I was in the running for the Sullivan Award that year, nineteen sixty-one."

Ingrid frowned.

"What's the Sullivan Award?"

"Oh, it's given to the nation's top amateur athlete. I guess I was close but in the end the great swimmer, Don Schollander won it. And he deserved to, but I was so proud to have even been considered."

"All right," Ingrid cut in politely, "you left USC in 'sixty-one, so how did you make it to Tokyo three years later?"

Gwen laughed.

"Just more hard work. My degree was in physical therapy...how ironic is that," she shrugged, looking down at her legs, "so I stayed at USC in the athletics department. That allowed me the time I needed to train and up my game. The school was always very supportive of my efforts.

"I managed to make the Sixty-four team and headed out in October for Tokyo. The moment seemed so magical and unreal but everyone told me I'd earned my place. All they wanted in return was for me to bring home a medal."

"So, you're in Tokyo, at the biggest event of your life," Ingrid pressed, "and you're only twenty-five. Give us a feel for the experience?"

"Oh, well, there were so many fantastic ones. Let's see...the opening ceremony for a start. Marching with all the athletes into a stadium full of thousands of screaming people. The different colors of the uniforms and flags. The momentous feeling that for a while we were all joined in innocence and happiness. I mean, you just had to shake your head and pinch yourself that it was really happening to you. Everyone seemed so friendly, just overjoyed to be a part of the pageantry. Sadly, that atmosphere doesn't seem so noticeable these days. By the end of the meet I'd made so many new friends, some of whom I still write to.

"And then being able to travel to the other venues and watch world-class folk compete. That was a thrill. The swimming; equestrian; boxing, oh, and gymnastics. Just fabulous the whole experience."

"Tell us about your own competition – the high jump?"

"Athletics didn't begin until the second week so I was able to get in really good shape and psych myself up. The prelims were one day and those in the top twelve made it through to the finals. That's when the competition heated up.

"After the first round of finals I was in fourth place. The then world and current Olympic champion, Iolanda Balas of Romania was first. She was something else and we all knew we couldn't get close to her. So, essentially we were fighting for silver or bronze. Incidentally, Iolanda was the first woman ever to clear six feet in a meet.

"Ahead of me were Michele Brown of Australia and Taisiya Chenchik of Russia. Of course, we all knew each other and were really good friends, but competition is still competition."

"Any nerves being at the Olympics in front of all those cheering spectators?" Ingrid asked, trying to get a sense of Gwen's state of mind at that moment.

"You're just in a zone," Gwen replied, plainly. "Block everything out and focus. It's the only way. And my only focus was to bring home a medal for the U.S."

"Guide us through what happened next," Ingrid urged, trying hard to hide her curiosity.

"All right," Gwen began, doing her best to sit upright. "Iolanda had already cleared six feet, so she had the gold tied up. Michele cleared five ten, but Taisiya and I were having trouble with five nine.

"You only get three tries at each height and we both had knocked the bar off twice. On her third try Taisiya barely cleared it but the bar held. So, now she was in for the bronze.

"I talked to the coaches and we made the decision to have the officials raise the bar an inch. If I cleared it that would put enormous pressure on Taisiya. But five ten was high for me, not impossible, but hard. I took a long time in prep, focusing, seeing myself jumping over the bar, just really psyching myself up.

"I took a deep breath and started off really strongly. But just before I got into my jump I felt a twinge in my hamstring, the one I'd injured. I should've stopped right there, regrouped, had it taped and tried again. But I didn't and it cost me the bronze. I actually cleared the bar going up but on the way down my trailing knee just nicked the bar. I turned just in time to see it hitting the sand."

Gwen shrugged and smiled, but Ingrid saw her reliving the moment as if it had happened yesterday.

"It still hurts, doesn't it?' she offered, kindly.

"You know, I've often thought about that moment, the moment I decided to risk everything, and I would do the same today. No regrets. None at all. In my mind, I was still a winner. An Olympian. Not many people can say that. And I was happy for Taisiya. She'd had a hard life in Russia, so if her winning the bronze somehow made her life easier, then that was okay by me.

"She offered to give me her medal, but I refused. She'd won it fair and square. The nice thing was, we remained good friends right up until her passing in two thousand thirteen. I appreciated that. She was a gem of a girl."

Ingrid concluded the interview with a few more questions before giving Gwen a long, warm hug she hoped might, in some small way, convey her admiration and appreciation. Ingrid vowed that this woman and her story, both of which had made such an impact upon her, would never be forgotten.

After lunch, Ingrid sat with Zach discussing Gwen's amazing story when they heard tapping coming down the hall. Within seconds, Clyde Weaver appeared in the doorway asking if he was in the right place.

Ingrid jumped up whilst quickly apologizing for not coming to meet him.

"Oh, no apology necessary," Clyde answered. "I know my way around this place like a blind man," he continued, as he laughed at his own joke.

Ingrid and Zach didn't quite know how to react to Clyde's humor.

"I can see that, Mr. Weaver," was how she responded, before guiding him to his seat.

"Now, let's get one thing straight," Clyde said, as soon as he settled down, "it's Clyde, not Mr. Weaver. Okay?"

"Perfectly," Ingrid replied, raising her eyebrows in Zach's direction. "Clyde, it is. And I'm Ingrid and my cameraman and all around tech person is Zach."

"Documentary film maker eh?" Clyde said. "Well, dear, you have a great voice for it. So, what d'you want to know?"

"We'd love to record your story. I have a strong feeling there's more to you than meets the eye!"

"Very funny, Ingrid," Clyde responded. "Now we're on the same wavelength."

"So, I'll ask you some questions and I'd like you to respond in your own words and for however long you like. Later, Zach and I will cut and paste your contribution into the whole documentary."

"Very good. Let's go!"

"You were the mayor of a town in New Jersey. Which one?"

"Bridgeburgh. Population around fifteen thousand give or take a few."

"And you were first elected in your early forties?"

"Forty-three, to be exact. Would have been nineteen seventy-six. And they re-elected me every year thereafter until I retired five years ago. Guess I must've done an okay job," Clyde finished, with a laugh.

"Ten straight elections," Ingrid countered, "if my math is correct. Very impressive. Now, I understand things in the town weren't always pleasant. You had some problems; some hard times."

Clyde's demeanor change immediately from light-hearted to serious.

"That's correct.," he answered, shaking his head.

"How so?" Ingrid pressed.

"After my first term, I was re-elected in the November. I was feeling kinda smug, that perhaps I'd hadn't done so bad. Then in February, all hell broke loose in the town."

"What happened?"

"Bridgeburgh was settled around eighteen sixty-five by a couple of wealthy mill owners. They built stores and houses for their work force but the quality wasn't exactly first class. They liked making money so the less they had to spend on materials the better. Of course, there weren't too many building codes back then. But, to their credit, they did a lot for the community.

"As the years rolled by more buildings and homes were added. Codes were updated but most of the older construction was grandfathered, and there were a lot of older folk who just couldn't afford the updates. So, now it's early nineteen eighty and some of these structures are over a hundred years old, with wiring and utilities to match."

Ingrid held out her open hands in front of her.

"I know. I know," Clyde sensed, "what could possible go wrong? A fire, that's what! Not just a fire but a conflagration that engulfed half the town.

"At the time, I was the Assistant Fire Chief. Got the call about two in the morning. So we loaded up and headed out. Now remember, it's an early morning in February and the temperature's hovering around fifteen degrees. Hoses are freezing up; water's turning to ice quicker than a blink and half the town's buildings are ablaze.

"We called for backup from seven local companies but by the time the sun came up there was only devastation. And I'm the mayor of this mess."

"So, basically," Ingrid surmised, "half of your town is gone. What about injuries and fatalities?"

"Fortunately, no one died but several folk had broken bones, smoke inhalation and minor scrapes. The lads saved a lot of people that night."

"Including you, right?" Ingrid offered, trying to guide Clyde into revealing how he'd lost his sight in the fire.

"Yup, including me. Lost my eyes but saved a kid," he replied, shaking his head.

"Would you mind telling what happened exactly 'cause that sounds heroic to me?"

"Nah, just part of the job. But I will tell you. Two of us were called to a two story house that was fully engulfed when we got there. A woman stood outside screaming to us that her two kids were inside, upstairs.

"Bill Gibbs, the other firefighter, grabbed a couple of masks and we went inside. The front of the house wasn't too bad. We got to the stairs, raced up and started searching. The kids were yelling but their shouts came from the back, which was going pretty well.

"Bill took one room while I made my way down the hall to the other. I found a kid, a boy about five, I guess, laying on the floor gasping for breath. Quick as I could I secured him to me and took off down the hall. I saw Bill disappear down the stairs with a young girl in his arms.

"I followed and was grateful to see him exit the building. Just as I reached the bottom stair a huge ball of flame came hurtling towards us from the kitchen area. I protected the kid from it but I couldn't turn my face back quick enough.

"The flames seemed to surround my head but I still managed to make it out with the kid safe and sound. The medics quickly took the kid away and then helped me. I was on the ground and all I could see was a bright light. That soon faded and everything went black. At first I thought it was due to the smoke, but my eyesight never came back. The explosion from the kitchen tore the retinas apart. From that day on I was blind."

Ingrid could find no words to express her astonishment at Clyde's heroism. She looked at Zach who stared back with his mouth wide open. *What the hell can I say,* she thought, *to someone who gave so much for a stranger?*

Finally, she reached across to Clyde and held his hand. He gripped hers back and nodded, understanding how difficult it was for her to say anything appropriate.

"I know. I know," he reassured her. "It's okay. It was a long time ago now. I've had a good life. No regrets, honestly."

"Your recovery," she began, tentatively, "how on earth did you cope?"

"My dear wife, God rest her, and the whole community couldn't have done more for me. I was never alone. Anything I needed I got. And slowly life picked up again. I started attending town meetings and, as I said, was re-elected so many times. I've been blessed, really, I've been blessed."

"And the town itself?" Ingrid asked. "Did it recover, too?"

"Took almost three years, but, yes, we rebuilt the town hopefully better than it was. I managed to secure state and federal funds, but most of the work was done by businesses and a lot of dedicated volunteers. We had an unveiling when most of the re-construction was complete. The governor came and cut a ribbon which was special beyond words. So proud of everyone, I was."

Ingrid finished the interview with a few wrap-up questions before walking Clyde back to his room for a well-earned rest. Meeting up with Zach again she once more found herself speechless.

"Yeah, I know," Zach said, "I don't know what to say either. These stories are like uncovering a gold mine. You think you've seen and heard everything then Gwen or Clyde pop up out of nowhere. I'm telling you, Ingrid, you've discovered a *real* gold mine here."

"Yeah, it's all a bit overwhelming to tell the truth," Ingrid answered, honestly. "And, we haven't even begun to finish with Josephine yet. You've got to promise to help me not screw any of this up, pal. Okay? Just make sure I don't ruin this for everyone."

Chapter Nineteen

During the early summer of nineteen fifty-two, an excited twenty-three year old Josephine Benson looked into her future and saw only happiness and love; caring and sharing. She had a wedding planned with Milton when he came home on leave sometime towards the end of summer, as well as an enduring and satisfying career with the Count.

One of the other singers in the orchestra had left and hadn't been replaced, so Josephine now found herself always front and center in performances. Her confidence was such that she relished the spotlight while being careful to respect her privileged position.

After the orchestra's engagement in Los Angeles it moved back to New York for a series of shows around the city. The Count Basie Orchestra began a period in American jazz history of innovative, ever-changing musical styles which solidified its place as one of the premier bands of the era.

Josephine, at this point in her life, had no clear idea of where her musical talents might take her. All she knew was the freedom it gave her, so living in the moment consumed her more than what might lie ahead.

The Village still invigorated her each day with its ever expanding wave of artists, musicians, writers and actors filling cafes and venues like never before. But despite the festive, lively mood of the area, Josephine found herself, at times, with empty feelings only seeing Milton again could assuage. She now ached for him every day in a way that surprised her. Absence, indeed, did make her heart grow fonder.

Josephine's spirits were raised when in early July she received a letter from Milton. It was an infrequent occurrence. This letter he actually wrote in May. But, although it took over two months to reach her, her joy and relief knew no bounds. She read and reread his words over and over;

Dear Angelface,

I'm so sorry I haven't written sooner but as you can imagine things out here are crazy difficult. First I have to tell you how much I'm missing you. I carry your picture with me all the time. It's a real comfort for me, oh yes, you have no idea how just looking at your pretty face makes me feel so much better. I hope you look at mine sometimes 'cause I feel they bring us close together.

We managed to get through the harsh winter but it was no fun I can tell you. We're supplied very well but everyone here misses home. I've made a lot of new friends including Australians and British. When we're not dodging the incoming we sometimes sit around and talk about home, family and all the things we miss.

I'm not allowed to tell you much about our situation but we're expecting the Chinese to make a big push real soon. Don't worry 'cause we're always ready for them and the North Koreans. Right now things have been quiet and it's like we're in a stalemate. There are supposedly some peace talks going on to settle this whole mess. I sure hope so since I just want to come home.

My next leave is still on for July or August and I can't wait to see and hold you again. I hope the wedding plans are moving forward, too. Just the thought of walking down the aisle with you by my side fills me with so much happiness. You will be the best bride a man has ever married.

I hope you are well, sweetness, and that you and the orchestra are still going strong. Some nights I close my eyes and can hear your lovely voice in my head. That sure helps get me through the long hours I can tell you.

I have to close now and hopefully catch the next mail plane out of here. Always remember how much I love and miss you and how often you are in my thoughts. You are, and will always be, my Angelface.

Until we see each other again real soon, be safe and keep singing!

All my love forever,
Milton

Soon after Josephine received Milton's sweet, touching and loving letter she began earnestly planning their wedding for mid-August in Los Angeles. She wired her father, asking him to set the wheels in motion. He actually responded by calling her on his newly installed telephone.

"Daddy, you have a phone?" she asked, surprised by the news.

"Indeed, I do," he confirmed, proudly. "Some of your mama's friends at the studio got it for me so I could talk with you in person. How do I sound?"

"Just like my daddy!" Josephine yelled. "Just like my daddy!"

"Okay. Good, but there's no need to shout, baby. I can hear you just fine."

Josephine apologized, explaining how excited she felt being able to talk with him as if he was in the next room.

"Oh, Daddy, I've got so much to tell you. I was so happy to get a letter from Milton. He wrote in May but as I said in my wire he's still coming home soon. I'm getting married, Daddy! I'm getting married!"

"I know, baby, and I've already got things moving. I'm not your mama, I realize that, but I'm doing what I can to pull a nice wedding together. Your mama's friends at the studio have been real helpful. They talked to Stanley and he's agreed to have the ceremony there, with some of his prop people setting up some kind of amazing chapel. They're not telling me much so I don't spoil it for you," he laughed, "but special is what you're going to get. Also, Stanley is throwing the reception…"

"What?" Josephine interrupted. "Stanley's what?"

"He wants to give you the reception, also at the studio. And I ain't arguing with that," he said, emphatically.

Josephine took a few seconds to process all this information

"Oh, Daddy, I'm so blessed with all these wonderful people in my life doing these things for me. You need to let them know how much me and my Milton appreciate everything."

"Already done that, sweetheart. You just like family to them. Now, we need to firm up a date. When does Milton think he'll be home?"

"Next month, Daddy. So please fix the ceremony for the middle of August. The Count said he'll get me there, no problem. He also told me he's bringing five or six members of the orchestra with him so they can play at the wedding. Oh, Daddy, I'm just so blessed."

Mr. Benson assured his daughter he would take care of everything for her. They moved on from the wedding so he could hear first hand the latest news on her singing career.

"Fine and dandy, Daddy. We are all one big family. The Count is so good to us and now he tells me he's planning a lot more trips abroad."

"And after the wedding?" Mr. Benson pointedly asked. "What you gonna do then?"

"I will discuss that with Milton when he's here," Josephine replied, coolly. "The Count has said he has a job with the orchestra when he's free and clear. So, either way, I'll still be singing. I'm sure Milton will want me to carry on. Now, Daddy, that's enough about me. How are you?"

Mr. Benson took his time in answering.

"Daddy," Josephine pressed, "you're not sick are you? And you better tell me the truth, d'you hear?"

"Ain't nothing for you to worry your pretty little head about," he responded lightly. "The doc says I should be easing up some. I'm getting older, sweetness, so I guess the man's right."

"That's not an answer to my question, Daddy, and you know it. Now, you tell me right now what's with you?"

"Just my heart's not as strong as it used to be. But I got me some pills and so long as I remember to take them I'll be fine."

"I'm coming home soon, Daddy, for the wedding and I will stay a while to look after you. I don't care about any singing career. All I care about is you."

"Honey, no. I'm just fine. You can check me out when you're here, but that's as far as it goes. You hear me?"

"Loud and clear, Daddy. If you're sure, then okay. But you can count on me talking with some people when I'm there."

Mr. Benson laughed at his daughter's promise.

"Oh, I know you be doing that," he agreed, with a smile she couldn't see. "I know you be doing that."

"Good. And now promise you'll call me anytime you're not feeling too good. Will you promise, Daddy?"

"I will, sweetheart. I will."

They ended the call tenderly and caringly. But after she replaced the receiver Josephine's heart became full of dread.

The days of July dwindled down with the last of the orchestra's engagements before Milton was due home for the wedding. She wasn't sure exactly when he'd arrive but she expected a wire any time. The war in Korea seemed at a stalemate, which she took as a good sign it might soon be over.

On a late afternoon in early August, Josephine finally received the telegram she'd been expecting for so long. It would tell her when Milton, her beloved Milton, would walk through the door and into her arms again.

Chapter Twenty

"If you're looking for Josephine, you'll find her in the large rec room," Sylvia Richards informed Ingrid and Zach as she passed them in the hallway. "She's directing her troops."

The pair had no idea what Sylvia meant so they quickly and eagerly headed downstairs to find out. The big recreational room usually used for movies, music recitals and the like, now contained about twenty residents scattered around facing the small stage. On the stage, Josephine and a younger woman addressed the crowd.

Ingrid and Zach respectfully stayed in the back but both were fascinated to discover what exactly was going on.

"We only have about four weeks," they heard Josephine say, pointedly, "so, no time to lose. Hard work and fun. Fun and hard work. Don't forget, we have our standards to maintain."

Ingrid frowned at Zach, who raised his eyebrows as if to say, *What the heck is this all about?* They continued to listen as Josephine introduced the woman sitting next to her.

"People, this is Elizabeth Carrington. Elizabeth, as some of you may know, is the daughter of one of our friends here, Peter Chadwick. Elizabeth just happens to be a high school music teacher and has graciously agreed to help me and all of us put on our annual 'Salute to the Musicals' evening. Obviously, she's no stranger to staging these types of performances and I, for one, need all the help I can get. So, without further ado I'll have Elizabeth say a few words."

The residents applauded politely before Elizabeth warmly outlined the steps she had in mind to make the evening a success. Afterwards, and for the next hour, she and Josephine put ten or more performers through their paces. Elizabeth, now at the piano, kept the mood light and fun, encouraging everyone with kind words and gentle hints. Ingrid, grinning and impressed, made a mental note to ask Sylvia if she and Zach could attend the event when the time came.

"Josephine, you never cease to amaze me," Ingrid announced, as she settled her down to continue the documentary.

"Why, child, what have I done now?" Josephine answered, coyly, as a cheeky smile creased her mouth.

"What was that in there? Are you directing some sort of show now?"

"Why, yes I am, with some help from Elizabeth. We put one on every year and, yes, it was my idea. You see, when I first came here I soon noticed folk were just kind of sitting around and not being too active.

"I thought some of them might enjoy doing a little singing and dancing. So, with my background, I suggested to Sylvia we put on a modest show. That was five years ago now and it's grown to a two hour performance. We invite family and friends, musicians and choirs. This time, Elizabeth is bringing her high school Glee club. Should be a lot of fun. You and your young man should join us.

"Of course," she playfully teased, "you probably won't know any of the song and dance routines. They're from shows like 'Guys and Dolls', 'My Fair Lady', 'Oklahoma' and 'The King and I'. But that's all right," she teased again, "you may actually enjoy a real song for a change and not that stuff you keep playing on that phone device of yours."

Ingrid feigned a pout before assuring Josephine they'd be at the performance.

"You said a moment ago '*with my background*' about pulling the show together. You meant your acting and singing background, right?" Ingrid inquired.

Josephine nodded.

"That and all the other skills I've gathered in my life, which I might tell you about at another time if you're a good girl," Josephine replied, with a wink and a twinkle in her eye.

"All right," Ingrid conceded, suitably admonished, "let's get back to… where… nineteen fifty-two? That summer, I think, is where we left it, right?"

The mere mention of the date entirely changed Josephine's demeanor. She went from sassy to sober almost instantaneously. Ingrid immediately noticed but chose to carry on.

"When we left off our last session you were recalling your excitement surrounding your upcoming wedding to Milton. Your father told you some of the plans Stanley and your mother's friends were organizing, and all that remained was for Milton to return from Korea. Then you received a telegram which you hoped would tell exactly when he was due home. Can you pick it up from there?"

Josephine took her time answering, trying hard to see the recollections clearly in her mind. Finally, she looked directly into the camera and began.

"Yes, I was over the moon to receive the wire, to learn when my Milton would be back. But life is strange and cruel sometimes. One minute you're on top of the world and the next…well…it all falls apart. That's how it was; that's what happened in the space of a few seconds."

"His leave was delayed?" Ingrid asked.

Josephine smiled wryly and shook her head.

"You could say that in a manner of speaking."

"Oh, Josephine, no. No. No. No. Are you…?"

"The telegram wasn't from Milton. It was from the military. He hadn't made it. He was never coming home to me."

"He died in Korea?"

"He did. Ironically, three days before he was due to ship out on leave. They didn't give many details just that he died fighting for his country. They'd already buried him out there, so I guess there wasn't much left."

"Oh, Josephine," Ingrid almost cried, holding back her tears, "I'm so sorry."

"I was just grateful they let me know. And that was due to Milton's thoughtfulness, too. He told me before he returned after his last leave that he'd given the military my name and address as one of his next of kin should anything happen.

"A few weeks later a sergeant, in full dress uniform, showed up at my apartment. He said some comforting words to me, handed me a folded American flag and gave me a box which Milton had asked be passed to me if he should die."

"His dog tags?" Ingrid guessed.

Josephine slowly nodded before ruefully shaking her head.

"I still have them to this day."

With the camera still rolling, Ingrid asked how on earth she had coped with Milton's sudden passing.

"The Count and everyone never left me for a second. Anything I wanted they were there for me. I didn't sleep alone for two weeks. Either the girls cuddled me or some of the band members stayed with me into the night just talking.

"But as much as I appreciated their kindnesses, the only person I really needed was my daddy. Even that wish the Count took care of, flying me out to Los Angeles and putting a car at my disposal."

"I assume you eventually went back to the orchestra," Ingrid surmised. "So, how did you manage to recover from such a devastating loss?"

"One word – Daddy. He let me wallow for a while, and I do mean wallow, before sitting me down and giving me some of his good ol' fashioned common sense. And that was so hard for him because I remained numb and almost unresponsive to...well...life in general.

"I wasn't eating or sleeping very well. My appearance went from normal to haggard and hollow-eyed. He saw what Milton's death was doing to me and I'm sure he thought the world didn't need another tragedy.

"So, one morning, he literally dragged me to the shower, turned on the water and shoved me inside. That moment, I have to say in all honesty, probably saved my life. Of course, at the time I thought he didn't understand what I was going through. Then I realized he'd experienced similar feelings when Mama passed. How stupid and self-centered was that?

"Daddy never referred to my bad behavior when we talked everything over. He just kept telling me he understood all my rollercoaster emotions. That was okay, he said, but he also kept repeating that my life wasn't over, that sometimes things are just meant to be, and I would come out of this on the other side stronger, more determined and eventually happy again.

"I stayed another two weeks, got myself together again, then headed back to New York and the orchestra. Once more, they were amazing, supporting and helping me get back on track. A lot of folks thought the Count was being insensitive by getting us out on the road again. He told me it was just what I needed and he was correct.

"We began a series in the city before heading to the mid-west. And I have to say how good it felt to be actually singing, laughing and having fun again."

Both Ingrid and Zach were mentally exhausted listening to Josephine's sad but riveting account of Milton's death. They imagined she felt the same, so Ingrid decided to cut the session short and walk Josephine back to her room to rest.

But Josephine hadn't finished her reminiscences for the day. Once in her room she asked Ingrid to go to the closet and retrieve an old brown suitcase.

"Yes, that's it. Bring it to me, child, if you don't mind?"

Ingrid placed the suitcase on a table and waited. Meanwhile, Josephine's bony fingers fished around inside her purse. She produced a small, brass key and proceeded to unlock the case. As she raised the top, she let out an audible sigh before beckoning to Ingrid.

"Sit, child. I have things to show you. Important things."

Ingrid, pulling up a chair, wondered what more Josephine could share that might be more important than her memories.

"I've watched a lot of documentaries in my time," Josephine continued, "and I'm always happy to see lots of photographs, letters and all sorts of souvenirs that help to tell a story."

"Of course," Ingrid agreed, nodding her head. "The more you can show the better the narrative."

"Exactly. That's why I need you see what's in here."

As Josephine spoke she began removing batches of photos together with bundles of letters. Soon the piles occupied a fair amount of space.

"And what are these?" Ingrid questioned, with a frown.

"These are my life," Josephine confirmed, "or, at least, the early part."

With great respect, Ingrid picked up a sheaf of sepia photos. As she looked through them, images of a very much younger Josephine stared back at her through the years.

There were shots of a smiling child, probably around eight or nine years of age Ingrid thought, splashing through a paddling pool, hugging her mother, reading or just goofing off. Another showed Josephine with an older girl, both of them laughing into the camera. On the back was a handwritten note: *Josephine and Judy 1937.*

Josephine saw Ingrid's astonished look and smiled.

"I wanted you to know I haven't been making all this stuff up. Now, shut the case and take it with. You can use whatever you want for your documentary. Just don't lose any of it," she giggled.

"Oh, Josephine, this is a goldmine," Ingrid effused. "And you're so right. These items will just add great visual evidence to your story. I will guard them with my life," she promised.

"Oh, we're not finished yet," Josephine informed her. "Now, go into my closet where all my dresses are hanging. That's it. Now, go to the far end of the left side."

"All right, I'm there."

"Do you see a long, black plastic bag on a hanger?"

"Yes."

"Take it out, please, and bring it on over."

Ingrid complied, laying the bag on the bed.

"Look inside," Josephine directed.

Ingrid carefully lifted up the bag from the bottom.

"Oh, my god!" she exclaimed. "Is this your wedding dress?"

Josephine nodded somberly. "The very same. Pristine. Never been worn."

"It's just so beautiful. I can understand why you've kept it all these years. But, Josephine, so sad, too."

"I could never bear to get rid of it. Stanley had it made for me by some of Mama's friends at the studio. They did a pretty good job, I'd say."

"This will also be in the documentary," Ingrid suggested, "if you agree. Such a moving story."

"And I have one more memento to share," Josephine said, reaching to undo a bracelet.

She handed Ingrid the silver chain adorned with what looked like charms.

"Take a look at this," she offered. "You might want to include this, too."

Ingrid took the object as if handling precious gold. She peered at the metal discs, turning them over and holding them close for a better view.

"You kept these for all those years," she said, staring at Milton's dog tags. "Oh, Josephine, I don't know what to say anymore."

"When you've met the love of your life," Josephine answered, with a resigned smile, "you have to hang on to whatever you can. Love, trust and loyalty don't just disappear when someone dies. He's been with me every day of my life since his passing. There have been no others."

Ingrid felt a chill run down her spine listening to Josephine's heartfelt, sagacious words. They would be words she would remember her whole life.

"Yes, I'd want to include these in the documentary, if I may. We'll film a segment later where you can repeat what you've just explained to me. Oh, Josephine, you've given me so much to think about."

"Then off you go now and do whatever it is you and your young man do. I need to take a nap or I'll miss bingo tonight," she giggled.

Later, in the quiet of her apartment, Ingrid and Zach opened Josephine's suitcase. They spent the rest of the evening into the early hours carefully sifting through the photographs, letters and other keepsakes.

"She hasn't embellished one single thing," Zach offered, as they began making separate piles of her life.

"I know," Ingrid agreed. "She's the real deal. We have her childhood; mother and father; her high school years; some great studio shots, candid and not, and all these of her performing with Count Basie. And look at the photos of Milton," Ingrid said with a sigh. "How handsome is he? So sad. So very sad."

"These, too," Zach answered, glancing through some of Josephine's letters from her father. "For a regular guy he must've been something special. He keeps giving her solid advice. No preaching like, 'listen to me, I know what's best for you' type of thing."

"That's right," Ingrid nodded. "All the items are a testament to her mother and father and how well they raised her. I could fill a whole section with them alone. But, we'll add them in where we think fit to make the narrative believable and touching for our viewers."

By around two o'clock Zach decided to call it a night. After he'd left, Ingrid made herself a cup of tea before curling up on the couch with Milton's dog tags nestled in the palm of her hand. Repeatedly turning them over, she tried hard to imagine how Josephine must have felt all those years ago when learning her beloved man wasn't coming back. Shivering, she pulled a blanket around her shoulders and wondered how on earth *she* would cope with such a loss. Those thoughts stayed alive with her until finally managing to sink into a peaceful oblivion.

Chapter Twenty-One

The rest of nineteen fifty-two and the whole of the next year eventually passed for Josephine with tremendous bouts of sadness, but also with major strides away from her grief and towards the light. It was, quite simply, a journey; one she needed to travel and navigate for herself if she was to find any sense of resolution and peace.

The dawn of nineteen fifty-four found Josephine immersed in The Count Basie Orchestra's exploding popularity. The performance schedule left her with little time to think, let alone wallow, as the visited venues and cities seemed to amass like a compendium from an atlas.

The orchestra now regularly appeared on the nascent television medium, which Josephine loved since it meant her father might catch a glimpse of her every now and then.

That summer, the Count wrote a lot of new music, experimenting again with different sounds and emotions, some calmer and smoother. The orchestra regularly backed Sarah, Ella, Lena and Billie Holiday, as well as sit-ins such as Charlie Parker, Miles Davis and Sonny Rollins. The whole experience for Josephine lifted her spirits to a point where she finally began to believe she could move on from Milton and live her life.

The next year she met one of her favorite and long admired singers, the twenty-eight year old sensation, Eartha Kitt. It was a thrill of almost unimaginable proportions for Josephine to provide back-up for her. Eartha, discovered by Orson Welles in Paris, burst onto the scene in the early Fifties. Josephine never forgot her magnetism and unusual delivery. Many of her classics, she always maintained, such as '*C'est si Bon*', '*Santa Baby*' and '*Just an Old Fashioned Girl*', could not have been sung by anyone else.

As much as Josephine enjoyed and prospered from her career with the Count, her life still occasionally felt the jolts and bumps of reality. During the early part of nineteen fifty-six, her father, her only living relative, suffered a serious heart attack while still working as a grave digger. He always joked to his wife that that's what would happen to him one day on the job – he would die while digging a grave, fall into the hole and be buried. They laughed about it then but now it seemed like a real possibility.

It did not happen this time. Co-workers called the medics and the hospital did the rest to save him. He waited three days before calling his daughter, but by that evening she was by his bedside.

"So, *now* will you retire, Daddy?" Josephine implored. "We've talked about this, haven't we? And it's this simple – I don't want to lose you." She squeezed his hand as she sniffed away a tear.

"Oh, honey, it's nothing really. Just got to rest up some and no more digging for a while. But I gotta work. I need the money. You know that."

Josephine shook her head as a determined look crossed her face.

"How much do you love me, Daddy?" she asked, plainly.

"Well, you know how much, sweetness," Mr. Benson offered, reassuringly. "You are my sun and moon."

"Then if that's the case, and I do know how much you love me, Daddy, you have to make some changes. If not for you, then do it for me."

"Know what your saying, baby, but it ain't that easy. I got bills to pay. They're not gonna take care of themselves."

"I understand," Josephine agreed. "And I want you to let me help you."

"Paying my bills?" Mr. Benson asked, incredulously. "No way I could let you do that. I'm a proud man and I take care of my own business."

"Stubborn more like," Josephine countered. "You and Mama always gave me what I needed. Now it's my turn to pay back some of your goodness. The Count's been very generous to me. He pays me well and I've always taken your advice to save what I can. That doesn't make me rich but I am very comfortable.

"Daddy, we have to make some changes. The work you're doing is killing you. It's much too hard on that ol' heart of yours. Now, I know you are a very proud man and part of that pride is going out every day and working. I get that. But I also want you around for a good long time."

Mr. Benson's face grew sterner and sterner by the second. The words coming from his daughter were not the ones he wanted to hear. But he also saw the passion and caring in her eyes. He realized, deep down, she was correct and that, indeed, his pride and dignity were clouding his usual good sense.

Reluctantly, he asked, "So, what exactly are you proposing here, sweetheart?"

"You need to stop working, Daddy. All your life, even when you were a little kid, you've been working at one job or another. Now…"

"But I *had* to, honey child," Mr. Benson desperately interrupted. "Weren't no other way."

"I know. I know," Josephine replied, softly. "But now things are different. You don't *have* to anymore. That's what I'm saying. You don't *have* to."

"And how am I supposed to pay my bills? Need money for that."

"I will take care of all your bills," Josephine assured him.

Mr. Benson vigorously shook his head.

"Ain't no way that's happening. I've always paid things myself. Ain't no way."

Josephine, squeezing her father's hand, put her face close to his, her eyes, fierce and strident, blazed into his.

"Do you want me to be an orphan?" she demanded, angrily. "Do you?"

Her tone and demeanor took Mr. Benson completely by surprise. Never before had he witnessed his beloved child behaving in such a harsh, biting way towards him. Taking a few seconds to consider her words, he quickly realized the pain he might cause her by not agreeing would forever break his heart.

He grasped her head between his massive hands, kissed her tenderly on her forehead and said, "Thank you, sweetness. Thank you. What would I do without you? How did you get to be so special and kind?"

"Only by what you and Mama taught me, Daddy. Both of you good teachers, that's how."

They spent the next two hours in closeness, discussing his future and how to make his new situation work. In the end, he accepted every piece of help and assistance she offered. Two weeks later she left for New York, satisfied her father would be well provided for and around for a good, long time.

Celebrities never turned Josephine's head. Over the years with the Count and his orchestra, as well as living in the Village, she met her fair share of famous people, some of them on their way up and others going in the opposite direction.

For quite a while she circulated in the orbit of singers, actors and writers, enjoying their company, marveling at their talent or, as with Judy Garland, considering her a sometime friend and confidante.

Josephine truly did not seek to become a household name. Her exposure to the lives of artists taught her two valuable lessons; that fame is usually fleeting and the damage it sometimes causes is often catastrophic. Added to those downsides was her own brief brush with stardom when she received her Oscar nomination. Her disappointment and loathing with an apparent corrupt process left her feeling empty and, at times, worthless.

Now she enjoyed the best of both worlds as an integral part of the orchestra. She had her moments in the sun while simultaneously fading into the background for most of the performances. It was a life that suited her personality and emotions.

Being on the road with the orchestra never ceased to produce surprises for Josephine. Whether it was a new city or a new country, each experience enlivened her spirits and gently reminded her how far she'd come and how lucky she was to have such opportunities.

One of the most special occurred towards the end of nineteen fifty-seven, when the Count took his orchestra on an extensive tour of the British Isles. Audiences were more than excited to see a true American jazz band of this stature grace their stages. Lines actually curled around the streets outside the theaters, such was the intense interest.

The countryside of England, Wales, Scotland and Ireland took Josephine's breath away. She had no idea places so lush, green and beautiful existed. Compared to growing up in California, the experience seemed like stepping out into another world.

But, in spite of those wonderful images, one other event eclipsed all others. In the middle of November the Count Basie Orchestra and singers played a Royal Command Performance before Her Majesty Queen Elizabeth II. On hearing the news, Josephine literally shook from head to toe. *The Queen of England! I'll be singing for The Queen of England! Oh my goodness! Oh my lord!*

The evening, a star-studded affair, included many of England's favorite performers, as well as international artists like Mario Lanza and Judy Garland.

When Josephine discovered Judy was also in the line-up she imagined someone was playing a trick on her. But at rehearsals, there she was in the flesh, just as warm and friendly as ever. Watching Judy from the wings as she practiced '*Somewhere Over the Rainbow*', Josephine fondly remembered their first meeting on the set of '*The Wizard of Oz*' twenty years before.

"Well, well," Judy began, as she spotted Josephine watching her, "if it's not my little chickadee. You come here right now."

The two embraced for the longest time before walking off arm-in-arm to Judy's dressing room.

"I should have remembered you'd be here with the Count," Judy said, holding Josephine's hand, "but I'm so frazzled some days I hardly know where I am."

Josephine shook her head as if it didn't matter. Studying her friend as she talked, she noticed how tired and ashen she looked. There was pallor about her face that suggested she might be sick; puffiness around her eyes Josephine could only feel sad about.

They caught up on each other's lives for the next hour before Judy abruptly said she had to leave.

"Dinner, eh? Tonight? I'll be in touch, my sweet. Now give me a kiss and tell me you love me."

Josephine did as she was told but the whole experience of meeting Judy again after so many years left her feeling bewildered and almost distraught at her friend's appearance and behavior.

The dinner never happened and she never heard directly from Judy ever again.

The Command Performance before the Queen was precisely choreographed due to the sheer number of performers. No act received more than ten minutes on stage apart from the main star, Mario Lanza, the most famous operatic tenor in the world, who sang for twenty.

The Count Basie Orchestra performed two numbers, one entirely instrumental and the other a great rendition of 'April in Paris'. They were on towards the end of the first set, which helped to ease Josephine's nervousness.

The staid audience gradually warmed to the music and by the time 'April in Paris' finished she noticed how rapt and attentive they were. The applause went on for what seemed like an age. Josephine actually thought the noise level increased when she took her bow. Sneaking a quick peek at the royal box, her heart rose as she saw the Queen smiling and clapping enthusiastically.

She managed to watch the rest of the show from the wings, laughing at the comedians, some of whose English jokes she found hard to follow, as well as taking careful note of how the singers performed under such a high pressure occasion.

When Judy took the stage the audience hushed to hear the voice of a legend and the star of one of the world's most treasured movies. Josephine, too, held her breath, fearing the worst but hoping for the best. Judy did not disappoint. She sang as if she was seventeen again, full of emotion, tenderness and spirit. For Josephine, the moment was magical but tinged with a sadness she found hard to fathom. Her friend had managed to climb the mountain once again, but for how long would she remain on top? Josephine quickly dismissed the morbid thought before joining in the thunderous applause.

At the conclusion of the event the main performers lined the foyer of the London Palladium to be acknowledged by the Queen and the Duke of Edinburgh. Only Count Basie represented his orchestra but Josephine watched the procession with pride and amazement.

The Queen, dressed in a long, flowing gown with a fur stole around her shoulders, moved effortlessly down the line, shaking hands and talking with many of the stars. A sparkling tiara adorned her head which Josephine thought made her very much the fairy queen of her childhood stories her mama used to read. Again, it was a magical and almost unbelievable moment in her life, and one she would never forget.

The next two years cemented The Count Basie Orchestra as the premier jazz and dance band in the land. Josephine relished the tours, visiting new cities and countries, recording albums and meeting up-and-coming talent.

One of the highlights of nineteen fifty-nine, apart from her thirtieth birthday, was the 1st Annual Grammy Awards. Josephine, along with the members of the orchestra, cheered as the Count became the first African American to win an award. In fact, he picked up two prizes – for Best Jazz Performance Group and Best Performance by a Dance Band. The awards were for the previous year's accomplishments and the Count celebrated by giving out generous bonuses and small replicas of the Grammy trophy.

In the meantime, Mr. Benson's health had stabilized with his daughter's help and financial assistance. She managed to visit him whenever the orchestra played in California. Late in nineteen fifty-nine she threw a 60th birthday party for him, held backstage after one of the band's performances. She had never seen him so relaxed and happy. Not one for public speaking, Mr. Benson managed to say a few words about his daughter and how fortunate he was to have her in his life. She cried in his arms at his touching compliments as the attendees applauded a moment that mattered.

Chapter Twenty-Two

"How are the rehearsals going?" Ingrid asked Josephine, as she settled into her chair to continue the documentary.

"Mighty fine, thank you. Mighty fine. Two weeks in and two to go. Got a good group of singers and dancers. Elizabeth has done such a wonderful job with everyone. No egos, just folk having a real good time."

"And are you planning on singing, too?"

"Of course," Josephine beamed broadly. "You're looking at the star of the show right here," she joked, giggling her head off."

"Is Miss Pearl behaving herself?" Ingrid inquired, with a sly grin.

"Like a baby. We are now the best of friends. Just shows what a little song and dance can do for a person. My, my," she mused, "how these shows take me back some sixty years."

"Time, then, to pick up the story again," Ingrid suggested. "Shall we? Nineteen sixty was where we were, I think."

"Ah, nineteen sixty, yes. So much happened it's a wonder I'm still alive and kicking," Josephine offered, with a laugh.

"You are now over thirty, your father is in a good place and you're still singing with Count Basie," Ingrid summarized. "Pick it up from there."

"Well, I'd had ten years with the Count - ten great years, I have to add - but I began feeling my own self was starting to get lost."

Ingrid frowned.

"Lost how?"

"I had no life except performing. And the touring started to get very tiresome. Living out of a suitcase, not laying your head on the same pillow for weeks on end became exhausting. I remembered Milton always saying how he wanted to make a difference somehow. To be of value not a success.

"So, after our last set of engagements in the summer of nineteen sixty, I told the Count I wanted to leave. Of course, he tried his best to persuade me otherwise, but my mind was made up.

"He and the orchestra dedicated my last show to me and there was a huge farewell party. Then, that was it. I walked away. That's what I did…I just walked away."

"To do what?" Ingrid asked, puzzled.

"I went back to the Village and simply relaxed for the first time in a long time. Then, by chance, I met a woman named Maxine Godfrey. And I saw in her my life for the next fifty years or so."

"Who was she?"

"Pure luck was how we met. Part of what I liked to do after my 'retirement' from the orchestra was to stroll around the city, particularly those parts I wasn't very familiar with.

"One day I happened to be in Harlem, passed by what looked like some run-down studio/store front, and found a woman crying in the doorway. Not only crying but sobbing her poor heart out. I was never one for ignoring tears in anyone, so I stopped and asked if there was anything I could do for her.

"I took her next door to a diner and over a cup of coffee she poured out her tale of woe. Now, let me remind you, dear, this was Harlem in the Sixties. The place was poor, the people were poor and the buildings were poor. There were public works projects ongoing, mostly to improve housing, but the atmosphere reeked of hopelessness.

"Kids weren't getting such a great education, which we know is so important to improving lives and the community. About seventy-five to eighty percent of students tested under grade level in math and reading. Add to that the chronic absenteeism rate and you had a recipe for disaster. But what Maxine had tried to do was give some of the kids an outlet."

"Like what?"

"She had artistic training and decided towards the end of the Fifties to return to her hometown and open a facility to teach singing, acting and dancing. Not many kids showed at first but word spread about the fun times inside the building. That was all down to her and her warm and giving personality. She also fed a lot of the kids and often provided a shoulder to cry on.

"But when I bumped into her she seemed to be at rock bottom. Her landlord raised her rent and wasn't fixing a lot of the building's problems. If she couldn't come up with a financial solution she'd have to close down.

"Child, they say when one door closes another opens. That's how it seemed to me, that I was destined to give her a hand." Josephine laughed at the memory. "Little did I know that helping hand was to last almost the rest of my life."

"And exactly how did you help Maxine?"

"I paid the rent for six months in advance to give her some breathing space. I also knew some guys handy with tools and such. They pitched in and fixed the place up. It seemed like a good start, but the more I got involved the more I liked the idea of actually teaching the kids some of what I'd learned.

"I began going down every other day, which became every day before I knew it. That went on for about a year before Maxine became very sick. I sort of took over for her and eventually, when it seemed obvious she wouldn't be coming back, she asked me to run the studio.

"And I loved it. The kids came in ever increasing numbers as the word went out about how much fun the programs were. I managed to get some grants and gifts from generous folk which allowed me to employ some really smart and artistic people. They were all from the neighborhood, so completely understood the hardships and problems most of the kids faced every day.

"Even the Count gave the music program a lot of instruments and over the years several members of the orchestra came by to coach and encourage the kids to pursue an interest in learning to play."

In her mind's eye Ingrid saw a building bubbling with life and laughter, with kids having some of the best times of their lives.

"What did you teach them?"

"Acting and singing."

"Did you tell them about your background?"

"Very rarely and only then if a kid needed an extra push to think he or she could really become something. But sometimes the word got out and I was quite the celebrity for a few days," Josephine offered, with a wide smile.

"Now, I imagine Harlem went through some tough times over the years," Ingrid surmised. "Did you ever think about just packing up and moving on?"

She watched as Josephine took her time in answering, seemingly running events through her mind like a movie.

"Never, even in the darkest moments. And there were some, let me tell you."

"Like what?"

"School boycotts, like in nineteen sixty-four, when about ninety-two per cent of the students stayed home. But the worst were the riots in the summer that year."

"Riots? Over what?"

"A young man was shot by an off-duty policeman and one thing led to another. Five days we endured that until things quieted down some. There was violence on both sides and plenty of looting. But my building never was touched, so I guess I must've been doing some good in the neighborhood.

"There was so much wrong in those days. People were poor, mostly unskilled and with few opportunities. That's why my efforts were so important. And then we got a lot of help from the Johnson administration. Project Uplift offered work programs and such to give the young people a way out of poverty.

"Other artists came along, too. Arthur Mitchell, who danced with the New York City Ballet, established the famous Dance Theater of Harlem as a school and classical ballet training center in the late Sixties. The Harlem Boys Choir began in or around nineteen sixty-five. That was a fine education program for many young boys. And eventually the Girls Choir came along in Eighty-nine. So there was an awful lot of goodness born out of that area."

"And you said you ran your program for over fifty years? Josephine, that's just incredible."

"With a lot of help. Could not have done one tenth without all that support."

"Where did the money come from? I mean, you never charge a fee did you?"

"No, never," she replied, shaking her head. "The money? Ah, well, that's a bittersweet story."

Ingrid saw the nerve she'd touched upon, hesitated to pursue it, but quickly realized whatever the pain it was still part of Josephine's story.

"I know you've said you had savings but I imagine running the studio was fairly expensive. Were you singing on the side or something to make ends meet?"

"No," Josephine answered, plainly. "The money came from my daddy in a manner of speaking."

It was only then Ingrid knew the sensitive spot she'd stirred within Josephine.

"What happened?" she gently asked.

"I'd seen Daddy a few times since our 'talk' and he appeared to be behaving himself, enjoying his friends, getting regular check-ups and making the most of his new hobby – growing flowers and vegetables. He had a big chunk of land.

"We talked quite often on the phone so I thought nothing of it when it rang one morning. But it wasn't Daddy, it was his close neighbor. He began hesitantly before telling me Daddy had passed away."

"Oh, Josephine, not again?"

"I asked what happened and he told me he'd found Daddy in his garden. He'd gone, apparently from a massive heart attack. I quickly made arrangements to fly out, but," she continued, resignedly, "that was that. I was indeed the orphan I never wanted to be.

"We had a lovely funeral and buried him beside Mama. I stayed at the house in Westville for weeks just crying, moping about and really feeling sorry for myself. It felt hard knowing you were now on your own.

"After a while I realized I had to get back, that although the studio was in good hands, I needed to be productive and involved again. So, I packed up some boxes of items from the house I wanted, mailed them to the Village and put the house and land up for sale."

"How difficult was that?" Ingrid asked. "I mean, it was your childhood home. It must have been wrenching to sell it after all those years."

"All of those things, yes. But then I looked at it another way. I felt Mama and Daddy left me a legacy, sort of like an inheritance to see me through. Times had changed a lot around Burbank. The whole area had exploded with folk wanting houses and land. When the real estate lady told me how much I could get for it…and we had over six acres…well, I was stunned. More money than I thought in the whole world," Josephine said, laughing.

"And what did that mean to you moving forward? Buy another house? Bigger apartment?"

"I did get a nicer apartment, yes. That's one move I made. But what I really wanted to do was secure the future of the studio. There was always something needing fixing in the building and the landlord wasn't the quickest jackrabbit around. So I asked him to sell it to me. To my surprise, he agreed. Bit more than I wanted to pay but we cut the deal.

"And with a chunk of the money I started a non-profit foundation so that all the running costs came out of that. Interest rates on savings were pretty high back then so we had no problem paying the mortgage. In fact," Josephine continued, proudly, "that note was paid off in ten years."

"Money smart, too" Ingrid commented. "Impressive. Now, the future of the studio is safe. You, unfortunately, have no more commitments in California, so your life is what, totally focused on running the studio?"

Josephine sat back, took a deep breath and smiled.

"Yes, child, that's what I did. For the next fifty years I had the time of my life. For me, giving back was all I could do to honor my mama and daddy. And, oh my, did we have some fun times. Shows, plays, recitals… you name it and we did it. Enrollment went up every year, so much so we almost had to turn kids away. Never came to that, though, 'cause we always found a way to find the space, time and help."

Ingrid smiled, too, truly believing she was now in the presence of a saint.

"Apart from the Count and some of his band, did you ever hear from any of your old running pals?"

"I did and many came and either performed or held classes. Of, course, the one person I reached out to was Judy. But I never heard from her. I didn't take offence since I'd heard she was going through difficult times. Her career had more or less stopped due to the drink and drugs. She tried several comebacks, the last one was in London, I believe. That's where she died. So far away from home."

"When would that have been?"

Josephine needed no time to answer.

"Nineteen sixty-nine. Clear to me as yesterday. Heard it on the news one morning and it stopped me in my tracks. Her passing was so hard to hear, let alone believe. But as the morning went on, more and more details came out." Shaking her head, Josephine continued, "She meant so much to me. Her kindness, love and friendship. Judy never played the movie star with me. It was big sister, little sister all the time. I've missed her being there for me so much."

Shaking her head again, she said, "Only forty-seven. What a loss. Despite her troubles Judy was still loved by her fans. At her wake, at Frank Campbell's Funeral Home, they said over fifteen thousand mourners came by to pay their respects. I was one of them, too. I remember she was dressed in a silver lamé gown. It was all very sad. Even the flowers were weeping."

As Josephine reminisced, Ingrid recalled an earlier segment regarding Judy's funeral.

"You told me before you repaid Judy in some way for her kindness when your mama passed. What did you do?"

Josephine stared off into the distance as if not wanting to share the details. She then looked into the camera and said, "Judy was broke and I simply wanted her to have the best send off possible. So, just as she had done for my mama, I paid for her funeral. It was the least I could do."

Chapter Twenty-Three

With the formal interviewing of Josephine now over, Ingrid and Zach spent the next two days following and filming her in her daily routine around the facility to give the viewers of the documentary some sense of her life now.

The footage picked up Josephine's day at breakfast in the communal dining room and ended as she closed her door at night. In between, there were shots of her on the walking trail, in the beauty salon, enjoying a glass of wine at 'Happy Hour' with some of her friends, playing bingo – and winning – and, of course, helping Elizabeth Carrington direct the song and dance routines for the upcoming concert.

For Ingrid and Zach the moments filled them with quiet joy. They laughed alongside the residents and marveled at how these supposedly forgotten folk not only lived full, happy lives, but managed to always conduct themselves with dignity and pride.

Both of them vowed, even when the documentary was over, to continue in some meaningful way to remain a part of this community.

"I mean, Zach, I can't just say 'thank you' and walk away. Most of these people are now friends. They're like grandparents to me. God, I've learned so much. I have to find a way to keep connected and helpful."

Zach nodded enthusiastically.

"Know exactly what you mean. The word I'd use is humbling. We bitch and moan because our latte hasn't been served up just as we like it. Or, worse, our phones are running too slow and having trouble keeping up with our inane demands. Honestly, sometimes I felt ashamed just listening to them and how easily and quietly they deal with the troubles in their lives. And I do mean troubles."

"And we shouldn't forget the staff and caregivers. I'm going to talk with Sylvia to get her permission to follow some of them around, too. Focusing on them will not only highlight their selfless, tiring work, but also fully round out the documentary in a meaningful way."

"Oh, I've been noticing them a lot since we've been here, Ingrid. Talk about dedicated and caring. And it's day after day. If anyone deserves a raise it's these folk. My suggestion to you would be to include a separate section at the end of the film, honoring them for all they do."

"I like that," Ingrid agreed. "Let's do it."

The filming, the easy part, had now ended. What followed for Ingrid and Zach was tedious and time-consuming work. Editing a documentary involved hours, days and months deciding what footage to include, what to exclude, whose contributions to use and which to omit for one reason or another.

Ingrid's earlier decision on a two-part documentary still prevailed. The first would showcase the six residents' stories and the two family members of Alzheimer's patients, while the other would concentrate solely on Josephine. She set the running time for each at two hours, which meant so much editing to create a smooth, explanatory narrative.

In addition to the editing of Zach's footage, there were television archive films to chase down, as well as historical photos depicting actual scenes from Josephine's life, some of which needed copyright approval. In all, the task was daunting but Ingrid and Zach accepted the undertaking by always keeping in mind the bigger picture. As Zach told her once, *'This is a goldmine, Ingrid'*.

"Ingrid," Sylvia Richards began, "Josephine asked me to call to invite you and Zach to the concert next Thursday afternoon. We really hope you'll be able to make it. I've seen some of the rehearsals and let me tell you...wow! So much fun. And the energy in the room...amazing."

"Try keeping us away," Ingrid joked. "Not only will we be there but how about we film the whole event? Not only would it be great for the residents to watch themselves performing, but I'd like to include parts of it in the documentary. What a tremendous opportunity to showcase another aspect of what your facility is offering."

"Oh, I like that. Yes, go ahead. I'm sure no one's going to mind. And you're right – a golden moment in more ways than one."

The main recreation room filled so quickly for the concert extra chairs were brought in to seat the capacity audience. Residents, staff, family and friends waited eagerly and expectantly for the performance to begin. Their lively pre-concert chitter-chatter produced an almost festive atmosphere, reminiscent, Ingrid thought, of a carnival or joyful family gathering.

Shortly after two o'clock Sylvia stepped onto the stage to welcome the guests and get proceedings moving.

"This is a celebration," she said, "of hard work, talent, enthusiasm and appreciation. The performers have worked so hard over the past five or six weeks. Their talent will become obvious to you, as will their enthusiasm for singing and dancing. But more than all that, they just so appreciate being able to stand or dance and express themselves in ways that I'm sure will surprise you.

"But before we begin, I have to acknowledge two people who have made this show possible. First, Elizabeth Carrington, daughter of our dear Peter Chadwick, who you will see presently. Elizabeth is a high school music teacher and has graciously given her time and expertise to help in all areas of the production. She will also be providing the piano accompaniment for the acts. So, a big round of applause for Elizabeth, please."

The audience clapped and hooted before Sylvia raised her hand.

"And, second, we owe such a debt of gratitude to our very dear own Josephine Benson. It was Josephine's idea five years ago to begin these concerts and over that time they have grown into what you will see today. She has been the heart and soul of the program. Without her experience and drive these concerts would not have seen the light of day. So, again, your applause for our Josephine."

Thunderous noise filled the room as Sylvia left the stage to the performers.

Betty Harper, who had lip-synced to *'Material Girl'* on karaoke night, was first up. Dressed in hand-me-downs, she sauntered on stage along with six dancers, similarly clad, giving a touching, wistful rendition of Eliza Doolittle singing *'Wouldn't It Be Loverly'* from *'My Fair Lady'*. She managed a respectable Cockney accent, even if regressing now and then into her native tongue. The audience immediately fell in love with her sentiments, joining in and for a while being lost in the moment. Betty received a standing ovation when she exited the stage. The show, then, was off to an amazing start.

Next up was Jack, the resident gardener. His rendition of *'Hello Dolly'*, accompanied by a stylish Grace Norman, who strutted around the stage as if she owned it, was straight Louis Armstrong. Gravel voiced and sporting a colorful handkerchief, with which he continually mopped his brow, Jack gave the rapt audience a performance for the ages. For many he brought back fond memories of another time, when 'good feel' songs still meant something. Jack, too, received a standing ovation and three encores, which he played up to the hilt.

After a brief pause to set the stage for the next act, the curtains opened on Pearl Lister sitting alone on a stool, staring off into the distance. As Elizabeth began her introductory chords, Pearl started her plaintive version of *'Tomorrow'* from the musical *'Annie'*.

The audience fell silent as Pearl raised her voice, singing hopefully of the future and what she hoped it might be. Elizabeth smiled broadly at her stunning effort as the final bars softly meandered away. As the crowd clapped enthusiastically, Pearl lowered her head, arose and quietly walked off the stage leaving a powerful, lasting impression for all those watching.

For Elizabeth, the next resident to grace the stage held an extra special place in her heart. As her father, Peter Chadwick, strode confidently across the boards, she felt the adrenaline course through her body. To actually play for her father, well…what could be better than that?

Well rehearsed, the two began simultaneously, as his still powerful voice launched into *'Some Enchanted Evening'* from *'South Pacific'*. Again, the audience fell silent as his deep baritone sound and cadences rang out over the room. Halfway through the song Peter turned his complete attention towards his daughter and sang the rest of the words to her and only her.

Elizabeth found it difficult to continue, deciding she could no longer look at him for fear of completely falling apart and ruining his moment.

At the conclusion, Peter left the stage, making his way over to his beloved daughter, where the two hugged for the longest time as the guests cheered and applauded. His number was a showstopper to say the least.

The six dancers took to the stage next, strolling around as if searching for something. Before long, Grace Norman appeared from the wings, dressed as a cat. The room deathly hushed as her music filled the auditorium. Walking among the dancers, seemingly lost, she began to sing *'Memory'* from *'Cats'*. Her voice, haunting and clear, not only did adequate justice to the iconic tune but enhanced it beyond measure. There was hardly a dry eye in the place as she finished. The lyrics, most people realized, were apt and true for so many of the home's residents.

Sylvia announced a fifteen minute intermission where drinks and snacks were served by the staff. Ingrid immediately sought out Zach.

"Are you getting some good footage?"

Zach, after sipping a soda, beamed as if he'd just won the lottery.

"Maybe you should stretch the documentary to include all of this. I mean, Ingrid, who'd have known the talent in a place like this? If I'm enjoying tunes I've never heard of, can you imagine what regular people would say? Think about it, Ingrid. Remember what I said – you've got a goldmine here."

Ed Westlake was a large, avuncular man, whose ever-present smile infected all those around him. Ed seemed to be the resident comic at the nursing home, always ready with a joke or to cheer someone up with a witty line or two. He also liked to sing and could often be found strolling the halls serenading anyone who'd listen.

After the interval, Ed was next on deck. He appeared wearing a false beard and a jaunty cap and carrying a fiddle. The dancers returned behind him and as soon as they were in place Elizabeth began playing *"If I Were a Rich Man'* from *'Fiddler on the Roof'*.

With his booming voice, Ed soon convinced the audience he really was Tevye, the musical's main character. Prancing, dancing and stomping around the stage, Ed pulled out all the stops, evoking a gamut of emotions from hope to sadness.

The audience, quickly picking up the song's tempo, clapped and joined in the chorus which only served to urge Ed onto further heights of over-the-top tom-foolery. In the end, the whole room seemed to rock with deafening singing and laughter. Ed, ever the ham, took his time leaving the stage, returning time and time again to take his bows. Again, it was a moment for the ages.

Everyone in the rec room took a while to calm down before Eleanor Freeman took to the stage alone for a sweet, touching rendition of *'People Will Say We're in Love'* from *'Oklahoma'*. Eleanor, nervous to be performing for the first time, charmed the crowd with her surprisingly gifted voice, graceful gestures and facial expressions. To say she had the audience in the palm of her hand would not have been an overstatement. Bowing graciously, she blew kisses far and wide, the nerves now apparently vanquished.

'Seventy-Six Trombones' from *'The Music Man'* was Clarke Price's contribution. Most of the cast joined Clarke for a rousing version of the beloved hit, which again brought the crowd to its feet in joyful appreciation.

Dougie Bird continued the rip-roaring event, with an outrageous, flowing, orange wig and a pink tutu over his pants, to lead the whole troupe in a corny, razzle-dazzle romp through *'There's No Business like Show Business'* from *'Annie Get Your Gun'*. Elizabeth played her heart out on the piano while desperately trying to keep up with the wild antics on stage. The audience whooped and cheered so much that Sylvia hoped none of them would suffer serious medical problems. None did. They simply enjoyed the song for all it was worth.

Now, only one performance remained. The lights dimmed as the curtains opened on Josephine Benson sitting alone in an easy chair, a spotlight illuminating her like an ethereal spirit.

Elizabeth's intro, haunting and mournful, took the audience to a totally different place. Breaths were held as Josephine started to sing. Her choice of song, *'Send in the Clowns'* from *'A Little Night Music'* was the perfect selection to end what had been a little afternoon music. She delivered each line with such skill and artistry, feeling and pathos, and with a voice both calm and telling. At the conclusion, many in the crowd were close to tears, with some realizing that perhaps this afternoon was not the end of the beginning but rather the beginning of the end.

Chapter Twenty-Four

Long days and late nights, fueled by endless cups of coffee and convenient fast-food take outs, became the norm for Ingrid and Zach until the documentary was completed. The labor of love, while exhausting at times, provided them with many touching moments and fond remembrances of the residents they came close to for a while.

But, finally, after five months the documentary was ready to be shared with the world. It emerged as originally envisioned by Ingrid, with the addition of the two family members of Alzheimer's patients, as well as footage from around the nursing home, including the staff, karaoke night and the big musical concert.

Josephine had the second part to herself. Ingrid and Zach expanded on her interviews with additional material highlighting the times of her life. To say they were overjoyed with the completed documentary would not have been accurate; they were ecstatic. The final result exceeded Ingrid's wildest dreams as she recalled how it all innocently began with her grandmother's recommendation she visit *The Sweet and Comfy Nursing Home* almost a year before.

Now, the other hard part loomed before her; finding a market to purchase the documentary and widely distribute it. Her agent, Glen Griffith, already warned her of the rough road ahead. Documentaries these days, he told her, needed to be special beyond words to have any chance of seeing the light of day.

"Send it over," he requested. "Let me take a look. No promises."

Three days later Ingrid answered her phone to hear an emotional and excited Glen almost screaming at her, telling her he wanted her in his office the next day.

When she arrived the following morning Glen greeted her as if she were another of the celebrities he represented.

"Come in! Come in!" he commanded, hustling her into his spacious office.

Ingrid, taken aback by the special treatment, quickly sat, folded her arms and waited for the bad news.

"You, young lady," Glen began, now somewhat calmer, "have produced one fucking masterpiece!"

Surprised, Ingrid raised her eyebrows and looked Glen directly in the eye.

"What? Did you say a 'masterpiece'?"

"You heard me," he confirmed. "Now, why the hell didn't I know about this until three days ago?"

"Sorry, Glen," Ingrid quietly answered, shrugging her shoulders. "It took a long time, that's all."

"I'm just rattling your chain," he replied, smiling. "But this is gold and we need to get on it right away. I'm already talking with some Public Television folk, as well as a number of other independent outlets. And Hollywood, too. Got a lot of good friends out there who maybe will want to take a look. Jesus, Ingrid, this is fucking gold!"

Calmer now, Ingrid answered, "I just want the widest audience possible, Glen. I'm passionate about this film. It means a lot to me and the residents. And I will do whatever it takes to get it on air."

Before the meeting ended Glen laid out his strategy, which included Ingrid making promotional appearances to endorse the film.

"Keep your phone handy, sweetheart. This ain't gonna take long, believe me!"

As good as his word, Glen Griffith proved his worth as an agent. Within two weeks he sold Public Television on Ingrid's documentary.

"There's still a few hoops to jump through but that's my problem not yours. They absolutely fell in love with the film and its subject matter. Said they'd never seen such a moving documentary. They'd need you to introduce it, you know, discuss it with the viewers either before or after it's shown."

"Oh, wow, Glen. This is so unexpected and overwhelming," Ingrid replied, genuinely surprised by the rapid acceptance of her work, but thrilled nonetheless.

"It's the reason you went to film school. Take the accolades while you can. They're few and far between in this business. Now, I have another piece of good news for you. I'm glad you're sitting down because this might blow your mind. Ever heard of Marvin McCullen?"

"Of course," she scoffed. "Who hasn't?"

"Well, my dear Ingrid, he's a good friend of mine and wants to meet you."

Ingrid's eyes opened wide.

"Wait. *The* Marvin McCullen? Director of two of my favorite films."

"Let me guess – 'One Monday' and 'Riddle'?"

"Exactly. Golden Globe winner and Oscar nominated."

"Right. Well, he wants to meet with you as soon as possible. When can you fly out to LA?"

Ingrid hesitated, still recovering from the shock.

"Er...tomorrow?"

"I'll call and let him know you'll be there. Text me your flight times. He'll have someone pick you up at the airport."

"I still don't understand why he wants to see *me*," Ingrid said, frowning. "Did you say something?"

"Not only said something but sent him the documentary. He loved it and the rest is history, as they say."

After landing at LAX at around noon, a uniformed driver met Ingrid at the arrivals, took charge of her carryon and escorted her to his limousine. Within minutes they were winding their way through the streets of downtown LA, finally arriving at The Beverley Hills Hotel.

Several minutes after freshening up in her room, the front desk called to say Mr. McCullen was in one of the conference rooms and would like Ingrid to join him when she was ready.

"Ms. Strauss," Marvin beamed, as Ingrid entered, "so good of you to come all this way at such short notice. Please, sit down. Can we get you anything?"

Ingrid asked for iced tea before making herself comfortable. In attendance with Marvin were three other people, who he introduced as a producer, his casting director and his personal assistant.

"I don't know how much Glen filled you in on why I asked you to come out," Marvin began, "but I have a number of proposals I'd like to present. First, though, my congratulations to you for producing an amazing documentary. It was spellbinding to say the least. All of us watched in awe."

For Ingrid, this moment of being told by one of Hollywood's foremost movie directors that he was in awe of her work just seemed totally unreal and baffling.

"I don't know what to say," she answered diffidently, truly not knowing what to say in response to such high praise.

Marvin grinned.

"I understand completely. When I directed my first movie and people actually liked it – well, yes, you kinda have to pinch yourself, don't you. Then you need to realize that, in fact, you may actually deserve the accolades because you knew what you were doing all along. And let me tell you, Ingrid, I would never have guessed in a million years this was your first documentary. So take the praise, please."

This time Ingrid smiled.

"I will, then. Thank you."

"Now, there are two other reasons I asked to meet with you. Right now we're almost ready to begin work on my next movie. We start shooting soon in New York. My question to you – and I don't expect an answer today – is…can I coax you to be an assistant director on the film?"

Again, Ingrid was nonplussed. *Wait,* she thought to herself, *the Marvin McCullen just asked me to work on his next film with him! No. No. No. This must just be some sort of weird dream.*

Trying hard to keep her composure, she replied, "Me? You want me as an assistant director?"

"Correct. But before you even consider the offer let me give you a quick synopsis of the story. Basically, it's about an African American family facing, and trying to deal with, many trials and tribulations within their ranks. Lots of distrust, anger, conflict and, hopefully, resolution.

"Not a large cast, and I won't tell you who we have on board, but you won't be disappointed. As I've said, don't give me an answer now. We'll let you have a copy of the script so you can look it over tonight."

"All right. I can do that. Can you tell me what the movie's called?"

"Yes, but first I need you to know the whole concept has been in the works for over three years. Sonia, here, our main producer, came to me with her suggestion, which I absolutely loved. Fast forward to today and we're ready to go. So, three years ago Sonia wrote a brief outline of a movie she was willing to produce. She titled it – and this is why I prefaced my remarks by saying all this occurred three years ago – as *'The Good Woman of Harlem'*."

Ingrid laughed.

"Are you kidding me, Mr. McCullen? The movie's actually called *'The Good Woman of Harlem'*?"

"Ain't life strange sometimes," Marvin suggested. "But, yes, that's the title."

"Certainly right up my alley," Ingrid agreed. "Let me think about it overnight."

"Very good, but I do have one other matter to bring up which may sway your decision. For this, I will need all your persuasive help."

"Sounds intriguing," Ingrid responded, now more comfortable with the group. "Ask away."

"I'm going to turn this part over to our casting director, Sissy Daniels. Sissy?"

"Ingrid, we've cast every role except one. Screen tests galore but no one we think really embodies the part."

"Which is?" Ingrid asked, quite curious now.

"The matriarch of the family, specifically the grandmother."

"Okay. And how can I help with that?"

"The second part of your documentary concentrated on the life of Josephine Benson…"

"Wait. Wait. Wait," Ingrid interrupted. "Are you seriously considering Josephine for the part?"

"Well, after a test, yes we are," Sissy replied, firmly.

"Oh, now hold on a second. Josephine is ninety-one years old. She hasn't acted in…what…seventy years. Are you really, really serious about this?"

"Deadly," Sissy answered without hesitating. "We've all seen her performance as *Desdemona in Othello*…"

"Yes, which was back in Forty-nine," Ingrid interrupted again. "Now she lives a quiet life in a nursing home for goodness sake. I hate to say it, Ms. Daniels, but Josephine is *old*. She enjoys her bingo and helping with some concerts, but acting, I don't think so."

Marvin jumped in to calm down the situation.

"Ingrid, all we're asking you to do is to put the offer out there. You now know her better than almost anyone. She will listen to you. All I will say is we'd like her in the film not because we want to exploit her story in your documentary, but because, clearly, she's the only actress who can bring the level of authenticity we're looking for to the role. It's as simple as that."

As Marvin spoke his piece another, more sinister, thought crossed Ingrid's mind.

"I hate being a conspiracy theorist here," she began, "but is why you offered me a job as assistant director on the movie contingent on my being able to get Josephine to say yes to you?"

"Absolutely, one hundred per cent, no!" Marvin replied, forcefully. "I want to work with you because I see myself in you some twenty years ago. Let me tell you a little story. Like you, I'd graduated from film school at USC and proceeded to make a couple of short, Indie, films. I had no agent and no one to see my work. I was working as a janitor at …well, I won't tell you which studio…when Spielberg walked by.

"I introduced myself, told him about those shorts and asked if I could drop copies off to him. To my surprise, he said yes. I just thought he was being polite and kind to some idiot wanna-be. Anyhow, he got them and I didn't hear another word for at least two weeks.

"I'm pushing my broom around the cafeteria when Spielberg comes in, sits down with me and offers me a job. By this time I'm thinking this must be some huge joke, but it wasn't. I became one of his assistant directors on his next film.

"Not only that, but during filming he says to me, *'Okay, kiddo, this next scene is all yours. Don't screw it up.'* He let me direct a scene, which I might add I did extremely well, because he thought I could do it based on my previous work. In other words, he gave me a chance. He became my mentor.

"It's the same with you, Ingrid. I see from the way you directed your documentary you have a natural affinity for film making. Whether you get Josephine Benson to come on board is not contingent on you becoming my assistant on the film. You've got the job, period."

Ingrid listened intently, feeling slightly guilty for doubting Marvin's intentions, while at the same time knowing what she suspected needed to be said.

"Thank you for your faith in me," she offered. "I just didn't need to be a charity case."

Marvin grinned broadly.

"No way, Ingrid. I know talent when I see it. You, young lady, have it in abundance. Now, tonight, I want you to think over everything we've discussed. Talk with Glen and anyone else you need to. I'll meet you here tomorrow for breakfast before your flight home and you can give me your decision. Okay?"

Ingrid agreed, feeling she'd left the meeting a completely different person from the one who'd entered it.

The only person Ingrid spoke to was Zach. She caught up with him later that evening as he downed his usual Chinese take-out.

After patiently hearing her story Zach made only one comment, bluntly and to the point.

"Take the effing job, Ingrid. You'd be nuts to turn down an opportunity like this. They don't come our way very often, so take the effing job!"

"Okay, but what about Josephine?"

"What the hell are you worried about? Make her the offer and let her decide. If she wants to do it, she will. If not, then no one's worse off. But I don't think you have the right to make that choice for her."

Ingrid knew she could count on Zach for good, level-headed, advice. Afterwards, lying in bed, staring at the ceiling, she knew he was right. Josephine should decide this for herself.

The next morning, over breakfast, Ingrid told Marvin she would accept his job offer.

"So, pleased," he responded. "You'll go a long way in this business, Ingrid. We'll let you know about schedules and all the rest, but I want you to know I'm very happy to have you on board."

"No, thank you for giving me such a great opportunity. Just don't expect too much first time around," Ingrid chuckled.

"And Josephine?" Marvin asked.

"I'll put it to her," Ingrid offered. "She definitely needs to decide this for herself. All I can do is ask."

Marvin opened up his hands.

"That's all I can hope for. Just tell her it'll be like winning bingo a million times over!"

They both laughed and left it at that.

Chapter Twenty-Five

As fate would have it, Ingrid's opportunity to approach Josephine with Marvin McCullen's offer of a role in his new movie coincided with the unveiling of her documentary at the nursing home.

Sylvia, excited as a first grader, set aside one afternoon for the event, inviting family, friends as well as everyone in the facility. She alerted all the local television news stations and several sent crews to record the showing and interview some of the participants.

The expectant atmosphere steadily built inside the recreation room as the residents and guests took their seats. As the chatter grew louder many of the featured folk speculated on how they would look on the big screen, and whether or not they'd made complete fools of themselves. They needn't have worried on both scores.

Sylvia welcomed the audience with her usual upbeat introduction.

"I know we have all been waiting for this moment ever since Ingrid began the documentary. So much has gone into its production and so many of you have been gracious with your time and memories. My hope is that it will make you laugh, cry and remind you of your value and importance to those who know and love you.

"I'd like to ask Ingrid to step up for a moment and say a few words. Ingrid?"

Ingrid, along with Zach, faced the crowd, broadly smiling and waving.

"Hello, everyone! Gee, what an amazing audience. So many people. I just need to tell you a few things which have meant so much to Zach and me since we started coming here.

"All of you opened your hearts and minds to us in a manner that truly surprised us. Getting up close and personal is not easy, but you managed to give of yourselves cheerfully and without reservations. For that, we are deeply honored.

"Over the past months we've been amongst you, we have grown not only to know you and your stories but come to regard you as close friends and, indeed, family now.

"We pray you will find the documentary a true and authentic record of lives well lived. We are so proud of the final result and hope you will be, too. Thank you again for sharing yourselves with us."

The audience stood as one, clapping and hooting, throwing kisses and hugs towards the pair. Bowing gracefully, they left the stage with tears welling in their eyes.

The documentary proceeded at a leisurely pace with the residents' stories intersecting with scenes depicting daily life in the nursing home. Ingrid intended the film to speak for itself without the need for extraneous explanations. As the footage unfolded she felt strongly that goal had been met.

As their stories filled the screen, the featured residents grinned, nudged ribs and watched intently as those around them offered amazement at learning so many previously unknown details of their friends' lives. They now seemed to be held in a different, higher light than before.

The section on karaoke was a big hit. Laughter and screams of hilarity filled the room, with Jack even standing up to take an exaggerated bow from his fans. For most of the performers this was the first time they'd seen themselves in the limelight. Some sheepishly buried their heads in hands, while others took the ribbing with good humor. All in all, the record of that afternoon only confirmed what a fun place the nursing home was at times.

Three of the residents' stories particularly resonated with their friends, family and staff members. Pearl Lister, Josephine's one-time nemesis, but now firm friend due to her involvement with the musical concert, intrigued the audience with her tale of the leather sewing kit with the mysterious initials MGS stitched on top. They sat rapt with attention watching the footage as Pearl slowly divulged the astonishing information.

No one in the room guessed the outcome that Pearl Lister's great, great, great grandmother and father were none other than Mary Shelley, author of *Frankenstein* and Percy Bysshe Shelley, one of England's greatest poets.

Clyde Weaver's part in the documentary probably touched the audience the most. Apart from the residents and staff, few at the event would have suspected this unassuming man was totally blind.

Ingrid's interview with him ran in almost complete silence as the crowd heard first hand his act of true heroism. The rescue of a five year old boy from an inferno gripped everyone, but to have lost his sight in the process – well – that was just a stunning tragedy.

How glad were they to learn of his service to the town of Bridgeburgh, New Jersey, as its mayor for so many trying but wonderful years. At the end of his piece, everyone truly felt this was a man of the people, for the people. His contributions earned Clyde a standing ovation, which he could not witness but felt blessed all the same. Many tears were shed over his story. Many held him in a new light.

At the conclusion of Betty Harper's interview, her daughter, Marion, the doctor, held her for the longest time. Hearing her mother's description of the family's life, including the trials and tribulations, fun and laughter, along with the expectations and hopes for all her children, filled Marion with so much love and gratitude.

She never fully understood until now the enormous sacrifices her parents made to give her, David and Grace the opportunities to be everything they ever dreamed. That her father was not around to witness the amazing chronicles Betty now revealed saddened Marion beyond measure. He, too, was their rock and guide, their hero and friend.

In the documentary, Betty continually spoke so highly of her children. She took no praise for their amazing accomplishments, but rather credited them for forging their own paths in life. Marion knew that wasn't the truth, tearfully remembering her mother's generous, encouraging, loving and mostly unassuming character. And, to this day, she remained so very, very proud of them all. No mother, in Marion's eyes, was ever better.

Before Josephine's segment aired the audience took a half hour break.

It gave the local television reporters a chance to mingle and hold their own interviews with the residents. Most devoted at least five minutes in their evening newscasts to the event, which amused the residents to actually see themselves on television.

"Eat your hearts out, grandchildren!" Jack yelled at the screen. "We're famous now!"

As the guests retook their seats, Josephine quietly made her way to the rear of the room, found Ingrid and Zach, and sat with them. Ingrid smiled warmly, before taking Josephine's hand and kissing it.

"Ready kiddo?" she asked. "It's amazing. Truly."

For the next two hours the guests watched in almost disbelief as Josephine's incredible life unfolded before their eyes. They experienced so many different emotions – warmth, happiness, tragedy, despair, hope, disappointment, resilience, perseverance and strength among others that wrenched their hearts, yet also filled them with joy.

None could believe one among them had led such a life, but here before them was the evidence, bravely and unselfishly told. And to think she still continued on at ninety-one…well, that was just an incredible bonus.

The reaction of all in the room at the end of the documentary varied not at all. People clapped and cheered more loudly than any Ingrid heard before. The response filled the rec room with such a reverberating sound she swore the building actually shook.

As her friends and staff gathered around Josephine to congratulate her, Ingrid whispered to Zach to not wait for her because she intended to approach their friend with Marvin McCullen's offer of a role in his latest movie.

As the crowds thinned and the television personnel packed up their equipment, Sylvia cornered Ingrid to express her grateful thanks.

"I really don't know what to say," she began, beaming, before hugging Ingrid. "All the adjectives seem totally inadequate. So, I'll just say on behalf of everyone here, thank you from the bottom of our hearts. We will never forget what you've done for us."

"Right back at you, Sylvia. None of this would have been possible without your cooperation and encouragement. This place is so lucky to have you at its head."

Twenty minutes later, Ingrid found Josephine relaxing on her bed, enjoying a well-earned glass of wine.

"Can I come in?"

"Of course, my dear. Grab a glass. We need to celebrate."

"Are you all right?" Ingrid asked, as the welcome red liquid slid down her throat.

"A little overwhelmed to say the least," Josephine replied, slightly turning her head and raising her eyebrows.

"I think they liked it, don't you?"

"All thanks to you, sweet child."

"Josephine, it's your story. I merely told it."

"Yes, but without you where would we be?"

"Okay, I'm not going to argue the point," Ingrid responded, lightly. "Let's just say we did good."

"Perfect."

"Now, are you too tired to talk for a while?"

"Never too tired to talk with you. I'm anxious to know what you're up to now the documentary's finished. You sold it to Public Television?"

"Yes. Very exciting. Not sure when it's going out, but hopefully soon. My agent also showed it to a Hollywood friend of his," Ingrid continued, gingerly broaching the subject she wanted to get to. "And in a way that's what I want to discuss with you."

Josephine frowned at the mention of Hollywood.

"Oh?" she questioned. "And why might that be?"

Ingrid took a deep breath before finally saying, "Because this friend, Marvin McCullen, is just about to direct his latest movie and he wants to know if you'd like to be in it."

Chapter Twenty-Six

"Hallelujah, sweet Jesus!" Josephine declared at Ingrid's suggestion. "That's one crazy man! Me, acting again at my age? No! No, child!"

"Don't you even want to know what the part is?" Ingrid responded calmly, after anticipating Josephine's response. "It might surprise you."

"No, I don't, because I'm not doing it," Josephine answered, firmly.

"He's seen your Desdemona."

"Who? Who's seen my Desdemona?"

"Marvin McCullen. They all have. The casting director, the producer, and they know what you can do."

"Yes child, seventy years ago! I don't see and hear so well now and remembering lines…no, no, it's impossible."

"Josephine, I've just watched your life story with you. One thing that struck me above everything else was your willingness to adapt and change, to always push forward and try new things. Nothing seemed to deter you. Nothing scared you. You got that from your mama."

Josephine leaned forward to catch all of Ingrid's perceptions of her.

"Now you're telling me you can't do this and you can't do that for one reason or another, but what I'm really hearing is that you're scared. And I fully understand that. But what I can't accept is you not doing something just because you're scared. You were not raised that way at all and I have the footage to prove it.

"If you don't want to do the movie because you're too tired or sick

or something along those lines, then I can agree with you. Otherwise…
well…I'd just be really disappointed."

Ingrid saw the wheels turning inside Josephine's head. For the longest
time her friend just stared at her with eyes fixated in a sort of trance.
Finally, she sat back, folded her arms and grunted.

"You think I'm scared of some young uppity film director?"

"I do, yes."

"Well, young missy, I most certainly am not!"

"Then what is it?"

"I'd be worried I'd be making a horse's ass out of myself, that's what!"
Josephine answered, quite plainly.

Ingrid couldn't help but laugh.

"Josephine, you're ninety-one years old. If you can't make a fool of
yourself now, then when, for goodness sake?"

Ingrid's suggestion made Josephine giggle, too.

"And, by the way," Ingrid continued, "there's no way you'd be making
a fool out of yourself. You got an Oscar nomination, didn't you? And they
don't give those out to fools.

"Now, I'm not going to press you any further today. But what I will
do is leave you a copy of the script to look over. Please, please consider the
offer carefully. I'll stop by tomorrow and if your decision's the same we
will say no more about it. Okay?"

Reluctantly, Josephine nodded.

"Don't expect me to change my mind, child, because I won't."

"That's fine," Ingrid agreed. "I'll see you in the morning." As she
reached the door she turned and said, "Oh, by the way, just thought you'd
like to know the title of the movie is *The Good Woman of Harlem*. Sleep
well."

"She's not going to do it," Ingrid told Zach later that evening. "Thinks
she'll make a horse's ass of herself."

"She said that?"

"Her exact words. That's what she's scared of."

"Doesn't sound like the Josephine we know but she is…what…ninety-
one? I'm sure just getting out of bed some mornings is a problem."

Ingrid immediately pooh-poohed that idea.

"She behaves like someone twenty years younger, Zach. I just think she's scared she can't act anymore."

"Which is completely reasonable from her point of view. Nineteen forty-nine *was* a long time ago now. Maybe you should let it go and let her have her memories."

"That's what I'm expecting tomorrow. Marvin's gonna be so disappointed."

"Sounds as though you'll be, too."

"Of course. He's given me the chance to not only work on a movie but to work with her. That would've been the gift of a lifetime but…oh well."

"I'm sure he'll cast someone else who'll be just as good."

"I'm sure he will, too, but it won't be the same."

"You just gotta look at it like it was never meant to be. Enjoy your time on set and leave it at that."

"Always the sage," Ingrid said. "Always the sage. Goodnight."

The next morning Ingrid was greeted with a strict order from Josephine.

"Sit yourself down right there, child, and don't say a word."

Ingrid did as asked, waiting patiently as Josephine went to her closet and put on a large, floppy hat. She then sat across from Ingrid, frowned and pointed her finger.

"I have lived a good, long life. You have not, yet. So, I want you to listen to me and heed my words."

Ingrid also frowned, not at all understanding what or where Josephine was going with the conversation. She went to respond before Josephine jabbed her finger in the air towards her.

"No! No! I don't need you to talk right now, just listen. I've been hearing some things that I don't like to hear. You are now old enough to be responsible for your actions."

This time Ingrid raised her eyebrows as if to say *I have no idea what you're talking about and if you carry on like this I will interrupt you.*

"You are a member of this family," Josephine continued, unabated, "whether you like it or not. That means there are certain rules that need to be followed. I follow them, your mama and daddy follow them and your siblings follow them. You are no different. Am I making myself clear?"

By this time Ingrid seemed completely baffled by Josephine's apparent ranting about her behavior until, suddenly, the penny dropped.

"You sly old fox!" she admonished. "You're going to take the part, aren't you? Those are lines from the script."

"How'd I do?" Josephine asked, coyly and with a huge grin. "Were you beginning to worry?"

Ingrid, jumping up, threw her arms around Josephine's thin shoulders and kissed her lightly on the cheek.

"Was I ever? This time I really thought you'd lost your marbles. But, yes, you did great. Now, what d'you think of the script?"

"Like it was written for me," she boasted.

Ingrid replied, glancing at the wall clock, "And no trouble remembering your lines, either. And that's good, because here's what we're doing next – calling Mr. McCullen in LA. It's only around seven-thirty but I don't care. He'll want to hear this."

Several minutes later a surprised Marvin listened to Ingrid's excited voice as she spoke hurriedly into the phone.

"Wait! Wait, Ingrid! I can barely make you out. Calm down and start again."

"She's agreed to do it. Josephine wants to be in the movie."

A huge sigh came through the wires.

"Fantastic! Did she take much persuading?"

"I just found out. Yesterday didn't look good but she read the script overnight and loved it. Said it must've been written just for her."

"When can I talk to her?"

"She's here with me now. Hold on." Quickly walking over, Ingrid whispered, "Mr. McCullen wants to speak to you," and handed over the phone.

"Hello? Yes, it's Josephine. Nice to talk to you, too."

"A distinct honor for me," Marvin said, deferentially. "Your Desdemona took all our breaths away. How you didn't win the Oscar is quite beyond me."

"Well, that is another story," Josephine stated plainly.

"You liked the script, then?"

"And the title. Both just meant for me."

Marvin laughed.

"Some of my crew and I will be in New York next week securing the house location in Harlem. We'll arrange to visit you there and do a quick screen test. Okay?"

"I'll be on my best behavior, promise." Josephine joked.

"I have very high hopes for the film and now having you agree to be part of it – well – just icing on the cake."

"Let's wait for the test," Josephine joked again. "Seventy years between takes is a long, long time."

"You'll do fine. I look forward to meeting you next week, Josephine. Now, could you pass me back to Ingrid?"

During their conversation, Marvin asked whether she'd told Josephine about the assistant director's job.

"No, not yet. Didn't want to influence the decision. But when we're done here I'll tell her."

After a few more details were ironed out Marvin took his leave, thanking Ingrid profusely for her help.

"See you next week. Ciao."

"He seems like a nice man," Josephine commented. "Just like Stanley."

"He is," confirmed Ingrid. "I liked him from the get-go. Now, Josephine, I have a secret I need to tell you."

"Oh, I like secrets," Josephine answered, clapping her hands like a two-year-old.

"Well, it's not like a real secret; more like a present for you."

"Even better. What is it?"

"Marvin asked me to go to Los Angeles for three reasons. He's promoting the documentary – number one. Number two, he asked me to try and get you into his movie…'

"Which you did. Thank you."

"Which I did. And, number three, he wanted me as an assistant director."

"You mean on the film I'm going to be in?"

"Yes."

"You'll be right there with me the whole time?"

"I will."

Josephine, although ninety-one, was still nobody's fool.

"Was that the price he paid to get me on board? Offering you a job?"

"Wait, what? No!" Ingrid quickly responded. "In fact, that was *my* first thought. But he assured me I was hired whether you agreed or not. He's honestly impressed with the work I did on the documentary. He looks at himself now as my mentor. I even signed the hiring papers before I left LA."

"Are you sure?"

"Yes, I'm one hundred per cent sure."

Josephine considered their conversation for a few moments before clapping her hands again.

"Then I could not be happier, child. To have you there with me... well...that'll be so special."

"As long as you pass the screen test first," joshed Ingrid.

"Oh, they'll all be eating out of my hand before I've finished with them," Josephine joked back. "He's not coming all this way to say no. You'll see."

"I'm so excited for us, Josephine. To think a year ago we were strangers and now this. Who could've guessed?"

"I might have done," boasted Josephine. "My whole life has been full of surprises one way another. But despite the ups and downs it's been a blessing. Just to imagine when I was a little bitty child that I would get to do all the things I have – well..."

"And you're still surprising yourself," interrupted Ingrid.

"Mostly by just being alive," Josephine joked again.

"Now, I understand from Marvin the whole movie will mostly be shot in and around a house in Harlem. That's why they're coming, to finalize the exact location. Your scenes will take about two weeks. Are you okay with that?"

"Child, going back to Harlem will be like going home again. It'll be fun to visit the old neighborhoods, including The Village."

"Well, I don't care what anyone says," Ingrid replied forcefully, "but I will be right by your side every step of the way until we safely return you here. There will be rules, Miss Benson," she continued, playfully waving her finger. "Your well being is the most important aspect of this whole scenario. You must tell me when you're tired or feeling the least bit off color. If scenes have to be postponed then so be it. Are you good with that?"

"Suitably chastised," Josephine replied, sheepishly bending her head. "And I thank you for that. But I know I'll be fine and dandy. I just hope I'll be able to live up to this young man's expectations."

"Okay, then. Now, you need to rest up for a while before I whisk you off to Harlem. Be good. Promise?"

"Promise, child. Oh, this is going to be such fun!"

Chapter Twenty-Seven

Marvin McCullen entered Josephine's room with an armful of fresh flowers and a smile as wide as the Grand Canyon.

"Miss Josephine Benson, I presume," he offered, in an amusing, over theatrical manner. Kissing her outstretched hand, he continued, "This is indeed the highlight of my life."

Both Josephine and Ingrid giggled before Josephine attempted a dramatic curtsey in return.

"Very pleased to meet you, Mr. McCullen."

"Oh, Marvin, please, since we're destined to create such magic together."

"Josephine's obviously a little nervous this morning, Marvin," Ingrid confided. "She's anxious to get the screen test over with."

"Oh, that! It's not a screen test, my dear. You already have the part. It's more for me to observe you under different scenarios and emotions so I'll know how best to direct. Absolutely nothing to concern yourself with."

Ingrid squeezed Josephine's hand before saying, "See, didn't I tell you he's already a fan?"

Josephine carefully took in Marvin's features and nature while the other two spoke.

"You remind me so much of Stanley," she finally said. "Kind but firm."

"Stanley who?" Marvin asked.

"Stanley Masters, of course. I thought you said you saw my Desdemona?"

"Oh, *that* Stanley. Yes, indeed. One of my director heroes. I can't believe I'm here talking to someone who actually worked with him. Excuse the pun but he was definitely a 'master'."

"Indeed," agreed Josephine, "but don't worry yourself, I won't be judging you by his standards," she teased.

Marvin feigned wiping sweat from his forehead.

"That's a relief. Thank you. Now, I have a car outside, so if you're ready we can head to the hotel where everything's set up and waiting for you."

In a small conference room, Sissy Daniels, the casting director and Sonia Myers, the producer of the film, were waiting. Both jumped to their feet and smiled broadly as Josephine entered.

Marvin made the introductions before outlining his intentions. Before long, Sissy handed out copies of the script while Marvin, with Ingrid's help, positioned Josephine for the session. There were no cameras since all Marvin needed was to get a real feel for Josephine's style and mannerisms.

"Okay," he began, "this first scene involves you being considerate, kind and understanding. It comes early in the movie before you've really had a chance to assess the difficult situations the family are facing. You are talking to the teenage son, so I'll play his part. Ready?"

Josephine nodded confidently before consulting her script.

"She doesn't understand me," Marvin began. "All she does is yell. I can't do anything right. Still treating me like I'm a little kid."

Josephine, knowing this scene well, looked directly at Marvin as she spoke.

"From what I've heard about you, Michael, you respect your mama and daddy real well. Am I correct?"

"Yes, ma'am."

"And you're working hard in school?"

As Josephine asked the question, she tilted her head down slightly and to the side, as her eyes held Marvin's without blinking.

"Do my homework and everything, yes."

"All right, then. So what is it you're doing that causes your mama to be at you all the time?"

"Not coming home when I'm supposed to, I guess."

"Not coming home. I see. Is that a rule in this house?"

"Yes, ma'am, it is."

"So, you disobeying your mama, then? Correct, Michael?"

"Guess."

Before uttering her next line Josephine smiled, wryly.

"So, you would agree your mama has a right to pull you up on that?"

"Guess so."

"Let me tell you, Michael, how you ought to be handling this situation, and I have a lot of experience with raising your mama…"

At this point, Marvin stopped the scene to give Josephine and his crew his feedback.

"That was so good, Josephine, particularly when you dropped your head and held my gaze. Where did you learn that?"

"Oh, just a little trick Stanley taught me. He had a million."

"You also had great command of the situation. Right amount of empathy for Michael, but firm, too. Okay, next scene is with your daughter, Michael's mother. In this one you're angry with her while still trying to set her straight. Sissy'll read the mother's part."

Ingrid found the spot in the script and handed it to Josephine.

"That boy! I tell you, Mama, he's headed in the wrong direction! No matter what I say, he does the opposite."

Josephine folded her arms, set her jaw and caught Sissy's eyes.

"Is that a fact? And what exactly have you been saying?"

"Oh, Mama, c'mon now. You know how Michael is sometimes."

"I know how you are sometimes and sometimes it isn't pretty. Now, what you been saying to him?"

"I want him home at a certain time, that's what and, he disobeys me."

"Uh huh, and you always give the boy a chance to explain where he's been, right?"

"Well, not all the time, because I get so mad at him."

Josephine shook her head and wagged her finger at Sissy.

"Over this, child? Listen, he's a young man just starting to grow up. Will he always do what you want? No, he won't, just like you didn't with me."

"I'm not having him disrespect me, Mama. I will not have that!"

To everyone's surprise, Josephine left her chair and stood directly in front of Sissy.

"Oh, you won't eh? Then you're a fool! He's trying to find his own way and whether you like it or not, he will. Now, you can help or you can hinder. Your choice. But let me tell you there are some battles you cannot afford to lose and some you can. This, child, is one you can."

Again, Marvin stopped the scene, feeling he'd seen and heard enough.

"Perfect. Just perfect. I got goose bumps just listening to you."

"Thank you, young man. I'm trying," Josephine joked.

"You have lost *nothing* of your acting skills, Josephine," Marvin continued. "It's as if your last movie finished yesterday. Now, one last scene. This comes towards the end of the film. You are on your death bed and your grown granddaughter is visiting, perhaps seeing you for the final time. Ingrid, can you play her?"

"Of course," Ingrid replied, slightly taken aback but honored, all the same. She found the scene and pointed it out to Josephine.

"Okay," Marvin said, "let's go."

"Take my hand, child. Lift it to your face."

"You're so cold, Gramma. I'm so sorry you're sick right now."

Josephine sunk low in her chair as she slowly shook her head.

"Just my time, sweet one."

"Are you scared?"

"Scared? What of dying? No, child, no."

"D'you have a favorite memory? Something I can always remember you by."

Josephine paused, lifting her head and eyes to the ceiling.

"Oh, so many. So very many. Let me see."

She paused again, turning towards Ingrid and smiling weakly.

"When I was a young girl my mama and daddy told me I was the prettiest thing they'd ever seen. And I have always believed that. Now I'm telling the same to you – you are the prettiest thing I've ever seen. Take that with you, child, always. You promise?"

"Promise, Gramma."

"Oh, my word, Josephine!" Marvin cut in. "So good. You brought tears to my eyes. That's it! We're done here. You've given me so much to think about."

Over lunch, Marvin carefully laid out his plans for the shoot, including dates, schedules and how much time Josephine would need to be in Harlem.

"You have six scenes, for a total of twenty or twenty-five minutes. Doesn't sound like a lot but we should plan on you being there for about two weeks. Is that okay?"

"Just fine," Josephine replied. "As long as I get time off to visit the old neighborhood."

"I'll put a car at your disposal," assured Marvin. "Also, if you need more time for your scenes, we'll accommodate that, too. We all want this to be the best experience for you. As I told you before, I have high hopes the movie will be leading the bunch of new releases next fall.

"The crew will be arriving in a month to set things up. Then I'll be out two weeks after that. I don't like doing a lot of rehearsals so the shoot should go fairly quickly and smoothly. Any questions?"

"Stanley always talked to me privately the day before my scenes. I liked that. I liked that I had a clear idea of exactly what he expected from me. Is that the way you'll be, Mr. Marvin?"

Marvin smiled broadly.

"Oh, Josephine, you'll soon know what I expect of you, believe me. But, yes, if that's what you want then that's what I'll do. I will do anything to secure your best performance. And Ingrid will be there to keep me in line, too."

After a few more discussions, Sonia, the movie's main producer, produced a contract for Josephine to sign. It was a simple one-page form liberally extending Josephine any courtesy she wished in exchange for basically having her act in the movie. Her fee was set at one hundred thousand dollars plus an additional hundred thousand if the film grossed over one hundred million dollars.

"My, oh, my!" she exclaimed, as she scratched her signature on the dotted line. "Now I don't have to play bingo anymore!"

Chapter Twenty-Eight

Five years is a long time to be away from your home of over fifty years. The world changes so fast and nothing stays the same. The only constant is memory; remembrances of what was and who we were.

Six weeks after meeting Marvin McCullen, Josephine found herself back in Harlem and Greenwich Village. Ingrid brought her down two days before the film's shoot was to officially begin so she could see her old neighborhoods and, perhaps, even reconnect with some dear friends.

For Josephine, the trip back in time was bitter/sweet nostalgia; milestones in her extraordinary life but also tinged with sadness. But despite her sometimes distressfulness, she reveled in showing Ingrid where and how she lived and worked for so many wonderful years.

Some of the cafes and nightclubs where she appeared with the Count were still there and thriving. They stopped in many of them to reminisce with the new owners who were fascinated to hear her story and amazed to actually meet a performer from that golden age in The Village.

But the highlight for Josephine took them back to her old performing arts studio in Harlem, where she nurtured, trained and encouraged thousands of young boys and girls to follow their dreams.

The new owner, Carmen Gordon, had expanded the place since Josephine's departure, but the atmosphere remained the same; full of energy, life and fun.

"I cannot believe my eyes!" Carmen exclaimed, as Josephine and Ingrid appeared in the main practice room. "Is it really you, Miss Josephine?"

"Just checking up on you, Carmen," Josephine joshed. "This is a friend of mine, Ingrid Strauss."

The hugs and kisses soon gave way to endless chatter, mostly by Carmen who wanted to know how Josephine was and what she was doing with herself.

"Oh, not a lot, child. This and that. Playing bingo and enjoying my wine."

"And I know that is *not* the truth by half. Why, you are a star on Public Television. I saw the documentary, Miss Josephine, so don't tell me you've been doing nothing! I never knew any of that stuff about your life."

"That was all Ingrid's idea," Josephine said, turning to her friend. "She directed the whole thing."

"Then you are one talented lady," Carmen told Ingrid. "And all those other folks' stories…my, my, who ever would've guessed?"

"Thanks," Ingrid answered, bowing her head. "Glad you enjoyed it so much. The film's gotten very good plays and reviews."

"As well it should! Now, would you like to look around? As you can see, I've jazzed up the place a little but the premise is still the same – give any kid who wants it a chance. And we couldn't do half what we do without your continued generosity, Miss Josephine. You are gold and so treasured."

For the next hour they toured the facility, listening to songs and music being performed by the novices, as well as watching a few dancing and acting classes. Josephine, thrilled that her work and vision still served the neighborhood, promised Carmen her financial assistance would continue long after she, Josephine, had passed.

"My mama and daddy would be so proud of what their humble beginnings helped achieve here," she told Carmen. "Ingrid is on the board of the foundation and so will do all she can to make sure your doors never close."

Carmen sniffed back her tears upon hearing Josephine's promise.

"To hear you say those words, Miss Josephine, well…your name will live forever, too, over those very same doors."

Before Josephine and Ingrid left, Carmen asked how they came to be in the neighborhood.

"Go on," urged Ingrid, to a diffident Josephine. "Tell her your great news."

"What this young hussy is referring to," Josephine began, with a rolling of her eyes at Ingrid, "is I'm about to be in a movie."

"What? Are you joshing with me again, Miss Josephine?"

"She's not," interrupted Ingrid. "Go on, tell her!"

"You heard of Marvin McCullen?" she asked Carmen.

"Sure have. The director, right? *One Monday. Riddle.* Great films."

"He's directing a new one called *The Good Woman of Harlem* and I'm playing the good woman, I guess."

"No way! Oh, my god, that's fantastic, Miss Josephine."

"Only been seventy years since my last one," Josephine teased.

"I saw the clip in the documentary. You played Desdemona, right?"

"Yes, and now I get to be in my second film. What a career!" Josephine giggled.

"I expect to be invited to the premiere," Carmen said. "Oh, wow. You wait 'til I tell this story to my students. They're never going to believe it."

"I have a hard time believing it myself," Josephine replied. "And me, nearly ninety-two."

"Just goes to show you're never too old."

After a lot of tight farewell hugs and kisses, Josephine and Ingrid took the car back to their hotel. It had been a whirlwind two days of recollections, connections and brand new memories. The past is, indeed, kind sometimes.

The next day was the first day of the shoot. After dropping Josephine at costume and make-up, Ingrid put on her assistant director's hat and found Marvin busily making last minute changes to the script.

He outlined the day's schedule which included introducing Josephine to the other cast members. Her daughter in the movie, Broadway star Tarteel Adams, had flowers for Josephine as an ice-breaker, as well as a rapid pulse in anticipation of their meeting.

Tarteel's film children, both young television stars, were equally anxious and nervous to be working with Josephine, as was legendary movie icon Tyrone Robinson, Tarteel's movie husband.

"You know her better than anyone," Marvin suggested, as he and Ingrid went over the first scene between Josephine and her movie grandson,

Michael. "I don't want too much rehearsing, but they haven't even been introduced yet."

"Personally, I think that's a good thing, Marvin. In the movie, they haven't seen each other in a long time. Not exactly strangers but certainly distant. I think it'll give the scene just the edge you're looking for.

"Same with the other actors. After all, Josephine's character is supposed to be visiting the family after not seeing them for quite some time. She's been leading her own life and they, theirs. It'll be good tension, I think."

Marvin considered Ingrid's comments and nodded.

"All good points. All right, let's briefly introduce everyone and get to work."

Over the next two weeks the cast came together as a close family, unlike the one portrayed in the movie. Josephine's down-to-earth manner and good humor made everyone leave their healthy egos at the door. They treated her with due respect and not a little awe, yet felt comfortable teasing and pulling the odd practical joke or two on her. She, in return, gave as good as she received.

Josephine's last scene, the touching moments she spends on her death bed speaking with her granddaughter, was silently witnessed by the entire cast and crew.

Marvin precisely set the stage, explaining exactly what he wanted from the two actors. Then, he took Ingrid aside and gave her some good news.

"I'm going to tell you now what Spielberg said to me on the set of my first film with him. Okay, kiddo, this next scene is all yours. Don't screw it up!"

"You want me to direct this?"

"That's what assistant directors do sometimes. So, yes, I want you to direct this scene. I won't watch because that'll only make you more nervous. I'll check the rushes later. Go on," he urged. "You can do this."

When Ingrid told Josephine the news, the actress seemed nonplussed.

"It's about time he gave you your chance," she said, plainly. "You're more than ready, child. You tell me and Ariana how you'd like it played and we'll do the rest. Oh, I'm so happy for you. This will be so special for me."

With the set prepared and Josephine and Ariana in place, Ingrid delivered her first instructions as director of a major movie.

"You both know the scene backwards, so the danger here is just going through the motions. I need you, within the parameters of the lines, to surprise each other with whatever you feel will add that element of unexpectedness. Hand movements, facial features and the rest. Make the scene sad but ultimately uplifting.

"All right. Positions. And go," Ingrid ordered.

Ariana entered her grandmother's bedroom gingerly, almost afraid of what she might find.

"You awake, Gramma?"

"Is that you, sweetness? Yes. Yes. Come in."

"Can I do anything for you?"

"Sit. Just sit for a while."

"You look nice, Gramma. Are you warm enough?"

"Tell me something special you did today, child. Make me smile."

"I nearly made a fool of myself."

"How so?"

"I met a new boy and he took me out for a cup of coffee. Then I spoiled it all by spilling some down the front of me. He was nice, though. Got me a damp napkin. He didn't seem to mind but I was so embarrassed, Gramma."

"That did make me smile, honey. You all right now?"

"Yes. He called later and set another date, so I guess I didn't ruin anything.

"Take my hand, child. Lift it to your face."

"You're so cold, Gramma. I'm so sorry you're sick right now."

"Just my time, sweet one."

"Are you scared?"

"Scared? What of dying? No, child, no."

"D'you have a favorite memory? Something I can always remember you by?"

"Oh, so many. So very many. Let me see. When I was a young girl my mama and daddy told me I was the prettiest thing they'd ever seen. And I have always believed that. Now I'm telling the same to you – you are the prettiest thing I've ever seen. Take that with you, child, always. You promise?"

"Promise, Gramma."

"One more thing you have to promise me, child."

"Anything. Just tell me."

"Your family needs help. You do know that?"

"I do, yes."

"Good, because I'm going to be relying on you to take my place."

"Take your place how, Gramma?"

'You are old enough to say your piece, even to your mama and daddy. Do not be afraid to say your piece. Your brother, Michael, he needs your help the most now. Talk to him. Guide him. Give him hope. Can you do that, child?"

"I'll do my best."

"No. No. You have to do more than your best. Listen to me, come closer. Your mama is struggling to find the right way. She needs your help, too. But with her it's different. She's your Mama and she will not take kindly to you speaking your mind. But you must. You must be the peacemaker between those two."

"But how, Gramma? What if she won't listen?"

"By showing her a better way. Your way. Oh, it will not be easy, child, I can tell you that. But in the end you will succeed. You will be the one to calm the waters. Now, can you do that? Will you try?"

"I will, Gramma. I will."

"Just put me inside that pretty head of yours and do the work. Now, go to my dresser and bring me my jewelry box."

"Here, Gramma. Let me help you sit up."

"I want you to have this. It was a present to me from my own grandmother. You take it and keep it with you. And whenever you feel like giving in, touch it and think of me. This will give you the strength you need."

"So beautiful. Thank you, Gramma. This'll mean so much to me."

"Now, child, lay me down and let me kiss you. Be good and remember what I've said."

"I will, Gramma. I will. Promise."

"Cut!" Ingrid yelled. "Perfect. So good, you two. The movement. The pauses. The interchanges. All of it, perfect. Thank you."

Later that evening over dinner, Josephine shared her thoughts with Ingrid.

"Mixed emotions, that's what I have."

"Yeah, I understand," Ingrid sympathized. "But, hey, you did it. You made a movie."

"So happy but sad it's over."

"I know. How did it feel after being away so long?"

"Just like riding a bike. Some things you don't forget. I thank Stanley for that. He instilled so many good lessons in me. But what I really want to tell you is having you direct my last scene made me treasure you even more than I did before. The moment was so special, child. Happy doesn't even begin to tell you how I feel."

"Right back at you, Josephine. Just to have the opportunity to be with you on set was one thing, but to actually be a part of your last scene...I'm almost totally speechless. Those moments and memories will stay with me forever, however sappy that sounds."

"Good, child. That's good you feel that way because memories make a life. You should always remember that."

"I will. Promise."

Chapter Twenty-Nine

Marvin McCullen's movie *The Good Woman of Harlem* wrapped up its on location shoot in two months after Josephine's scenes were finished. Ingrid became an integral part of Marvin's crew, directing a few more minor scenes while becoming enamored by the whole process. She now knew for sure where her future lay; directing movies would be her passion and life's work.

Two months later Marvin, she and the editors finished the final cut. That process she found to be tiresome but necessary; time consuming but revealing in how effective editing could make a good film great.

The movie's scheduled release was set for early fall. Marvin insisted its premiere be held in Harlem and secured The Apollo Theater. He asked Ingrid to inform Josephine.

On her next trip back east, Ingrid stopped by the nursing home to surprise Josephine with the news.

"At The Apollo? Oh, my, how wonderful!" Josephine responded. "I haven't been there for so long."

"Marvin says you can invite whoever you want. The premiere's in three weeks and I would love to escort you there."

"Please, because you're the one who's made all this possible."

On a beautiful September evening in Harlem, with The Apollo Theater festively decked out, Josephine and Ingrid arrived for the premiere of *The Good Woman of Harlem*.

In the weeks leading up to the first showing Marvin's publicity team played every angle to ensure the movie received all the hype and attention it deserved. The main focus point was, of course, Josephine's appearance in a movie for the first time in over seventy years.

After Ingrid told her about The Apollo, she also asked if she would be willing to meet with the media.

"Of course, child. That will be fun."

"Good," Ingrid responded, "because we've lined up seven interviews this week alone."

"My word," Josephine answered, surprised. "I'd better go get my hair done."

During that week, all the major network entertainment shows sent reporters to get their stories. Newspapers, too, joined the bandwagon; national, local and international. After a while, the parking lot at the nursing home became like a circus.

Josephine, with Ingrid's help, handled the notoriety with calmness, humility and dignity. She answered all their questions with good humor, honesty and patience considering reporters wanted to know the same details repeatedly. She was actually a little sad when the excitement finally died down, but grateful to have her old routine back once more.

Now, as she stepped out of the limousine with Ingrid, Josephine remembered a similar night some seventy years before when she attended the premiere of *Othello* with her daddy.

"I bought him a new suit for the premiere," Josephine whispered to Ingrid.

"Who? Who did you buy a new suit for?" Ingrid asked, confused.

"My daddy. When we went to the premiere of *Othello*. I bought him a new suit with some of the money I earned."

"Oh, yes, now I remember you telling me that. What else do you recall?"

"Judy came to support me. That was very kind of her. Oh, that was such a night!"

"And this will be, too. C'mon."

Ingrid led Josephine past a line of photographers, television cameras and press. People were shouting her name, calling for her to turn this way and that. She waved at a massive crowd of onlookers who cheered and clapped when she appeared. It seemed like madness to her, but a good kind of madness.

In the lobby of the theater, Marvin, Sonia and Sissy rushed forward, greeting Josephine with smiles, hugs and flowers. Josephine's fellow cast members waited respectfully until their turn came to welcome her like family. Soon after, Sylvia Richards from the nursing home and Carmen Gordon from the performing arts studio, both Josephine's guests, offered warm embraces and words of awe for their friend. Obligatory selfies were taken by everyone until Marvin ushered them all into the theater.

"Welcome, one and all, to this truly special and, dare I say, historic, occasion," Marvin began, as he introduced his film. "For me, the premiere of one of my movies is always gratifying personally because it represents the culmination of many years of planning, writing and execution.

"But this time, with this movie, my feelings go way beyond the normal. And they do that for one simple reason – and her name is Miss Josephine Benson."

The audience interrupted Marvin's speech with thunderous applause.

"If you don't know her story, and you must've been living under a rock not to have seen Ingrid Strauss's wonderful documentary, then let me briefly recap. At the age of twenty she appeared as Desdemona in Stanley Masters' *Othello*, a performance so powerful, moving and expressive that she was nominated for an Academy Award for Best Supporting Actress. That, ladies and gentlemen, was in *nineteen forty-nine*, I think, so some seventy odd years ago.

"Josephine never made another movie mainly because of the bias towards African American actors in those days. She honestly believed she would never truly be accepted into the world of Hollywood. So, she abandoned acting, became a renowned singer with The Count Basie Orchestra before leaving that profession to spend the next fifty years or so mentoring and teaching young boys and girls in Harlem. Her performing arts studio still thrives today.

"When I thought about casting this movie I immediately realized only one person could adequately portray the family matriarch. With Ingrid's help, we managed to persuade Josephine to take on that role. The result is what you will see on screen in a few moments. To say it is a performance for the ages simply does not come close. In my humble opinion, it is a performance for all time.

"So, without further ado, sit back and enjoy the film and Josephine's remarkable performance. Thank you"

And so, for the next one hundred, twenty-six minutes, the audience in the Apollo Theater was treated to a drama unlike any it had seen before. All the roles were near perfection in a story full of resentment, distrust, resolution and poignancy. At the conclusion, the crowd rose as one to applaud the movie in general and Josephine in particular. With Ingrid's help, she slowly arose, bowing and waving to the audience. The applause lasted a full ten minutes.

Sylvia Richards took Josephine back to the nursing home but not before Ingrid had the chance to get her reaction to the evening's proceedings.

"Quite the star, aren't we?" Ingrid teased, as they found a quiet spot to talk.

"Oh, I suppose you want my autograph, too?" Josephine kidded right back.

"Tell me how you feel now you've seen the movie?"

Josephine put her hands together, prayer-like, before taking Ingrid's in her own.

"Blessed. Lucky. A little overwhelmed. So grateful you talked me into taking the part."

"And what did you think of your performance?"

"Not bad for an old broad!" she joked again.

"No, really. What did you think?"

"That I couldn't have done it any better. I was fearful of my last scene, that I would finally let everyone down, but with you there, directing, it went as smooth as silk. You were…you are…my angel. My guardian angel."

"Now all we have to do is await the reviews and the box office."

"I hope for Marvin's sake and the rest of the cast it's a success because they all worked so hard. For me, just being a part of it has been enough. If no one goes to see it, I'd be okay with that."

To everyone's surprise, *The Good Woman of Harlem* took in over thirty-four million dollars in its first weekend's release. Marvin reacted ecstatically, calling the cast and crew with the astounding news. The last person he spoke to was Josephine.

"And it's all because of you, princess," he offered warmly. "Your performance, your strange history in this business has just fascinated people. I'm thinking they all went to see it to get a look at you. Whatever the reason, I owe you a lot of thanks."

"Nonsense, young man," Josephine scoffed. "The film tells a wonderful story. That's why. They have been moved by the trials and tribulations of this family. It will touch home with so many folk. My part was small but I'm glad you feel I helped a little."

"You are more than kind and generous, Josephine, but I know the real truth."

"Now," Josephine asked, matter-of-factly, "are you planning to keep my guardian angel, Ingrid, working for you?"

"Of course. Why d'you ask?"

"Because, if it turns out you only used her to get me on the film, I will come after you with my stick!"

"I already told you and her that was not the case and I meant it. In fact, I'll let you in on a little secret I have for her. My next project is all lined up. Sonia is producing again and I'm going to ask Ingrid to direct the whole movie. But you have to promise not to say a word until I tell her myself."

"Oh, wow, Marvin, that *is* wonderful news. She will be just thrilled. Having faith in people is so important. She won't let you down."

"No, I know. Ingrid is destined to become a marvelous director. She has that instinct you just cannot teach. I'm breaking the news to her tomorrow. So, stay tuned. I'm sure you'll be the first person she calls."

Marvin was absolutely correct. The following afternoon Josephine received the call.

"Josephine," a breathless Ingrid began," you will never guess what just happened."

"What, sweet child?"

"I just got off the phone with Marvin and, guess what?"

"What?"

"He wants me to direct his next movie! Me! By myself! Can you believe it?"

"Well, of course, child. Oh, that is so wonderful. He sees so much potential in you. I even told him myself he'd be a fool to let you go. Give yourself a big pat on the back."

"I'm going to try to wangle a small cameo in it for you, if you'd like."

"Oh, no. No, child. I am done and finished. This is your time. Your moment. But I thank you for thinking of me."

"Are you sure?"

"One hundred per cent. You go and make your film and invite me to the premiere. I'll come to that."

"All right. If you're sure."

"I am, sweetness. I am."

After four months *The Good Woman of Harlem* grossed over one hundred, fourteen million dollars. On a cold but sunny afternoon in December, Ingrid came to the nursing home with a surprise for Josephine.

"You are a sight for sore eyes," Josephine said, welcoming Ingrid with smiles and hugs. "Just in time for some wine."

"Perfect."

Ingrid poured them both a glass.

"So, child, what is new with you?"

"Only preparing to direct my first movie," she answered, exuberantly.

"And I assume it is going well?"

"Very. Oh, Josephine, you have no idea how it feels to be completely in charge. Overwhelming at times with so much to do but so, so satisfying."

"Good. That's good, child."

"But that's not why I'm here."

"Oh?"

"No. I have some very good news for you. Do you remember the contract you signed with Sonia?"

"Yes, vaguely. Why?"

"Well, the contract stipulated that if the movie grossed over one hundred million dollars you would receive an additional one hundred thousand dollars. Do you recall that?"

"If you say so."

"A few days ago the gross reached more than that. So," Ingrid continued, reaching into her purse and pulling out an envelope, "Sonia asked me to give you this."

Josephine carefully tore open the envelope and retrieved a check.

"Oh, my word!" she exclaimed. "Oh, my word!"

"Congratulations."

"I don't know what to say," was all Josephine could offer in reply.

"Take it. You earned it."

Josephine stared at the piece of paper until a huge smile crossed her face.

"What?" Ingrid asked.

"I know exactly what I will do with the money."

"Good. We're all glad it'll help you."

"No, not me. I have enough for my needs. This," she continued, waving the check in the air, "will go to the studio. Carmen will never have to worry again."

"Oh, Josephine," Ingrid lauded, "that is so selfless of you. Are you sure?"

"I am. It can go into the foundation and you can see it gets used for the studio."

"Lots of unknown girls and boys will thank you. You're the best."

Josephine pooh-poohed Ingrid's compliment with a shrug.

"Just paying it forward, child. Just paying it forward."

Chapter Thirty

As the year drew to a close, two important events took place at the nursing home; Christmas and New Year's Eve. Of the two, Christmas was by far the most exciting and joyful for the residents, families and staff.

The whole facility, beginning in early December, took on a colorful, festive atmosphere, which many of the folks joined in to create. Decorations and lights began appearing in all the units in a friendly competition to see which group could outdo the other.

Josephine, ever the organizer, corralled Betty Harper, Jack and Pearl Lister to help her and some of the staff bring a few unusual touches to their display. Their theme, of Christmas around the world, included such customs as nativity scenes from Poland, paper chains from Germany, hand-painted terracotta figurines, called santons, from Italy and Christmas Crackers from England.

Many of the items came courtesy of their families; pieces that were, in fact, family heirlooms cherished by the residents throughout their lives.

Jack, the gardener, provided the floral touches to the display. Holly branches, red amaryllis, boughs and a few poinsettias, a native plant of Mexico, brought color and freshness. All in all, it was a minor work of art.

Another of the favorite activities centered on decorating the numerous trees around the halls, rooms and entrance ways. Ornaments were hung, garlands draped and lights carefully arranged before a star was ceremoniously placed on top of each.

Many of the residents loved to walk or ride around the facility to take in the various trees once they'd been completed. Happiness and smiles reigned at this time of the year.

Ten days before the actual day, a Christmas lunch was held. Family members joined the residents to celebrate a wonderful traditional meal provided and served by the staff. Turkey, ham, mashed potatoes, vegetables, gravy and all the fixings gave everyone a real sense of the season and togetherness. Pies, fruit cake and plenty to drink rounded off a veritable feast.

Afterwards, music and carols were performed by the choral choir from the local high school, while an entertaining magician thrilled and bemused everyone with his amazing tricks and sleight of hand.

Santa and Mrs. Claus, though, made the afternoon complete, as they suddenly appeared to greet each resident with handshakes and warm hugs, filling the room with so much laughter and good cheer. The event left all those present in high spirits and with overflowing cheerfulness.

Another part of the Christmas season that Sylvia Richards particularly enjoyed was when she personally took groups of residents around the local towns to see the display of lights. For Sylvia, this was a magical time, as she slowly drove by houses drenched with colorful lights that turned neighborhoods into wonderlands, if only for a while.

Christmas is about memories; making them and remembering them. Sylvia hoped, by taking folks on these special journeys, she might plant some new ones while also, perhaps, having them recall some of the good times past. The comments she always received afterwards made her happy both goals had been met.

Late on Christmas Eve, when the residents were hopefully fast asleep, the night staff visited each room to leave a gift or two. These gifts, purchased through kind donations and with the staff's own money, awaited folk as a surprise the next morning.

As much as possible, the hard-working and thoughtful staff made every effort to match the gifts with the preferences of each resident. They were colorfully wrapped and accompanied by cards signed by Santa.

When Josephine awoke she found two gifts on her side table. *My, my,* she thought. *I wonder what these are?*

With the excitement and expectation of a child, she carefully unwrapped her first present. Sylvia happened to be passing and heard Josephine giggle.

"Merry Christmas, Josephine," she offered brightly, poking her head around the door. "You sound in good spirits this morning. What've got there?"

Josephine proudly held up a framed gold star with an inscription underneath that read: *Movie star extraordinaire! Josephine Benson.*

"That is so cool. Santa really got it right that time," Sylvia beamed. "What's in the other package?"

"Probably a lump of coal," Josephine joked. "Let's see."

It wasn't a lump of coal but a beautiful butterfly brooch, with a note from Santa that read, *Still spreading joy after all these years.*

Sylvia thought Josephine was about to cry as she sniffed into a tissue.

"So blessed," was all she said, but her words meant the world to Sylvia who would share them later with the staff.

Meanwhile, Jack found a new trowel and gardening gloves in a stocking left by the staff. He'd been heard complaining for weeks about his urgent need for them, so was thrilled to actually find them. Santa's note read, *Keep sowing, growing and making the world a better place.*

The home's resident 'librarian', Pearl Lister, unwrapped her gifts alongside her friend, Betty Harper.

"What's that?" Betty asked, as Pearl opened a box set of her favorite paperbacks. An avid reader, Pearl seemed thrilled with the present.

"These'll keep me busy for quite a while," she admitted. "They know what I like. Now, Betty, open one of yours."

Betty removed the pretty wrapping on a soft package.

"Oh, yes, I love it!" she exclaimed, showing Pearl a beautiful, silk scarf. It was the perfect gift since her doctor daughter, Marion, and she always seemed to have a friendly competition as to who could wear the smartest scarf whenever Marion visited. "This will put me ahead when she pops in later," Betty said, mischievously.

"And what is this?" Pearl wondered aloud, as she tore off the paper on her other gift. "Would you look at this, Betty, a new cribbage board. How thoughtful of Santa. He must've known I'd lost my other one. Real wood, too. Beautiful."

A box of her favorite chocolates was Betty's other gift and made her day.

"And I can certainly help you eat those," Pearl offered, as Betty responded by poking out her tongue.

Christmas lunch, amid family and staff, was full of lively chatter and lots of laughter. One surprise for the residents was the appearance on each of their placemats of a festive-looking, colorful tube, twisted at both ends. No one had any idea what they were except to say they made beautiful table decorations. As some folk began fidgeting with them, Sylvia announced, as kindly as possible, they were not to be touched until after lunch was over.

"All right," she began, "now the fun really starts. The funny looking tube objects are called Christmas Crackers, a tradition which comes from England, which I learned from one of your displays.

"Here's what you do – hold your cracker by one end, have a partner, guest or one of the staff hold the other, and on the count of three...pull as hard as you can. There is a popper inside that will make a 'cracking' sound. Once the cracker comes apart you will find a prize, a paper hat and a joke. Then, you must help your partner pull their cracker. Everyone good? Okay, find your partner and on the count of three, go."

Very quickly and excitedly the residents found partners and waited for Sylvia's countdown.

"Three. Two. One. Pull!"

The room erupted into near chaos as popping sounds crackled all around. Prizes, hats and jokes spilled onto the floor and tables, which just made everyone laugh more. The staff helped collect the novelties, handing them to their rightful owners.

"Okay," Sylvia shouted above the din, "time to pull your neighbor's. Ready? Three. Two. One. Go!"

Again, the contents spewed from the crackers amid more hilarity. The prizes included plastic rings, watches, games and small photo frames. The paper hats were unfolded and worn with comical pride. And everyone told their joke to whoever would listen. The introduction of the crackers was a big hit with the residents, family and staff.

To top off the afternoon's festivities Santa made his customary appearance, mingling and spreading more good cheer. By the end of the lunch a lot of happy, tired folk retired to their rooms for a nap.

The other main event, New Year's Eve and the dropping of the home's ceremonial ball, took place earlier in the evening. But it was a joyous occasion tinged with sadness that another year had passed.

Drinks and snacks were served and noisemakers given out so that when the big moment arrived everyone could celebrate as loudly as possible.

Josephine and several of her other musically gifted friends got up and sang *Auld Lang Syne* as the countdown began and the ball slowly began to drop. By nine o'clock most of the residents were in bed, no doubt wishing the coming year would be as good and kind as the one just passed.

Chapter Thirty-One

It was Marvin McCullen who first suggested the possibility to Ingrid. They were working on pre-production details for his up-coming movie, which Ingrid was to direct, when he offered her some startling news.

"Now," he began, cautiously, "I don't want you jumping the gun but I've heard some strong rumors which would be amazing if true."

Ingrid put down the second draft of the shooting script which she'd been going through with a fine tooth comb, took off her glasses and gave Marvin her full attention.

"Okay, I'm always skeptical of hearsay," she answered, "but I do like to be in at the beginning."

"What's coming up in early February?" he asked.

Ingrid searched her mind but drew a blank.

"Valentine's Day?" she responded, with a shrug.

"No, you idiot," Marvin said, frowning. "The Oscars."

Ingrid's eyes widened.

"Oh, yes. Sure," she acknowledged, as the penny dropped. "Dah! Stupid me. But, so what?"

"Well, I've heard from a couple of people who are on the inside of these things that there might be a huge surprise coming down the pike."

"What, Marvin, you're getting a nomination?" Ingrid almost screamed at him. "Oh, my god, that's great!"

"Not me, dumb ass!" he scowled, in good nature, "although that would be nice."

"Then who?"

"Only Josephine Benson! That's who."

"Oh, no, your friends must've got that wrong," Ingrid replied, doubtfully. "Josephine? Really, at her age? I don't think so."

"Only telling you what I've heard through the grapevine."

"Wow, that would be *so* cool. When are they announced?"

Marvin looked at his phone.

"Next Monday. January seventeenth. One of the morning shows usually carries it live from LA."

"Then I'm going. Sorry, but this'll be too awesome to miss."

"Going where?"

"To be with Josephine. If there's even the remote possibility of her being nominated, I want to be with her."

Ingrid never told Josephine she was coming to see her. The day before the Oscar nominations were set to be announced, Ingrid nonchalantly called to inform Josephine she was in town for a few days. Would Josephine have breakfast with her at the home?

"Of course, child. Haven't seen you for so long. That would make an old lady's day."

"Great! Let's say eight o'clock. See you then."

Bundled up against the cold and snow flurries, Ingrid set out from her hotel with a flutter in her heart she hoped would not be crushed a short time later. Just to *imagine* Josephine being nominated for another Academy Award some seventy-odd years after her first seemed totally unreal; the stuff of make-believe.

And yet, on the flight from LA, she replayed Josephine's role in *The Good Woman of Harlem* over and over in her mind. She saw her friend's command of the script, her nuances of movement and facial features, her profound, meaningful emotions and the ultimate belief she brought to her part. So, Ingrid, thought, *Why not?* Why should she not be nominated for such a performance just because she was ninety-two? What difference did age make in the process?

As she entered the doors and made her way towards Josephine's room she spotted Sylvia Richards making her usual early morning rounds.

"Why, Ingrid! What a lovely surprise. And to what do we owe this honor?" Sylvia asked, with a hug.

"I'm in town for a couple of days and thought I'd pop in and see Josephine. Is she okay?"

"She is now all the attention's died down from the movie. She likes a quiet life and I think she's glad to be back to that."

Well, just you wait, Ingrid thought to herself. *That may only have been a dress rehearsal for what's hopefully coming in a moment.*

But instead, she invited Sylvia to join her.

"Come with me," she offered. "I think you'll want to see this."

Sylvia shrugged, not having any idea what Ingrid alluded to, and dutifully followed her to Josephine's room.

"There's my girl!" Ingrid exclaimed, as she rushed over and embraced her friend. Standing back, she continued, "You look so good! How have you been?"

"Behaving myself, as usual," Josephine answered. "That right, Sylvia?"

Sylvia nodded and smiled.

"We haven't had to call security for quite a few months now," she joked.

"Can we eat breakfast in here?" Ingrid asked, hopefully. "I'd like to catch up without too much distraction."

Sylvia made the call and in less than ten minutes someone brought in three trays.

As they talked, Ingrid kept glancing at the wall clock. When the hands approached eight-thirty, she asked if they could turn on the television.

"You come all this way and you want to watch television?" Josephine complained, with a laugh.

"There's a program coming on I think you might like to see," Ingrid countered. "That's all."

Sylvia hit the remote and the screen burst into life. The popular network morning show was back from commercial and one of the anchors began an announcement.

"Now, as promised, it's time to head out to Los Angeles to hear the nominations for this year's Academy Awards. Let's listen in as Brea Colton and Max Ringer make the announcements."

Ingrid took a sneak peek at Josephine as she watched the screen, frowning and apparently bemused.

"And we're watching this program why?" asked a puzzled Josephine.

Ingrid just beamed at her, indicating she should turn and listen in. After about ten minutes when several of the non-acting categories were read, Brea Colton took the next list from Max Ringer.

"And now we come to the nominations for Best Actress in a Supporting Role. The nominees are:

Rachel Baylis for *The Answer*

Tamara Lewis for *Two O'clock Somewhere*

Faye Salatini for *Flowers and Wine*

Rosario Guerrera for *Beautiful Eden*

And, oh, my word, Josephine Benson for *The Good Woman of Harlem*"

"Josephine! Josephine!" Sylvia yelled across the room. "Did you hear that? You've been nominated. Oh my word!" she continued, briefly covering her face with her hands. "There's your picture on the screen."

Ingrid, beaming, went over and hugged her friend for the longest time.

"You did it, beautiful. You actually did it!"

Josephine, speechless for a few moments, just kept shaking her head.

Finally, she said, "They like me. They really like me!" as she echoed Sally Field's memorable quote.

Sylvia and Ingrid immediately broke up.

With a frown, Josephine turned to Ingrid and asked, "Did you know about this?"

"Only a strong rumor. Marvin told me he'd heard something. That's when I knew I had to be here with you just in case."

"I can't believe this. Must be people felt sorry for me."

"That is definitely *not* the case," Ingrid responded firmly. "The process is vigorous. Only the best five out of many get through."

As she spoke, the morning anchors responded to the news. Sylvia hushed the other two to listen.

"The most surprising name on the list for Supporting Actress is obviously Josephine Benson," Mike King, one of the anchors began.

"And she has an amazing story," Chloe Davis, his fellow anchor, continued. "Briefly, she was nominated in nineteen fifty, at the age of twenty, for the same award but lost out to Mercedes McCambridge. Then she had a great singing career with The Count Basie Orchestra until giving that up to work with under privileged kids in Harlem for over fifty years. I mean, Mike, what a story? Even Hollywood couldn't make this up."

"Indeed, and we'll hope to get her on tomorrow morning for an interview. Meanwhile…"

As good as their words, within an hour, Sylvia received a phone call from a producer on the morning show requesting an interview. Josephine already told Sylvia she would agree as long as Ingrid was there, too. The producer inquired about Ingrid and, as soon as she understood her importance in Josephine's later life and success, welcomed her to be on the show.

Early next morning, Ingrid arrived as the cameras and lights were being set up in the same room she and Zach used to film their documentary. Josephine's hair had already been done earlier by a kind and willing member of the salon's staff. As they waited with a producer to go on live, Josephine took Ingrid's hand.

"I'm going to tell them none of this would have happened without you. And you must speak up for yourself. Don't be modest. Let the people watching know who you are and what you've done."

"But Josephine, this is your day; your achievement. They want to hear your story, not mine. But thank you, anyway."

"Oh, we'll see about that, child," was all Josephine replied, as the producer ushered them before the cameras.

The segment lasted a full ten minutes. Chloe Davis, ever gracious and informed, guided Josephine to speak about her life and what the new nomination meant to her. She particularly picked up on Josephine's comments about her first nomination and how she felt about the then bias prevalent in Hollywood.

But, good as her word, Josephine spent a considerable amount of time praising Ingrid for all she'd done for her.

"She is the one responsible. This sweet child sitting right next to me," she continued, grabbing Ingrid's hand. "My story was only told because of her."

"How do you feel receiving such a tribute from a legend?" Chloe asked Ingrid.

"It was *her* life and work. All I did was chronicle it with her permission," Ingrid answered, deferentially. "But in doing so, I will tell you that I've gained an amazing friend. Someone who's spent most of her life being of value. I can only hope to aspire to her level."

After a few more questions, Chloe thanked them both and wished Josephine good luck at the Oscar ceremony in February.

"All our hopes are with you, Josephine. We'll be keeping our fingers crossed."

Before Ingrid left to return to Los Angeles, she asked Josephine about attending the Oscar ceremony on Sunday, February thirteenth.

"Of course, we all want you there, but it's a long way. Marvin says the studio will send a plane and, of course, I'll be right there with you the whole time. Please, please say you'll come."

"Wouldn't miss it for the world, sweetness. Wouldn't miss it for the world."

Chapter Thirty-Two

The studio's Cessna Citation XLS private jet touched down on runway 8 at the Hollywood-Burbank Airport, formerly known as the Bob Hope Airport, at two o'clock in the afternoon. On board were only two passengers, an attendant and two pilots. Soon after, the two passengers, Ingrid Strauss and Josephine Benson, walked down the short flight of steps into a warm, Los Angeles, February sun.

In the limousine on the way to The Beverly Hills Hotel, Josephine raved about the flight from New York.

"An airplane all to ourselves," she gushed. "Can you believe that?"

"Well, yeah," Ingrid nodded. "I was there with you after all."

Josephine playfully swatted Ingrid's arm.

"That was so kind of Marvin. He's really spoiling me."

"He just wants to make this moment as special as possible. He knows how much you contributed to his movie and its success."

"Still and all, he didn't have to be this kind."

"Marvin's only too pleased to do it, Josephine. Like me, he now thinks of you as family. Now," Ingrid continued, changing the subject, "is there anything you'd like to do or see while we're here? Your old neighborhood and where your house was? Anything at all?"

"No. No, dear. That's all right. The house is long gone and I know the area has changed completely. I'd rather remember it as it was. That's the vision I always have in my mind and that's the way I'd like it to stay. Mama running around the yard after me, and Daddy always fixing something or other. That house was a lovely place to live and that's how I want to remember it."

After another minute or two Josephine did ask Ingrid for a favor.

"Mama and Daddy's graves. I'd like to visit them."

"Of course. Let's do it tomorrow, because Sunday is the big day."

"I won't be disappointed this time," Josephine said, matter-of-factly.

"About what?"

"Not winning, of course. It hurt so much last time. But now it's all fun and games. Those other actresses were a lot better than me."

"Josephine," Ingrid countered strongly, "that is so *not* true. You have been nominated because you *deserve* to be. The only reason you are in that elite group is for your outstanding performance. Just like them. No, you may not win but that doesn't diminish what you've done."

Josephine smiled and closed her eyes.

"It would be kind of amazing though, wouldn't it," she said, almost to herself.

"Yes, it would," Ingrid agreed. "But hold that thought because we're at the hotel."

As the limousine headed off Sunset Boulevard and up the driveway to the hotel, Josephine glanced out the window at the palm trees, the manicured lawns and the landscaped gardens full of bougainvillea and hibiscus.

"How beautiful," she declared to Ingrid. "And we're staying here?"

"Oh, you ain't seen nothing yet," Ingrid replied, with a laugh. "Wait until we go inside."

They were met at the entrance to the lobby by a bell-hop who greeted them warmly, as the chauffeur handed him their bags. He led them up a red carpet into the grand lobby with its distinctive black and white striped ceiling. Josephine, surprised to notice a fire roaring in the ornate fireplace, asked the bell-hop about it.

"Oh, it's one of the hotel's traditions," he answered, pleasantly. "There's a fire going every day of the year."

While Ingrid checked in, Josephine marveled at the luxury surrounding her and the warm, predominantly pink and green color scheme. To her, it seemed as if she'd just stepped into some sort of magical wonderland.

Marvin had booked them into a two bedroom suite at Ingrid's insistence, so Josephine could feel safe. The suite, spacious, luxurious and, again, decorated in pinks, greens, apricots and yellows, also had a balcony with a distant view of the Pacific Ocean. After their bags were delivered, Ingrid asked Josephine how she felt.

"Like a princess. All of this is overwhelming. I'm so glad you're going to be with me."

"Me, too. Now, let's freshen up and head downstairs to the Polo Lounge for lunch."

The Polo Lounge, the world renowned 'place to be seen', had a peachy pink and dark green booth waiting for Ingrid and Josephine. Word must have leaked to fellow diners that here, in their midst, was an Oscar nominated actress by the way heads turned and chatter increased ten fold.

The waiter, who brought a carafe of sparkling water and menus, offered a friendly greeting to both women.

"Miss Benson. Ma'am. It's an honor to welcome you to The Polo Lounge. And for me, personally, an honor to serve you. May I start you off with a drink?"

"Let me, Josephine," Ingrid cut in. "I think you'll like this." To the waiter, she said, "We'll have two watermelon vodkas, please. Light on the ice."

The waiter nodded and left.

"You seem to know your way around," Josephine commented, with a smile. "Watermelon vodkas? At my age?"

"Specialty of the house. You'll love it. And, yes, I do know this place pretty well. Marvin brings the crew here all the time."

In the background, a pianist began playing softly and unobtrusively, yet pleasantly enough for his music to create a warm, cozy atmosphere. Josephine almost started to sing along.

The waiter returned with their drinks, setting them down with graceful precision.

"If you're ready, may I take your luncheon orders?"

Again, Ingrid spoke for them both, knowing Josephine's restrictive diet.

"Yes. We'd each like a Caesar salad and a side of fresh fruit. Bread, too, please."

"Very good, ma'am. Thank you."

Before lunch finished Ingrid brought up the subject of Josephine wanting to visit her parents' graves.

"We really only have tomorrow morning or afternoon since there's a dinner in the evening for all the nominees. How about we go around eleven?"

"I don't mind, dear, as long as we get there some time."

"All right, then. Eleven it is. Now, what was your town called?"

"Westville, a few miles outside Burbank. It's still there, too. Mama and Daddy are buried in the town's cemetery, but I don't know if that's still there."

"I'm sure it is, Josephine. We'll find it one way or another."

Before they left The Polo Lounge, a young couple approached their table, hovering diffidently until Ingrid asked if she could help them.

"We're so sorry to interrupt your lunch but are you Josephine Benson?" the young woman politely inquired.

"Indeed," Josephine replied, with a quizzical look.

"Oh, great!" the young man butted in, excitedly. "We thought it was you. May we get your autograph?"

"Of course," Josephine shrugged.

The man produced a napkin and a pen, handing them to Josephine. While she scribbled her signature, the young woman spoke of seeing *The Good Woman of Harlem*.

"We loved it so much. And you were just so wonderful! We hope you win the Oscar on Sunday."

"That is very kind and thoughtful of you," Josephine answered, as Ingrid beamed. "It certainly would be nice."

The young couple took the napkin and memories away, smiling and hugging each other as if they'd just won the lottery.

"My. My. That was a surprise," Josephine commented. "Fancy people wanting my autograph."

"Josephine," Ingrid replied, astonished, "why wouldn't they? You're a twice Oscar nominated actress. You've had a successful documentary about your life broadcast all over the country. And folks, by now, recognize your beautiful face. I'm just surprised more people haven't come up to you."

The rest of the day was spent relaxing and sleeping, getting ready for the hectic time ahead. At one point in the evening Ingrid left Josephine in the suite, found a quiet spot and called Marvin. She needed his help with an urgent matter and, as usual, he came through with flying colors.

Back in the suite, the pair of them watched a little television before turning in for some well earned rest. It had been an exhausting day, full of surprises, but one well spent.

The next morning they left the hotel by ten-thirty to briefly cruise the neighborhood and head for Westville cemetery. Josephine recognized nothing of the outskirts of Burbank, an area she once knew so well. Back in the mid-Sixties, when she sold her parents' house, she well understood it was the beginning of the end for the place she'd so long called home. She didn't mind and the views did not make her sad; she had her memories and always remembering her town as it was left her feeling as if somewhere out there it still existed. And that gave her comfort.

Westville cemetery seemed largely unchanged except for the encroachment of more urban civilization. The facility, surrounded now by houses, stores and a nursing home, looked like an oasis in a suburban nightmare. But the sacred land, now fenced in with black wrought iron, had escaped to remain a true resting place as ever.

Josephine couldn't quite recall the exact location of her parents' graves. The chauffeur guided the limousine through the wide paths as if by divine intervention.

"Yes!" Josephine squeaked, "they're around here somewhere because I remember that big mausoleum over there. Judy asked me if I'd like something similar for Mama. I said no thank you. She wasn't that type of person."

In the front, Ingrid whispered to the driver to pull over and stop. They had arrived. She helped Josephine from the car and slowly led her to a sheltered corner of the cemetery. Two graves lay before them, side by side and seemingly calling out.

"Oh! Oh!" Josephine gasped, grabbing Ingrid's arm. "Oh, my!"

The grass around the site had recently been mowed, the marble headstones polished and shining in the weak sun, and fresh flowers adorned each grave.

Turning to Ingrid, Josephine said, "You did this, didn't you?"

"I spoke to Marvin and a couple of his guys volunteered to spruce things up. They were glad to do it, Josephine, and said they'll take good care of them from now on."

"Thank you and thank them. They look wonderful and I know Mama and Daddy would thank them, too."

"I'm going to leave you alone for a few minutes so you can spend some time with your folks. I'll be right over there with the car."

"That is kind. I would like a moment or two if you don't mind," Josephine replied, as her eyes began watering.

For the next ten minutes she whispered to them, telling her mother and father how much she missed them every day.

"I hope you can hear me. I hope you know how much I still love you. You both were so good to me, guiding me along, helping me when I most needed it.

"You set me on a good life, oh my, yes you did! Because of you I've been able to do so much, see wonderful places and meet so many fine people. I wish you could've been there with me, to share them and be a part of it all." Nodding her head towards the graves, she continued, "But you were. You were right there in my heart. I carried you with me through everything.

"Thanks to you both I've had a great life and," she said, nodding her head, "it isn't over yet. I got another Academy Award nomination! Yes, I did! So, what d'you think of that? At my age, your daughter is still going strong.

"I don't know when I'll get back this way again. I just know I will. So, 'til then, Mama and Daddy, you stay safe and know I love you and am always, always carrying you close to me. Bye. Bye."

Before she finished, her tears washed over her cheeks in both sadness and joy. She felt the loss and emptiness all over again while also thinking how proud they would have been of her. For Josephine, that mattered more than anything.

Ingrid held her close on their way back to the hotel, saying nothing because there was nothing to say. By the time they reached their suite, Josephine had recovered her composure.

"We should get some lunch," she offered. "I really need one of those delicious watermelon vodkas."

"You got it, sweetie," Ingrid answered, with a grin. "And then we have to get you ready for the nominees' dinner tonight. You're going to be the belle of the ball!"

The Grand Ballroom dripped film stars, fashion and fascination. The stars were there to acknowledge their nominations in fashions that wowed the eyes. But the fascination centered solely on Josephine Benson.

Escorted to her table by Marvin McCullen, she was seated with her fellow nominees Rachel Baylis, Tamara Lewis, Faye Salatini and Rosario Guerrera, who all stood in unison, clapping, as she approached. The applause was infectious; soon the entire room seemed engulfed in its appreciation.

Josephine bowed and waved as Ingrid helped her into her seat. She wore a full length, pale yellow gown, tailored to fit by the studio's wardrobe department. Her hair and make-up were also compliments of the studio. Her corsage, gifted by Ingrid, contained only her favorite white roses. She looked a million dollars and felt it, too.

The other actresses wasted no time in expressing their admiration and awe over Josephine's magnificent achievement.

"We all want you to win," Faye enthused, speaking for the others. "If we could, we'd all drop out right now!"

Josephine frowned then smiled, waving Faye's comments away as if swatting a fly.

"Oh, now child, that is just such nonsense," she countered. "I've watched all of your films and any one of you deserves to win. But, really, that's not what's important. Working hard and giving the best performance you can — that's what really matters. And all of you beautiful ladies did that."

Kisses were blown across the table and selfies were taken individually and as a group. The love fest for Josephine continued unabated throughout the evening as other, more established stars, stopped by her table to pay their respects. When she and Ingrid finally retired to their suite, she told her friend and companion it felt as if she'd already won.

"And you have," Ingrid agreed. "People just adore you for who you are and what you've done. My advice, just sit back and enjoy the fuss."

Chapter Thirty-Three

Preparations for the Academy Awards ceremony had been underway for months. Oscars, sets, presenters and a myriad other arrangements were now in place for Hollywood's annual night of nights.

In their suite at The Beverly Hills Hotel, Ingrid and Josephine tried hard to keep calm before venturing out into what they both knew would be a maelstrom of cameras, photographers, interviewers and a clamoring public eager to set eyes on one remarkable lady.

They ate a late, room service, breakfast and talked about the moment before them.

"Are you just a little bit nervous?" Ingrid wanted to know.

"Just a bit," Josephine answered, trying to smile. "I've never enjoyed a lot of fuss being made over me, but I understand the interest. I'll be good, don't worry," she teased. "I only hope I don't fall asleep!"

"That's why I'm with you, to keep on your toes."

"It is very strange, though," Josephine remarked, "how I'm finding myself back in exactly the same position as I was seventy or so years ago."

"Not just strange," Ingrid replied, "but extraordinary and almost unbelievable. I doubt anything like this will ever happen again."

"I am proud of the film," Josephine said, nodding. "It's nice that it will live on long after I'm gone. It's pleasant to think you might be remembered for something, that in a way you'll never die."

"Yes, that will be so cool," Ingrid agreed. "And for me, to be able to see your face and hear your voice," she added, shaking her head, "that will mean you are always with me." Ingrid then took hold of Josephine's hand and looked into her eyes. "While we have this moment together, and I don't want to sound melodramatic, but I want you to know what you've meant to me since we met."

"Oh, now, child, there's no need for any of this," Josephine began, before Ingrid cut in.

"Yes. Yes, there is. I need to say this, to let you understand how I feel. When I started the documentary we were strangers from different worlds. But you trusted this young upstart with essentially your life. You didn't question me or ask my motives. You just put your trust in me to do justice to your story.

"And over the past weeks and months I have come to love and respect you in a way that can't easily be explained, except to say, Josephine Benson, you have enriched my life beyond measure; beyond anything I deserve or ever dreamed of. You are now so much a part of me that I can't imagine what my life was like before you. You've simply been the best, that's all."

Both women cried in each other's arms until Josephine finally pulled away.

"Carry me with you, sweetness. Carry me with you," she whispered. "That's all I ask. Carry me with you."

"I will. I will. Promise."

The Oscars were due to begin in Los Angeles at five o'clock. After their late breakfast, Ingrid and Josephine had only three hours to get ready before leaving the hotel. Marvin again sent hair and make-up from the studio, as well as wardrobe to tailor dresses for them both.

"Just like Stanley," Josephine recalled, as her hair was teased and her eyes brightened. "He spoiled me, too, the first time around."

Ingrid, dressed conservatively in black, concerned herself only with making sure Josephine looked and felt like the star and legend she'd become.

When the assistants left she had Josephine stand before her for one last scrutiny. She looked at her from every angle, fussing now and then with a sleeve or pleat of her ivory colored gown.

"Perfect, except for some bling!' she exclaimed.

Josephine went to her purse and handed Ingrid a necklace.

"This is the only thing I want to wear. Can you?"

Ingrid placed the locket around Josephine's neck and set the clasp. "There."

"I want him with me…Milton. He's all I've ever really needed."

Ingrid nodded.

"He would have been so proud. So proud."

As they left the hotel for the Dolby Theater in Hollywood, several members of the staff lined the lobby to wish Josephine good luck. Outside, in the bright sunshine, twenty or so members of the public waited to cheer her on, too.

"It's starting," Ingrid whispered, as Josephine waved to the well-wishers. "Better get used to it."

Their limousine awaited them at the end of the lobby, impressive and shiny, with a smartly dressed chauffeur standing by.

Josephine stopped and frowned when she saw it, shielding her eyes from the sun, thinking it must be some sort of mirage.

"Oh, no! Oh, no, no, no!" she squealed, as Ingrid just grinned broadly.

In the driveway stood a shiny, 1931 cherry red Packard.

"Oh, my. This cannot be real. It's just like the one Mr. Hoyle drove Mama and me in when she took me to her studio."

Josephine gawked at the car's high sides, silver running boards, monster trunk, white-walled tires and the gleaming hood ornament.

"Goddess of Speed," she proclaimed. "That's what Mr. Hoyle said was her name. Now, don't you dare tell me…"

"It is," Ingrid interrupted. "This is the same car you rode in all those years ago."

"No. No. How can that be?"

"Thank Marvin, again. He thought it would be a neat idea for you to ride to the Oscars in the same car you first rode in when you were eight. There are lots of vintage car owners in LA, so Marvin asked around and eventually found it. The current owner still takes it out now and then and was only too happy to lend it for the evening."

"I just cannot believe it," Josephine said, ruefully shaking her head. "This is beyond belief."

She quietly walked to the front of the car, caressing the magnificent ornament as if to say *'You're as beautiful now as you were then.'*

The chauffeur produced a small step and helped Josephine up onto the running board and into the back seat. Ingrid joined her and, with a wave to the crowd, they were off.

The car brought stares and more waves on its three mile journey to the theater. Josephine, still dumbfounded by the surprise, could only think back to the first time she rode in the car.

"I told Mama when we were riding in the car that I felt like a princess. Now, well now I feel like a queen."

"And you look the part, too," Ingrid declared. "All you need is a crown."

The Packard slid silently to a halt a few hundred feet from the theater's entrance. Again, the chauffeur helped the ladies out of the car, telling them how much of a pleasure it had been to drive them and how he would be there later to return them to their hotel.

Upon their arrival, an Academy official bustled over and guided them to the red carpet, which, to Josephine, seemed to stretch for miles. Above the sidewalk, special balconies contained masses of people cheering and applauding the arriving stars. Photographers crowded every inch of space as television reporters also clamored to get interviews.

"This way! Over here! Josephine, here please!"

The photographers jostled each other to get their best shots as Josephine, guided by Ingrid, made her way down the red carpet, swiveling her head from side to side until she felt dizzy.

Just in time, one of the presenters from a network entertainment show gently grabbed her arm and asked for a few words.

"Quite a night for you, Miss Benson. How does it feel to be back after so long away?"

A startled Josephine said what she thought.

"Overwhelming. Just completely overwhelming," before adding, "but fun. Yes, a lot of fun, thank you."

"Now, nominated for Best Supporting Actress for your work in *The Good Woman of Harlem,* can you tell us what it was like to be acting again in a major movie?"

Josephine quickly glanced at Ingrid who just nodded and smiled.

"Wonderful. Marvin…"

"…Marvin McCullen, the director…"

"Yes. He was just so kind, patient and understanding. He reminded me so much of Stanley Masters, my first director. He made the whole experience so very special for me. And the cast and crew, too, just wonderful, wonderful people."

"And how do you plan on celebrating if you win?"

"Probably with a watermelon vodka and an early night," Josephine joked.

"Well, we wish you all the very best and hope you really enjoy your evening. Thanks for stopping by."

Two more interviews followed before Josephine and Ingrid finally made it into the theater where Marvin, Sonia and Sissy waited to greet them.

"There she is!" Marvin called out, rushing over to hug her. "We thought you'd got lost."

"It felt like that to me, too," Josephine replied, quick as a flash. "Now, young man," she continued, pulling on Marvin's coat sleeve, "a word with you if I may?"

Guiding her to a quieter spot, he bent and asked, "Is everything all right?"

"Yes, it is but here's what I need to say to you…thank you. Thank you so much for making an old woman smile and feel so very special. The hotel, the dresses…oh, my, and the car! I couldn't believe you did all that just for me. Now, let this old woman give you a proper hug."

Marvin embraced her as the rest looked on, grinning and happy to be a part of the moment.

Sonia Myers, the producer, noticing the time, gently urged everyone to move inside.

"We best get you seated," she said. "They run a tight ship with these events."

The group sat together, chatting and laughing, when an elegantly dressed woman made her way up from the front and across the row to where Josephine was sitting.

"I had to meet you. I just had to!" Meryl Streep exclaimed, reaching out for Josephine's hand. "I've never been more excited than now," she continued, squeezing Josephine's hand harder than she realized. "Really, I've seen the film and you were exquisite. Pure magic."

Josephine tried to rise but Meryl raised her hand.

"No. No. Please don't get up, and I'm so sorry to intrude but I just *had* to. You give me hope," she said, with a chuckle.

By this time, Josephine, recovering somewhat from the shock of being accosted by a legend, reached out and touched Meryl's cheek.

"You're just as beautiful in real life as you are on the screen. Thank you, child, for your kind words. From you, they mean everything."

Meryl kissed her hand, thanked her again and was gone. It was a brief moment in time but one that mattered so much to Josephine.

During the evening, Morgan Freeman, Oprah, Tom Hanks and others made their way to Josephine to pay their honest respects. Moments that mattered, all of them.

The ceremony was well into its second hour before Tom Hanks appeared on stage to present the Oscar for Best Actress in a Supporting Role.

"We have all seen the clips of their marvelous performances," he began, "so, without further ado here are the nominees for Best Supporting Actress...

> Rachel Baylis for *The Answer*
> Faye Salatini for *Flowers and Wine*
> Josephine Benson for *The Good Woman of Harlem*
> Tamara Lewis for *Two O'clock Somewhere*
> Rosario Guerrera for *Beautiful Eden*."

As Hanks read their names, the camera panned to each woman in turn. When Josephine's name was called, she clasped her hands in front of her and bowed her head. Ingrid couldn't help leaning over and hugging her in front of millions of television viewers, while slowly and carefully, Hanks opened the envelope.

"And the Oscar goes to..."

Chapter Thirty-Four

The studio's Cessna touched down at the Wyverne County Municipal Airport on a warm June afternoon with only one passenger on board. Ingrid Strauss stepped down from the plane and into a waiting car, which then whisked her the seven miles to *The Sweet and Comfy Nursing Home*.

At the entrance, a visibly somber Sylvia Richards greeted Ingrid with a hug and tears in her eyes. The two embraced for what seemed like an age before Sylvia guided Ingrid to her office.

"I can't thank you enough for coming all this way at such short notice," she began. "But I knew you'd want to be here."

"Of course. Of course," Ingrid replied, understandingly. "She's family, as you well know. But what happened? It all seemed so sudden."

Sylvia slumped into her chair as Ingrid pulled up another.

"It was, in a way. About two months ago she began complaining about pressure and some pain across her chest."

"Oh, she never told me and I spoke to her about once a month."

"Not surprised. She didn't like to talk about her aches and pains. Anyway, we had our doctor check her out. He diagnosed angina, gave her some meds, which she wouldn't take, and sent her for some tests. They came back indicating various blockages, which at her age wasn't surprising.

"There were options but none of them good. She decided against doing anything. Said she just wanted to live out however much time she had left as normally as possible. And quite honestly, who were we to argue?

"So, she continued her daily walks, ate whatever she felt like and, really, just carried on as normal. She rested whenever the discomfort got too much, but other than that it was still life as she knew it.

"Two days ago, after finishing her early evening bingo game, she had a drink and a few snacks before going to bed. One of the staff checked in on her around one in the morning and everything seemed fine.

"Then a member of the morning crew, Trish, who always got her up and going for the day, went in but couldn't wake her. She took her pulse then sounded the alarm but..." Sylvia recounted, trying desperately to hold back her tears, "...but it was too late. She'd apparently died peacefully in her sleep." Sylvia covered her face and sobbed uncontrollably.

Ingrid, crying too, rushed over to comfort her. If sadness could be measured then this was a ten.

"She has no family, does she?" Ingrid asked, almost in a whisper.

"No, none."

"When we were in Burbank we visited her parents' graves. She told me then it was her wish to be buried beside them."

"Yes, she told me that too. I had her put it in her will."

"I'd be honored to take her back and manage the arrangements."

"Would you? I'll make sure all the paperwork's in order."

"And I promise she'll have a great send off. Marvin and the crew will be there, I'm sure. There'll be room on the plane if you'd like to..."

Sylvia shook her head.

"No, but thanks. That would be too hard to bear. I'll remember her as she was, that's what I'll do. Besides, I still have a facility to run."

"Of course, I completely understand. And Sylvia, you've done so much for her over the years. She often spoke of you with respect and true love. Her last years were wonderful because of you and all the staff here."

"I keep wondering how I'm going to manage walking by her room every day and not seeing her there?"

"By keeping her in your book of memories, that's how."

They talked about Josephine for another hour until Sylvia went to her office safe, brought out a decorative box and handed it to Ingrid.

"She wanted you to have this. She said you deserved it more than she."

Ingrid frowned, puzzled, as she took the package and looked inside.

"Oh, my word! Her Oscar!" she exclaimed, carefully holding the gleaming, gold statue as if it might break at any moment.

"Yes. She insisted I pass it onto you. So insistent, in fact, she added the bequest to her will just to make sure. She wanted you to have something tangible to remember her by."

Ingrid, dumbstruck, just stared and shook her head.

"She's given me her *Oscar*?" she finally blurted out. "Her *Oscar*? Me?"

"I think she knew without your documentary none of the other stuff would've happened. And, she also told me, '*Sylvia, I can't take it with me.*' She knew you understood the importance of it to her, that you might be able to use it as a symbol to spur on others. In the end, she just wanted *you* and nobody else to have it."

Ingrid sat down, cradling the Oscar in her lap and, again, shaking her head.

"That evening was so precious," she began recalling. "The whole theater exploded when Tom Hanks read out her name. I wasn't sure if she'd even heard him so I leaned over and said, '*Josephine! Josephine! You've won! He just said you name.*'

"It was hard for us to get to the stage through the throng of people wanting to congratulate and touch her. And the noise, the cheering; it was deafening.

"I'd helped her write a short speech just in case and after she'd calmed down she read it beautifully. The most touching moment, of course, was when she thanked her parents…'*And Mama and Daddy, I know you're looking down on me and sharing this, too. You've always been my life since the day I was born. Never a day gone by without I haven't talked to you. You did this for me, I know. I love you, Mama and Daddy.*'

"For the rest of the evening almost every star you could think of came up to her, hugged her and told her what an inspiration she was and always would be. By the time the show ended she was exhausted, poor thing. Marvin wanted to take her to one of the numerous parties but she declined.

"So, we rode back to the hotel in the beautiful, red Packard, where, again, masses of people were there to greet her. I finally managed to get her to the suite at around eleven. Honestly, she flopped down on her bed, gown and all, and slept until morning.

"Of course, it all started up again with the early morning news shows interviewing her. That went on, believe it or not, for three more days before she asked me to bring her home.

"In our quiet times she said how happy she was to have won, but mostly because more people now would go and see the film. That was the most important part of winning for her; that more folk would see a slice of life they knew nothing about. And she was correct; on its second run the movie did another fifty percent. Amazing!"

"It was and so was she," Sylvia offered. "But when she returned I started noticing some subtle changes with her." Struggling to find the right words, she continued, "Almost as if she knew things were winding down for her. Her heart problems only seemed to confirm that. Oh, don't get me wrong, Josephine still led as full a life as ever. There was no depression, no feeling sorry for herself, just a…a resignation, I suppose.

"When she first began having symptoms and I suggested it might be time to see a doctor, she sat me down and explained her feelings about… about dying, I guess. She said she'd agree to see the doctor but if the news was bad and involved all sorts of treatments, then she wasn't interested. *'I'm ninety-three, dear child, and have lived a good, productive life. There's no shame in dying. All you need is courage. So I will face whatever time I have left with courage. My mama had courage. So did my daddy. And it was worse for them because they had me to worry and care about.'* And she ended our conversation by saying she couldn't wait to be with them again. Honestly, Ingrid, I couldn't argue with anything she'd said."

Ingrid nodded and smiled knowingly.

"Sounds just like our Josephine. Well, I will see she gets her wish. I'll take her back to Burbank and bury her with her folks. That seems like a perfect end to her story."

"Give me a few days to get the necessary paperwork in order. And thank you for doing this for her. Definitely fitting."

"Marvin already told me to do whatever it takes. He's also going to take care of the funeral costs and provide her with a meaningful ceremony. Are you sure you won't come?"

"Absolutely," Sylvia nodded. "Just let me know when and I'll carry the day in my thoughts."

Josephine's flower-laden casket left the funeral home three days later on its way to Wyverne County airport. At Sylvia's request, the hearse was slowly driven to the nursing home where a mix of residents and staff sat or stood outside to pay their final respects.

As it stopped at the entrance, Sylvia approached with a pillow shaped wreath, full of Josephine's favorite white roses. A member of the funeral home opened the back of the car and Sylvia carefully slipped the home's homage onto the coffin. Stepping back, she bowed her head and blew Josephine a touching kiss goodbye. As the hearse pulled away a ripple of somber applause filled the air.

At the airport, Ingrid watched solemnly as the casket was loaded onto the Cessna with due dignity. She took a few moments to thank the funeral staff for their help and compassion before taking one last look at the rear of the plane now cradling Josephine. With tears streaming down her cheeks, she slowly climbed the steps to accompany her friend on her last journey to join her parents.

The Hodges-Dixon Funeral Home in Burbank was founded by the current owner's grandfather in nineteen forty-five to help service and give comfort to some who paid the ultimate sacrifice in World War II. In the area, over the years, it became known for its extraordinary compassion and caring, often reducing costs or even waiving them for some families who found themselves faced with unexpected grief.

When Josephine's mother died they handled the arrangements, coordinating with Judy Garland, who paid for the funeral, as well as taking extra special care of a terrified fifteen year old. Years later, when her father passed, Josephine again contacted Hodges-Dixon to perform the funereal duties, which old Mr. Hodges told her would be an honor.

This time it was Hodges-Dixon that contacted the studio, specifically Marvin McCullen, to offer their services in any way possible as a token of the esteem in which they held Josephine.

The grandson, now the owner, put it this way to Marvin, "She was part of our family just as much as we were of hers. We all followed her career, beginning with my grandfather, and finishing now with me. A remarkable life, one well lived and it would be a tremendous honor if you would allow us the privilege of seeing her safely home."

Marvin, of course, agreed, before adding that all costs should be sent directly to him. Young Mr. Hodges told him they'd discuss that at a later time. In fact, Marvin never received a bill.

The Cessna touched down in Burbank on a warm afternoon that Ingrid barely noticed. Waiting on the runway was a full contingent of staff from Hodges-Dixon ready to take care of Josephine's casket on its final journey. Marvin, Sonia and Sissy were also there to acknowledge the somber moment and lend whatever comfort they could to Ingrid.

As the hearse drove away, the group hugged and cried like the bereaved family they were; empty and mostly silent. In the end, it was Sonia who spoke for them all.

"I'm just grateful I had the chance to get to know her for a while, to experience how a real lady carries herself and makes the most of what talents she's given. If I can be half the woman Josephine turned out to be then I'll be lucky and blessed."

The others nodded in agreement, tears and wry smiles spreading across their faces like clouds covering the sun.

Ingrid spent the evening before Josephine's funeral alone by choice. Earlier, Marvin took the whole group out to dinner, which he asked to be a celebration not a wake; joyous not somber in any way.

They told Josephine stories, giggling, laughing and remembering her as they felt she would have approved.

"She loved practical jokes," Ingrid explained. "She once told me about an incident while making 'Othello'. They were about to shoot a huge, pivotal scene when Stanley Masters handed her, out of the blue, a revised script in which she had a large part. He gave her no time to really read it, saying 'places' and 'action'.

"When Josephine reached her lines they were basically gibberish; a mixture of weird Shakespeare, German and French words and a liberal sprinkling of mild oaths.

"But since this was her first film and the director was Stanly Masters, she soldiered on regardless, spouting rubbish until the whole crew collapsed with laughter. She never forgave Stanley and vowed to get her own back one day.

"Fast forward to halfway through the shoot and one morning Josephine arrives on set with two suitcases and supposedly a train ticket in her hand. She then tells Stanley she's quitting the movie because his joke really upset her and she could no longer work for him.

"Now, remember, Stanley has a whole lot invested in the movie which is halfway finished. So, he pleads and apologizes, apologizes and pleads until Josephine starts to laugh. He, of course, wants to know what's so funny. She then pulls a calendar from her purse and shows him the date… April Fools Day! Man, did she ever get her own back!"

The dinner ended with Marvin proposing a toast to Josephine, group hugs and a definite feeling of profound sadness despite the earlier laughter.

Alone for the rest of the evening, Ingrid took time for herself to just think back over the relatively short span of knowing Josephine. She replayed every moment best as she could remember, hearing Josephine's voice in her head, seeing her still graceful movements and thinking all the while how fast it all went.

She ran Josephine's remarkable life through her head, marveling at how someone who started out with so little, except for a loving family, achieved so much and affected the lives of so many others.

If I live to a hundred, she thought, *I know I'll never meet anyone who meant as much as you did to me. And what I will try and do is to live up to your standards, to be as good a person as I can. That's a promise.*

Josephine's funeral took place two days later at Westville cemetery, at the site of her parents' graves. The small crowd of attendees, including her four fellow nominees, Rachel, Tamara, Faye and Rosario, watched, glassy-eyed, as the hearse slowly made its way up the gravel path and slid to a halt. Four members of the Hodges-Dixon staff, assisted by her four cast members from *The Good Woman of Harlem,* lifted the flower laden coffin from the back and placed it on a raised dais near the graveside.

The group then stood in a semi-circle as Pastor Richfield from the Benson's church in Westville welcomed them to the ceremony.

"Today is not the end," he began, "but a glorious beginning for our dear, departed sister, Josephine Benson. Here starts her final journey, a journey that will finally take her back to the bosom of her family."

The pastor continued his blessing for another ten minutes, lifting everyone's spirits with powerful, meaningful words that spoke truth to the character and to the woman Josephine had become. He then invited Marvin to give the eulogy.

"Who we are is what we leave behind. Who we are is what we leave behind," he repeated, forcefully. "And Josephine left so much goodness behind, so much that will endure and enrich our lives forever.

"Sonia, Sissy, Tarteel, Tyrone, Ariana, Seyvon and you four wonderful actresses," he continued, glancing at her fellow nominees, "and myself came into her life long after we were magically introduced to her by Ingrid, who managed, with her amazing documentary, to shine a light into what had before only been the shadows of her life.

"And what we learned through Ingrid's incredible story telling was a tale of which any Hollywood writer would be proud to own. Except this life wasn't fiction; it was true fact right down the line.

"Born of humble, but proud and responsible parents, she garnished an Academy Award Nomination at the tender age of twenty. Twenty! Imagine that? In my opinion, she should have won, but that's another story. After leaving acting, she had an amazing singing career with Count Basie, before deciding to become a teacher and mentor to hundreds of disadvantaged youths in Harlem, at a studio that still thrives today.

"And finally, she consented to appear in *The Good Woman of Harlem*, which she enhanced beyond measure with a performance for the ages. Her Oscar was not only well deserved, with all due respect ladies," he said, turning to the four nominees, "but way, way long overdue…seventy years, in fact!

"So, as we say goodbye to our dear friend, I want to remind you just what she leaves behind. A body of professional work that will live long in the memory. An on-going performing arts studio which, through her generosity, will stay productive and vibrant for many years to come. A reputation for kindness, fairness and thoughtfulness that also will live on in all of us. And, finally, the love and friendship she unselfishly and unconditionally gave to us while asking nothing in return.

"Who we are is what we leave behind. Now we well know exactly what it is she left behind. Rest in peace, dear one. Rest in peace."

The small congregation desperately wanted to applaud Marvin's eulogy, but out of deep respect for the solemn occasion declined to do so. Pastor Richfield gave Josephine a final blessing as her flower-draped coffin was slowly lowered into the ground.

Ingrid retrieved a dozen white roses, handing them out for each person to toss on top of the disappearing casket. When everyone had finished, she stepped forward and threw a single red rose as a symbol of all their love. It was a touching, poignant moment befitting the woman they honored.

Two day later, Ingrid returned alone to Josephine's grave. She was overjoyed to see the trimmed grass, the vases of fresh flowers and a shiny, marble headstone. She read the inscription, which she, herself, had written:

JOSEPHINE BENSON
February 6, 1929 - June 11, 2022

Beloved daughter, friend and mentor to many

Oscar winner, singer and teacher

A life well spent

Ingrid reread her words, smiling and nodding her head, kneeling and kissing her fingers before touching the cool marble.

Out loud, she said, "Miss Josephine Benson, I want you to know there is never a day I don't wake up being thankful you came into my life. While there's so much sadness inside my heart, like a sore that will never fully heal, I also know the happiness and love you showed me will always far outweigh the pain. I can hear you now saying, 'Listen, child, stop your crying, straighten your back and just have courage.' Now I'm laughing just thinking about that. But, as usual, you're right. I know I'll never be as good as you want me to be, but I promise you I'll try. Trouble is, Miss Josephine Benson, you've set the bar so high for me to follow, but I promise you I'll try. Whenever I feel like taking a short cut or not doing something because I just can't be bothered, I will remind myself, with a swift slap to the side of my head, of some of the hardships you suffered; your disappointments, your let downs and your losses. You will always be my shining example of how to live a kind and decent life. I know you're not alone now. You have your mama and daddy with you and that makes me so thankful. Whenever I need to see you, I'll watch the movie again and that will trick me into believing you haven't gone, that you're still out there somewhere, watching over me. I'm smiling again just thinking about that. So, anyway, don't worry about me, I'll be fine. I've had such a great teacher. Just know I will carry you with me 'til the end of my days. I will. I will. Promise."